CRIMSON
AMULET

CRIMSON AMULET

BY

ADRIANA GIROLAMI

BOOK TWO OF THE

TEMPLAR TRILOGY

Cover by Adriana Girolami

THE AUTHOR

 Adriana Girolami was born in Rome, Italy. Books were always available in her home and at an early age she was encouraged to read by her parents. Adriana's creative, artistic nature was apparent even as a child and she delighted in drawing pictures on the pristine sands of Italy's coast line during beach outings. She immigrated with her family to the United States following her father's untimely death and later attended The Art Students League in New York City. Soon she embarked on a satisfying career as a portrait artist and illustrator, but still longed for the freedom of the written word. The author remembered all those wonderful and exciting books that stimulated her imagination as a child. She favored distinguished, historical authors such as Sir Walter Scott and Adriana's personal favorite, Alexander Dumas. She wrote her debut novels, the "Knights Templar Trilogy" containing *Mysterious Templar, The Crimson Amulet* and *The Templar's Redemption*. Being a professional artist, she made the illustrations for the cover of the books. In her spare time she enjoys physical activities. Jogging faithfully, she plays racquet ball and has a black belt in Kenpo Karate. She loves to travel and has visited many different countries throughout the world. She currently lives in Florida.

ISBN-13: - 978-0-9971290-2-1 Print
ISBN-10: - 0-9971290-2-6
ISBN-13: - 978-0-9971290-3-8 E
ISBN-10: - 0-9971290-3-4

Timber Creek Press
Imprint of Timber Creek Productions, LLC
312 N. Commerce St.
Gainesville, Texas

ACKNOWLEDGMENT

The author gratefully acknowledges Mr. Ken Farmer and Mr. Buck Stienke for the publishing of the "Knights Templar Trilogy". Also Mr. Anthony Flacco, Mr. John Hennesy, Edith Kinsman and Mrs. Gloria Toder.

DEDICATION

This book is dedicated to my dear sister Silvia, who always believed in my writing abilities before I was even aware of them. Through her efforts I was exposed to my favorite authors, Alexander Dumas and Sir Walter Scott, who have inspired me to become a writer.

Contact Us:
Published by: Timber Creek Press
timbercreekpresss@yahoo.com
www.timbercreekpress.net
Twitter: @pagact
Facebook Book Page:
www.facebook.com/TimberCreekPress
214-533-4964

HISTORICAL FICTION WESTERN

THE NATIONS by Ken Farmer and Buck Stienke
Audio version: www.tinyurl.com/NationsAudio
HAUNTED FALLS by Ken Farmer and Buck Stienke
Audio version: www.tinyurl.com/HauntedFallsAudio
HELL HOLE by Ken Farmer
Audio version: www.tinyurl.com/HellHoleAudio
ACROSS the RED by Ken Farmer & Buck Stienke
Audio version:www.tinyurl.com/AcrossRedAudio
BASS and the LADY by Ken Farmer & Buck Stienke
DEVIL'S CANYON by Buck Stienke

SY/FY

LEGEND of AURORA by Ken Farmer & Buck Stienke
AURORA: INVASION by Ken Farmer & Buck Stienke

Coming Soon

MILITARY ACTION/TECHNO
BLACKSTAR MOUNTAIN - by T.C. MILLER
HISTORICAL FICTION WESTERN
LADY with a BADGE by Ken Farmer

HISTORICAL FICTION ROMANCE
THE TEMPLAR TRILOGY
TEMPLAR REDEMPTION by Adriana Girolami

TIMBER CREEK PRESS

CHAPTER ONE

LORENGARD-LORRAINE

Arsenio saw Polyxena at a distance. Her graceful figure strolled among the tree-lined pathways brimming with flowers in bloom. She was resplendent in a loose fitting purple gown with oversized sleeves lined in ermine. Her long, raven hair hung loose upon her shoulders and caught the sunlight. Arsenio was thoroughly enticed and approached her with a bright smile. When their eyes met, she extended her hands in greeting. He clasped them raised them to his lips.

In the closeness of the moment, he noticed an unusual glow radiating from her. It was so unlike her customary somber and dignified demeanor. He felt pleased and encouraged by the change in her.

"My lady, your smiling face brightens the beauty of the day. I am delighted to see you so cheerful."

Polyxena took a deep breath to control her excitement, and looked at Arsenio with joy. "I have received some wonderful news, my lord, and I am eager to share it with you." Her voice became softer. "I hope you will be pleased..."

"I am intrigued." he answered. "What is the news?"

"Yes. I have been informed by the court physician that I am with child. Of course the news is unexpected, but so very welcomed."

A shadow of pain crossed Arsenio's face before he caught himself and concealed his feelings. He offered her a comforting smile.

"My lady, this...is a blessed day that...brings forth such news. After much sorrow, you have reason to rejoice."

He took a deep breath, then looked into her eyes and added, "The noble Duccio will be much more than a loving memory, because his sacred blood will continue to flow unhindered through the child."

Polyxena gasped in delight. "Arsenio. Oh, thank you. Thank you for your kindness..."

"I rejoice with you, to see again that smile upon your face. After so much sadness for us both, there will be a great celebration of the coming birth of a new Prince or Princess of Lorengard-Lorraine."

But instead of showing him that smile, her face darkened. "Duccio's child is not of royal lineage my lord. I will not falsify a birthright and deny the father's name."

Arsenio felt as if he had just stumbled down a flight of stairs. "Forgive me Polyxena," he quickly replied. "I have no desire to usurp Duccio's rights as a father. He was my friend and I honor his memory. I only wish to bestow upon his child the protection and love he will not have otherwise.

"Please do not apologize, Polyxena. No explanation is owed for your behavior, considering all the suffering you endured. You placed your life in great peril to save mine. I am forever grateful to you."

"Thank you, my lord." She studied his face. There was a sensual, aristocratic demeanor in Arsenio, coupled with a warmth and approachability that was disarming. She moved closer to him and smiled, looking directly into his eyes.

Arsenio beamed and slid his arms around her waist in a warm embrace. "I am not your lord, Polyxena. I am your husband who loves you above all others. I also know that Duccio would want you to be happy. Please, allow me to share your life."

Passion and love were etched on Arsenio's face. Polyxena was startled, but the sight moved her. She felt as if she saw him for the first time, and was overcome by the same intense and sensual feelings that had struck her then. She responded to his embrace and pressed into him. He held her in his arms, caressing her with all his ardor and desire.

When her arms remained tightly wrapped around him, he dared to press his lips against hers, and when he felt her respond to his kiss, it stirred all his longing. He gasped and began taking fast, deep breaths while she returned the kiss with warmth. He reveled in the softness of her lips, ripe and full of promise.

Arsenio's desire remained bound by her delicate condition, regardless of Polyxena's tantalizing beauty. He could feel that the memory of the man whose child she was carrying still cast a long shadow over them. Nonetheless, he was elated that the woman he loved was in his arms once more after so long, responding to his passion.

"Polyxena, my wife, I love you so much." He immediately regretted saying it, fearing he had gone too far. But Polyxena's smile widened.

For her part, she had grieved alone for so long that she reveled in the comfort of Arsenio's arms. Coldness and sorrow were replaced by a deep glow of sensual warmth. "Arsenio," she whispered. "my husband…I love you, too."

Somehow, hearing herself speak such passionate words amplified her own emotions. She was finally able to release her pain and felt herself freed from the torment of guilt that she had not earned over betrayals which she had never committed. Such feelings had plagued her ever since Duccio was killed. Now she allowed herself to nestle in Arsenio's arms and drink of the comfort in his embrace. After so much time lost, she felt as if she and Arsenio had finally found one another again.

News quickly spread about the impending birth of an heir to the Dukedom of Lorengard-Lorraine. The people were overjoyed and eagerly awaited the blessed event. The birth of a new Prince or Princess was considered a good omen, a blessing from God that would assure peace and prosperity for the Dukedom.

For Polyxena, the months could not go by fast enough. She waited with great anticipation. Arsenio's reassuring presence and comforting words were always available during the stressful moments. The respect and affection she felt for her husband grew with each passing day.

She had been emotionally impaired, almost paralyzed, not just by the pain of loss, but by the fear of disrespecting the noble Knight's memory so soon after his passing. The secret she nurtured was the news that she was carrying Duccio's child had greatly relieved her torment with the knowledge that the man she had loved would live on through his child. The splendid interlude of passion that they shared for a fleeting moment had not been in vain.

Finally, the bell towers of the churches in Lorengard-Lorraine rang a festive sound that resonated throughout the Dukedom, tolling the news that the Dukedom now had a new prince.

Pandemonium ensued, and elated citizens shouted with delight, "Long live our new Prince. Honor to the noble house of Lorengard-Lorraine."

A massive crowd gathered in front of the ducal palace, waving banners with the crimson coat-of-arms of Lorengard-Lorraine. Their joy was palpable and the sound of their voices resonated throughout the walls of the palace, reaching the stately room where Polyxena cradled her newborn son in her arms.

Arsenio was by her side, beaming with joy despite the challenges of his wife's pregnancy with Duccio's child. The baby boy looked healthy and was sleeping peacefully, unaware of the excitement he was bringing to so many people.

"My lady," Arsenio said. "Our people rejoice at the arrival of their new Prince. After all the suffering they endured under Ludwig's evil reign, his little life is bringing needed joy. This is truly an eventful day."

He remained silent for a moment, then placed his hand gently on the infant head, intoning a heartfelt prayer. "Heavenly father, we thank you for all our blessings and the gift of this precious child. Endow him with wisdom and kindness; make him worthy of the high station in life that is his destiny."

He smiled at Polyxena and continued, "Duccio, this is your son that is given in my care. I promise to love him as if he were my own child. I pledge to protect him against harm and guide him in the righteous path, hoping he will be as noble and chivalrous as his father."

Polyxena took Arsenio's hand with gratitude and love. In that pivotal moment, peace and contentment filled her. The three of them were a family now and she rejoiced.

DUCCIO RETURNS

Nearly a month passed since the birth of the new Prince, and already Duccio's likeness was apparent on the child's face. Polyxena was keenly aware of it and secretly rejoiced that the handsome features of her first great love would live on through their son.

The young prince was named Alexander in honor of Polyxena's father, the Duke of Nemours, and Edward, in memory of Arsenio's father. Preparations were made for the stately baptism according to the tradition of Lorengard-Lorraine, with the festivities scheduled to occur in the infant's second month of life.

Young Alexander's nursery was lavishly decorated with delicate mahogany furniture, richly inlaid with semiprecious stones. The splendid ceiling frescos depicted mythological scenes of fawns and unicorns giving the room a whimsical allure. The golden crib was a priceless heirloom of the ducal family, crowned by precious Venetian lace. The privileged infant's comfort was of paramount importance, with a wet nurse always at hand and several handmaidens catering to the child's every need.

As a new, doting mother, Polyxena was at first reluctant to give Alexander's care to strangers, even if required by the court's etiquette. Despite her aversion, she finally relented, knowing it was a traditional and necessary requisite.

Because of her many duties as Duchess, the compulsory separation from her child was necessary, even though she spent every available moment with him and cherished the precious time they were able to share. Her nightly visits to the nursery were joyful, and she was always reluctant to retire to her adjoining bedchamber.

One evening, Polyxena found the separation from her child unusually challenging. Disturbing thoughts plagued her and she was unable to find solace in the luxury of her lonely room. She tossed aimlessly in her bed searching for elusive relaxation.

Finally, no longer able to endure her distress, she jumped out of bed, placed a dressing coat over her nightgown, and walked impatiently toward the tapestry that separated her room from Alexander's bedchamber. She felt herself filled with uncontrolled anxieties and yearned to hold him in her arms, searching for comfort in the warmth of his little body.

But when she was about to enter the nursery she was startled by the sight of Arsenio leaning over her son's crib and lovingly caressing the child. The tender scene filled her with warmth.

THE CRIMSON AMULET

She was gratified to witness this genuine affection for little Alexander by stepfather Arsenio. She had feared that his acceptance of another man's child was only due to his sense of gratitude toward her. Now she was finally certain that he truly loved and accepted the child as his own.

She eagerly entered the nursery and joined her husband, whose face brightened at the sight of his beautiful bride. He encircled her waist in a loving embrace and they stood together silently, gazing at the sleeping child.

When the time came to finally retire, Arsenio reluctantly escorted his wife back to her sleeping quarters. They were chosen for her because of the close proximity to the nursery, but Polyxena had dwelled alone in the lavish bedchamber since the birth of her child. Now the young Duke felt reluctant to leave her and return to his own lonely rooms.

Throughout their marriage, no intimacy had existed between them, and the situation had become difficult for Arsenio to sustain. However, dominated by his inflexible sense of chivalry and pride, he wanted her love to be freely given and passionate, not dictated by some sense of duty.

The closeness of her body accentuated his longing and erotic desires, but Polyxena remained silent without extending an invitation to join her in the bedchamber. Arsenio bowed and with reluctance prepared to leave her. But Polyxena surprised him by firmly holding his hand to stop him from departing. She gazed in his eyes.

"Thank you Arsenio," she finally said. "I am so grateful for all your generosity and kindness toward me and my child; you are truly my very best friend."

Arsenio could not hide his disappointment at the sound of those words. The offer of friendship hardly fulfilled his passionate nature and only added to his feeling of rejection. Polyxena noticed his reaction and moved closer to him, snuggling against his body and pressing her breasts invitingly against his chest.

"You are not only my best friend, Arsenio," she whispered. You are also my love." She blushed violently as she uttered those last words, while she brought her lips so close to his that he could feel the warmth of her breath.

Arsenio was stunned by the revelation and beset with desire. He placed his strong arms about her and caressed her curvaceous form. He kissed her lips with hunger. The ecstasy of the moment was volatile, overwhelming them while he lifted her off the floor and carried her in the bedchamber and closed the tapestry behind them.

Once inside, he placed her on the bed while their bodies trembled with desire and he kissed her once again with unbridled passion. Polyxena's response to his loving overture took his breath away. He had never been so much in love with any other woman before, and having her so receptive to his passion was almost unreal. Polyxena's body seemed untouched by the recent pregnancy and Arsenio reveled in the silkiness of her skin and the loveliness of her form. The intensity and heat their bodies generated in their passionate embrace was exhilarating.

For her part, Polyxena was stunned by the depths of her feelings. All the emotions and desire that her grief had stifled were resurging.

She wondered if she could be in love with two men at the same time. Was she being disrespectful to Duccio's memory? Or was she following his desire that she should go on living and fulfill the path of her destiny?

She had been fearful of being vulnerable to the pain of a loss if she ever allowed herself to love again, and yet in her husband's arms she felt the love and contentment that she never expected to feel again.

Strangely, the catalyst that brought them together was Duccio's son, since the child's eventful birth had been instrumental in giving Polyxena the necessary strength to go on with life. The child was the ultimate gift from the noble knight, and his message to her was to go forward with life, to once again open herself to love with a noble and proper person.

Great plans were in the making in celebration of the baptism for the heir apparent of Lorengard-Lorraine. Duke Arsenio spared no expense for the grand occasion. It was an opportunity to share the eventful day with the citizens of the Dukedom and they were eager to rejoice and celebrate after so much turmoil and suffering.

Arsenio was truly happy for the first time in his life. With the woman he loved by his side and the birth of a healthy new son, he felt grateful for all his blessings.

He doted on Polyxena and considered himself fortunate that this courageous woman was his wife. And so he showered her with lavish gifts and loving devotion, eager to please her and bring her joy in every possible way.

Polyxena was overwhelmed by the attention and reveled in the warmth of the relationship. Her passionate nature, long repressed, was finally reawakening and her romantic feelings toward Arsenio grew with each passing day, coupled with renewed respect and trust she had for him.

One afternoon, while busily performing her many duties as Duchess, Polyxena received an unexpected, but welcomed visit from Arsenio. He approached her with a bright smile, then placed his arms around her and lovingly kissed her cheeks.

"This visit is a pleasant surprise, my husband," she told him. "I thought affairs of state were occupying your time today."

"That is true, however, I have some wonderful and surprising news for you that I am eager to share without delay. This gift is truly special and I am certain it will bring you great joy."

"Thank you Arsenio, but you are far too generous," she said in a mock reprimand while caressing his face and rearranging an unruly lock of his hair. "You have already showered me with so many presents that I am overwhelmed and humbled by them."

Her voice became softer, alluring, "The greatest gift of all is your love Arsenio and I will not ask for more."

"I believe this is one gift you will not wish to return," he added with an enigmatic smile.

Intrigued, she replied, "Then please don't keep me in suspense."

"Your noble father, the Duke of Nemours, will honor us with a visit," Arsenio exclaimed joyfully. "He is already on his way and will soon be here. He is very anxious to meet his new grandson."

Polyxena threw her arms around Arsenio's neck and kissed him on the lips with joyful ardor, disregarding the court etiquette and the presence of nearby ladies-in-waiting. "This is such wonderful news Arsenio and the best present of all. When will he arrive?"

"In just a few days, according to his message, and he will remain with us until Alexander's baptism."

Polyxena laughed in delight. Nothing could have pleased her more than a reunion with her father. She savored the thought of introducing him to her son.

"But wait," Arsenio added. "I have one more surprise for you Polyxena, and although is of a different nature, I am certain you will be greatly pleased." He squired her without delay toward the adjacent reception room of the palace.

The stately chamber was crowned by splendid ceiling frescos and chandeliers brimming with a thousand lights, and as they entered, Polyxena noticed a striking man in his late twenties, dressed in a distinct Italian style. His appearance was refined and elegant, with an unusual flair. A flowing mantle draped his shoulders, and a black velvet cap topped his reddish brown hair. A long beard framed his sculpted features, and the face was highlighted by his piercing blue eyes.

The man exuded an aura that seemed benevolent, but also quite intimidating. The instant he saw her, the man removed his velvet cap with a sweeping gesture and bowed to the royal pair in courtly fashion. Arsenio introduced him.

"My lady, it is my pleasure to introduce to you, Master Leonardo Da Vinci, who has graciously consented to oversee the festival honoring our son's baptism. His artistic contribution represents a special gift from our friend and ally, Ludovico Sforza, Duke of Milan."

Polyxena walked eagerly toward the distinguished guest and extended her hand in greeting. "Welcome to Lorengard-Lorraine Master Leonardo. We are honored by the presence of such a great and distinguished artist. We joyfully extend our hospitality to you, and we are most grateful for your artistic contribution to our son's festival."

"Thank you for your warm welcome, your grace," Leonardo kissed her hand with courtly flair while his piercing eyes focused on her lovely face. He was silent for a long moment, then added, "Rumors of your beauty have been greatly understated my lady, I am overwhelmed by the grace and loveliness of your presence."

With those parting words, Leonardo bowed deferentially to the royal pair and exited the room.

After many days of eager anticipation, the arrival of the Duke of Nemours was welcomed with ceremonial splendor in Lorengard-Lorraine. He was accompanied by the festive sounds of trumpets as he strode by the ceremonial guards honoring his arrival.

No expense was spared to welcome the Duke. Arsenio was eager to honor his heroic father-in-law, who had been instrumental in saving Lorengard-Lorraine from an evil tyrant.

Polyxena was pleasantly surprised by her father's healthy appearance and relaxed demeanor, so unlike the usually stern and reserved man. She embraced her father and Arsenio warmly greeted him. They offered to escort the Duke to the comfort of his rooms, assuming after such an arduous journey he needed a proper rest. But to their surprise, the vigorous Duke dismissed the offer and professed his desire to meet his new grandson without delay.

Unable to dissuade the stubborn man, Polyxena and Arsenio acquiesced and squired him to their son's nursery, where he was finally introduced to the little Prince. The elder gentleman was overwhelmed; tears of joy blurred his vision at the sight of the beautiful child. He struggled to maintain his dignity and his face shone with delight. Polyxena felt as if she could glow in the dark while she placed the baby Alexander in his grandfather's arms.

The Duke gazed lovingly at the child, focusing on the striking beauty of the dark eyes and the perfection of his features. The excitement of the tender moment between father and daughter was palpable and Arsenio graciously left the nursery to allow his wife and father-in-law to share the wonderful occasion alone.

"This is one of the happiest days in my life," the Duke of Nemours finally said. "This precious child brings so much joy to us."

"Yes father, that is true," responded Polyxena. "Nothing could have been more helpful to heal the wounds in my heart than the blessing of his presence."

The Duke of Nemours remained silent for a brief moment, then exclaimed with pride. "My grandson has a brilliant future before him. As the heir to Lorengard-Lorraine, he will be groomed for his great destiny as the future leader of the people."

Sadness flashed across her face. The moment sagged. She turned away from her father, unable to face him while she spoke. The beauty of the moment was suddenly ruined by escalating emotions and deep seeded feelings of guilt. "My son is Duccio's child, father. He is not of royal lineage. It pains me to think of hiding that fact and denying him his true heritage."

Her father, surprised her when he smiled and lovingly placed the child in the crib. He embraced her and spoke in a soft voice, "I am aware of it, Polyxena. Even at this early stage of his life, the child's resemblance to the noble knight is apparent. Those luminous dark eyes and the perfection of his features tell the tale.

"However, my daughter, there is no need for distress in sharing this knowledge with me. I place no blame and have no desire to judge your actions. You have shown amazing courage and chivalry despite impossible odds and I am proud you are my daughter. In truth, I am happy because it will comfort you to know that the chivalrous Knight you loved will live on through his son.

"However," the Duke continued. "the child's welfare must be paramount. He is in need of a father. I believe Arsenio is the person to fulfill such an important task. He is a kind and noble man who truly loves you.

"Polyxena, you must remember that your marriage to Duccio was celebrated in secret and was never duly recorded by the church. Consequently, Alexander will be unfairly marked with the stain of illegitimacy. It will certainly complicate his young life. He will also be denied, through no fault of his own, the high station in life that I believe was willed to him by Destiny."

"But what about Duccio?" Polyxena interrupted. "Aren't we denying his son his true heritage?"

The Duke's response was stern. "He was a noble knight, and thus would have been in full agreement that the present course of action is the proper one. Unquestionably, his son's welfare would have been paramount to him."

Polyxena remained silent. Tears streamed down her face. She understood the wisdom in her father's words, and his understanding gave her comfort.

The Duke wiped away her tears. "The child is an immense source of joy to everyone and a precious gift of love. Cherish him without regrets. And if the occasion should ever arise, it will be your choice to determine whether Alexander's true heritage should be revealed."

"Thank you my father. With your wisdom and understanding you give me peace."

They remained silent for a moment, savoring the joy of their reunion, until Polyxena looked into her father's face and noticed concern in his eyes. The Duke moved away from her, cleared his throat, and addressed his daughter with concern in a tighter voice.

"Polyxena, did you share the knowledge of the Templar's treasure with Arsenio?"

"I did not. I swore an oath of silence and allegiance to the Knights Templar. It is a manner of honor."

"It isn't mistrust on my part, for I believe in your honorable nature. However, Arsenio is chivalrous in his own right and I thought, perhaps, you made an exception with him."

"I considered it, I must confess. However, I would never break a promise of such importance without your knowledge or consent."

The Duke was visibly relieved. "I am very glad you used discretion, Polyxena. Knowledge of the treasure would only place Arsenio in peril."

"How can there be danger, since no one knows of the treasure but us?"

"Over the past century, going back to the times of Wilfred the Valiant, many have had knowledge of the existence of a great treasure. We are the only ones who know its location…

"Enemies of our ancestor were aware that Wilfred took possession of the fabulous plunder from the holy land, but they never learned where it was hidden. For generations, a long list of ruthless people has been on the quest to find it. They have used barbaric means at times to achieve their aim. Through the decades, several heroic members of the house of Nemours were captured by our ruthless enemies, tortured, and even put to the sword. All of this was done in the search for the treasure."

Polyxena was overwhelmed by a feeling of dread. Her son was also a member of the house of Nemours.

The Duke put his arms around her. "This is the reason, Polyxena, why we must be vigilant in dispensing the wealth. We must not attract attention, since we are the direct descendants of Wilfred the Valiant. There are too many people who would do anything to possess such a treasure."

Polyxena finally said, "Why don't we try to find trustworthy individuals who are not connected with the house of Nemours to join our quest? They could help us dispense a greater portion of the treasure to needy people."

"Unwise…given the risk." Her father shook his head. "Wealth brings about great responsibilities. Even trustworthy people can be corrupted by the awesome power of gold."

"But with so much suffering out there, that treasure could do great good in many places."

"No, daughter. Involving more people who would have knowledge of the great treasure will bring too much danger. You must remember that the treasure rests within Nemours Castle and the Dukedom would be in grave peril if the secret became known to our enemies. We would be vulnerable to attack from every direction.

"Polyxena, I know the kindness of your heart and your generous nature. But if the secret becomes known and the Templar's great treasure falls into the hands of our enemies, it will be lost forever. We must be vigilant, in order to protect it.

"Much good has been done through the ages, dispensing the wealth successfully to thousands of needy people, while many evil tyrants have been toppled. To succeed in our quest, it is essential that we stay the course. The safety of the house of Nemours depends upon it. It would be preferable for the treasure to be forever lost rather than fall in evil hands."

"I see your reasoning and I bow to your wisdom, father. The present course of action is the right one. I pledge my life to the protection of the Templar's treasure."

CHAPTER TWO

THE FESTIVAL

The majestic center hall of the palace was the chosen place for the young Prince's celebration. For that day, the entire area was restricted. And there Leonardo weaved his special magic with his many helpers alongside him.

When the festive day finally arrived, throngs of excited guests filled the massive hall. They crowded each other to witness the amazing artistry of the great Leonardo.

At first glance, the unusual appearance of the palace hall surprised them. The majestic area was covered from floor to ceiling with a translucent gauze-like material. A large, imposing stage had been built against the far end of the stately hall, and the backdrop of the stage was decorated with cascading water images painted on long silken strips of fabric that stretched from ceiling to the floor. In the center of the makeshift stage stood a beautiful, circular fountain decorated with images of unicorns.

The entire area was brilliantly lit by striking lighting fixtures nobody had ever seen before. They were comprised of flaming torches encased in open-ended glass containers, that radiated and reflected their lights on strategically placed faceted mirrors.

Finally, Maestro Leonardo made his grand entrance on the stage, welcomed by thunderous applause. The artist was elegantly dressed in a purple cassock, topped by a velvet vest richly embellished with gold details. A flowing mantle and matching tights completed his ensemble.

He acknowledged the audience's enthusiastic applause with deference, and bowed with courtly manners to the Duke and Duchess.

Silence reigned while all eyes focused on the great magician. He remained motionless for a long moment, looking out at the audience with a hypnotic stare.

With a dramatic gesture, he lifted his arms toward the ceiling, and the lights dimmed in response. They imbued the great hall in a golden glow. A pungent aroma of lilac permeated the area with its sensual fragrance.

Slowly, as if by magic, the fountain on stage began rotating and came alive, spouting water. The gauzy cloth on the walls rippled in the reflected lights. Beautiful images of flowers appeared almost by magic on the diaphanous fabric, giving an enchanted appearance to the area.

Leonardo's notorious love of botany was apparent in the splendid imagery that brought the beauty of nature and the great outdoors in the confinement of the great hall. Sounds of delight were audible from the audience, none of whom had ever witnessed anything such as this. A sudden burst of wind erupted behind the water images on the silken strips, moving the delicate fabric in a swaying rhythm. The painted imagery came alive as a majestic waterfall and an ingenious form of motion picture. Special sounds effects rumbled throughout the hall, imitating the resonance of water crashing against the rocks. The overall illusion rendered the audience speechless.

The floor sprouted a burst of multicolored silken flowers, whose petals opened and allowed young girls to emerge, dressed in translucent lavender veils and with ringlets of flowers on their hair.

The flower nymphs commenced a graceful dance among the guests, throwing petals throughout the area. The hall was suddenly transformed into a Garden of Eden, brimming with beautiful flowers and cascading waterfalls. Graceful dancers took to the stage and encircled the fountain. Joining hands, they commenced to move around it in a circle while the fountain also began rotating with increased velocity. This was accompanied by thundering drumbeats, while the arcs of spouting water rose to greater heights and flashed under multicolored lights.

With a final burst of light and clouds of smoke, the fountain and the girls disappeared. It was as if they were swallowed by the stage floor.

For a long moment, there was no sound but the murmur of stunned spectators. The silence was broken by the resonance of a loud boom, and a globular image ascended from the depths of the stage, blazing with fire. The sphere projected multicolored flashes of light toward the vaulted ceiling, crowning the area with flickering lights and giving the effect of a starry sky.

The tiny beams of light projected from the globe cast the moon and familiar star formations, turning the ceiling into the sky. Then with a final thunderous sound and spectacular bursts of light, the globe disappeared from sight.

The audience sat awestruck by the inventive beauty of this spectacle. And still, when the lights returned, there was a final illusion to the spectacular show.

Because the great hall was now returned to its original pre-show state. The imposing stage, the unicorn fountain, the wall coverings, and all the stunning visual images had suddenly disappeared. It was as if none of it had ever really been there.

The title of the show made sense, now: The Festival of Paradise. For it truly was.

The spectators exploded in thunderous applause, drunk on amazement and crying out in honor of the brilliant Leonardo. An ecstatic aura dominated the great hall while guests immediately began recounting the spectacle to one another with delight.

Suddenly the voice of the Lord Chamberlain resonated above the din, silencing them all, "May I have your attentions, milords?"

He bowed with deference to the rulers of Lorengard-Lorraine as he announced. "The Lord Zanar Mutamin, Sultan of El-Cabir, requests the honor of an audience."

The Duke amiably signaled for the mysterious guest and his party to come forward. In response, a tall, strikingly handsome man in his twenties stepped forward with an imposing stride. Lord Zanar was elegantly attired in a black caftan and turban, with a crimson sash tightly cinched at his narrow waist. His bronzed complexion emphasized the brilliance and intensity of his eyes, while his bold demeanor exuded an aristocratic elegance.

He was closely followed by an entourage of six men dressed in Middle Eastern garb, but while he approached the Duke and Duchess, he signaled his men to remain behind. He bowed his head in greeting, touching his chest, lips, and forehead with a swift motion of one hand.

The Duke spoke first, "Lord Zanar, we welcome you to our house on this special day honoring our son. We extend our hospitality to you and your entourage."

The mysterious stranger smiled in response to the gracious welcome. "I thank you for your generous hospitality. My presence here is prompted by this auspicious occasion. I have also been honored with the task of bringing a special gift to the young Prince."

Lord Zanar gave a signal and immediately a member of the entourage approached him carrying an exquisite mahogany jewel box. It was richly detailed in gold and precious stones.

Lord Zanar moved toward Polyxena and bowed with courtly manners. He also gazed at the loveliness of her face with intense interest. She felt disturbed by the boldness of the stare and recoiled slightly.

Lord Zanar quickly regained his composure and placed the jewel box in her hands. "Your grace, I have been sent here on the occasion of your son's baptism to deliver a special gift for the young prince," he then added with a smile. "The offering is accompanied by my prayer that he will lead a long and happy life!"

"We thank you, my lord," Polyxena responded graciously in spite the unsettled feeling he gave her. There was an allure and magnetism in the intense, dark eyes of the stranger that could not be denied, but he also exuded a strong sense of danger.

She then addressed him in a polite but commanding manner, "It would please us to know the name of the generous person who sent this gift to our son."

"Unfortunately, I am not at liberty to say. The person in question wishes to remain anonymous, but sends the young Prince greetings and good wishes."

Polyxena and Arsenio were puzzled by the strange answer, but despite their apprehension they did not yet wish to offend him.

"In that case, please relate our thanks to the donor of the gift," Arsenio finally said. "Also express our gratitude for the generous contribution to our son's celebration." The Duke signaled his guards to give Lord Zanar free passage from the great hall.

The mysterious stranger bowed and exited the palace followed by his escort and soon disappeared amongst the surrounding crowd.

Silence and curiosity pervaded the great hall while all eyes focused on Polyxena, who held in her hands the exquisite jewel box containing the mysterious gift. She felt concerned by receiving an unexpected offering from an unknown donor, and hesitated for a moment in opening it. However, she also noticed the interest of the audience and felt unwilling to create an aura of concern. She finally lifted the cover and looked at the contents.

Her eyes widened with dread. She gasped and the color bled from her face. She nearly dropped the jewel box on the floor.

Arsenio was so startled by the reaction that he quickly removed the strange offering from her hands, anxious to see what had caused her such alarm.

And there inside the jewel box, resting on a silken bed of bright crimson, was laid an ivory skull, exquisitely detailed. Two splendid rubies were encased in the eye sockets and sparkled bloody red in the torchlight. There was an overall sinister appearance to the amulet and Arsenio was alarmed by this symbol of death.

He signaled his head guard to come forward, and related a stern command, "Find Lord Zanar and all members of his escort! They are all to be apprehended and detained for questioning!"

The guard bowed and hastily departed.

A thousand frightening thoughts crowded Polyxena's mind. The joyous day of her son's baptism was tarnished by the strange episode. Is Alexander in danger? She thought. Does anyone wish to harm him? Fear suddenly overwhelmed her.

The Duke of Nemours turned to her. "Don't be concerned about the gift. Arsenio's action in pursuing them is mere prudence. We should not reach conclusions without cause. Why, the human skull is regarded as a benign symbol in some cultures. A sign of good luck."

"Your father is right," Arsenio agreed, eager to dispel Polyxena's distress. "We are only investigating the situation to be on the safe side. It is quite possible the anonymous donor had benevolent intentions. The ivory amulet with the precious rubies is a splendid, costly gift and may be nothing more than someone's generous offering to our son."

Polyxena was comforted by the encouraging words, and attempted a more positive outlook. She waived to the surrounding guests and signaled for the festivities to continue. Soon laughter reigned again in the great hall.

In spite of the speed with which the men had been sent to search for the guests who had just left, the mysterious men were not found. Lord Zanar and his escort seemed to have disappeared without a trace. No one in the Dukedom had any prior knowledge of them or claimed to have seen them.

There was little else to be done.

Once the celebration played itself out and the festival ended, the brief but eventful visit of Duke Alexander also came to an end. His departure for Nemours saddened Polyxena and she unwillingly bid him goodbye.

"I shall miss you so much, father!" she tenderly said. "Your presence at little Alexander's baptism made my happiness complete...May God grant me the joy of seeing you again!"

The Duke embraced his daughter with great warmth and gently caressed her face as he responded. "You have always been my greatest blessing, Polyxena. And I am also thankful for the special gift of my new grandson. He has brought peace and contentment in my life, and a true feeling of joy I never hoped to experience again. I am truly grateful for all my blessings."

His voice broke, and father and daughter remained silent while they embraced each other. The bond of love enhanced the bittersweet moment.

Arsenio had remained discretely apart, and now joined them for his final goodbye. The Duke of Nemours embraced him with fatherly affection.

"Take care of my daughter and grandson, Arsenio. And may peace reign in your house."

With that, Alexander, Duke of Nemours, mounted his horse and swiftly exited the courtyard of the castle with his escort.

Polyxena silently followed his image until he disappeared from sight. Sadness overwhelmed her and she hurried back inside the castle.

Two weeks after the disturbing appearance of Lord Zanar and his delivery of a strange gift from an unknown source, the skull shaped amulet with the ruby eyes was a distant memory.

On this night, the dukedom was peaceful and moonless, shrouded in darkness. Only flickering stars and torches on the palace walls broke the surrounding gloom. Most of its citizens were fast asleep, unaware of impending danger and oblivious to the soft sounds of predatory footsteps on the palace battlements.

Slithering, ghostly images emerged from the shadows and moved through the darkness with stealth. In a few silent moments, the palace came siege. The heavily armed palace guards were swiftly overpowered by the unknown assailants, and their bodies hurled from the heights to hit the stony courtyard with a distant thud. The mysterious intruders continued their assault with practiced ability and coordination, thrusting forward into the castle keep.

Polyxena and Arsenio were peacefully asleep in the security of their palace until their slumber was interrupted by noises of movement. They were coming from inside little Alexander's nursery.

They both sat up on the bed, heart pounding with apprehension. Polyxena was overwhelmed by motherly concerns and started to rush toward the adjoining room, but Arsenio grabbed her by the waist and stopped her.

"We must keep quiet, Polyxena!" he whispered. "Do not move, while I summon the palace guards. We must not give warning to an intruder until we get help."

He squeezed her hand, then quickly left the bedchamber and disappeared into the darkened corridor. She felt terrified to be left alone in the gloom of the bedchamber, and paced the room trying to control her growing anxieties.

Suddenly, the unsettling silence was broken by her child's cry. The wailing sound was piercing and did not relent, as if no one was in attendance to relieve her baby's distress.

Polyxena desperately peered into the corridor, hoping to see Arsenio return with the palace guards. Only silence and darkness greeted her.

She could no longer control her distress. She donned a dressing gown from a nearby chair and quickly retrieved her sword. Moving in silence, she threw back the tapestry connecting her bedchamber to the nursery and quickly scanned for intruders.

The room was only lit with a few small candles. But as her eyes became accustomed to the dark, she recognized with horror that Alexander's wet nurse and several members of the staff lay lifeless on the floor.

She was given no time to absorb the shock. On the far end of the room, several strange men encircled her baby's crib. She was unable to see her son, but the loud cries from the little Prince comforted her by confirming that he was still alive.

Forgetting her own safety, she lifted her sword against the intruders and started toward her son. Unbelievably, the menacing strangers stepped to the side, allowing her full access to the child.

Polyxena retrieved her son from the crib and held him tight in a comforting embrace, kissing his face as if she were oblivious to the strangers. Like magic, in the comfort and safety of his mother's arms, the little Prince stopped his lament.

An uncomfortable silence reigned in the room for a few endless moments. Finally, the person who appeared to be in charge stepped boldly forward, and the enigmatic face of lord Zanar was revealed in the dim candle light. He bowed with mock deference to the Duchess. When he spoke, his sardonic tone sent chills down her spine.

"Our compliments your grace! We eagerly awaited your arrival and the allure of your presence!" He smiled while he continued. "We have expected you for some time, my lady."

Polyxena was confused by his strange behavior and recoiled from him, shielding the child in her arms. Her mind raced to make sense of this. "Who are these people and what do they want from my son?" she cried. "Lord Zanar! You will pay for this intrusion in my son's bedchamber, and the murder of all these innocent people! What madness drives you?"

Zanar again showed her that same sour smile. "Fear not my lady, no one has been murdered here! Your servants have been rendered unconscious for expediency. They were simply in the way. They will awaken soon enough!"

Polyxena felt relieved, though puzzled by the stranger who seemed to possess mysterious powers that enabled him access to a heavily guarded palace with little effort.

"But then," she continued with a voice made shrill by emotion, "if violence is not your intent, why have you invaded the sanctity of our home in this manner?"

Lord Zanar stepped closer to Polyxena. His dark and intimidating gaze bore into her eyes. He remained silent, as if to enhance the suspense of the moment, and to conceal the fact that he felt truly fascinated by this courageous beauty, who handled the sword with such panache and faced him in defiance.

"We do not want your son, my lady!" he finally said. "You are the only person of interest to us! We only used your son as a lure."

"You lure me with my son?" she responded, simmering with rage, "You must be mad! You and your accomplices are the ones who are entrapped in the castle, with no way out. And if any harm comes to me or to my son, you will surely die here!"

Suddenly, the silence was broken by loud hammering sounds, and the doors of the nursery gave way to Arsenio and the palace guards, who pushed their way through the locked entrance and erupted into the room, sword blades flashing.

They attacked the intruders without a word, and in an instant the nursery was transformed into a battleground. The little Prince was frightened by all the commotion's and screamed louder than ever and even Polyxena's comforting embrace couldn't pacify him.

But there was more oddness. The interlopers only used their weapons defensively, without attacking the guards in return. For some reason they allowed themselves to be captured with relative ease. It made no sense at all. moments later, with the struggle done, Arsenio ordered the guards to take them away and tend to the wounded.

The lingering question was not just the identity of the intruders, but more importantly, how did they manage to enter the nursery with such ease? The area was heavily guarded by well-trained soldiers, and yet they seemed to have had no difficulty in infiltrating the palace.

Arsenio turned to one of the guards. "Remove our son from the nursery. Place him safely in the hands of a maiden who will attend to his comfort."

The guard immediately responded to the command and bowed deferentially to Polyxena before removing the screaming child from her arms. She understood that they could not be certain the danger had passed, and so she reluctantly accepted separation from her son.

A creeping sense of evil plagued her. There was an ominous aura to the room that made her feel certain something dangerous was going on that she didn't quite understand. She felt like a prisoner in her own house, even if Lord Zanar and his men had been apprehended and disarmed. For prisoners, they seemed strangely in command of their emotions.

Arsenio was even more mystified by the ease with which his home had been disrupted. Rage flooded him over his wife's distress. Somehow, he had let them down and failed to keep them safe within the walls of the palace. He felt deeply frustrated and determined to find out why Lord Zanar and his men had come. He ordered his guards to place the prisoners in the palace dungeons and prepare them for interrogation.

The guards began to remove the prisoners from the nursery, while Lord Zanar began to struggle vigorously against their grip, calling out, "Please my lord! I beg you to give me a moment before you take me to my cell. I have something of great importance to tell the Duchess!"

"Whatever you have to say can wait until morning," responded Arsenio with a dismissive motion of his hand. He repeated the order to take all the prisoners away.

"I must speak now!" insisted lord Zanar. "It's a matter of life and death!" He then turned anxiously toward Polyxena, continuing his plea with urgency, "What I have to say, my lady, is of vital importance. I must speak now!"

"Very well. Speak openly. We are all listening," Polyxena replied, slightly alarmed but also intrigued by the request.

Lord Zanar noticed her receptiveness and regained some of his bravado. "My hands must be free before I speak, my lady," he dared to say. "Please order the guards to release me…"

Arsenio scoffed. "You will be speaking with your mouth and not your hands. Besides, you are not in a bargaining position. If you have anything of value to offer, you had better say it now, without delay. This will be your only chance."

"My hands must be free before I speak," Lord Zanar insisted. "Besides, you have nothing to fear. I am unarmed and surrounded by soldiers, with no possible way out!"

Zanar turned once again toward Polyxena, continuing his desperate plea, "It is truly a matter of life and death, my lady. Time is of the essence. I must speak now or it will be too late!"

"My lord," said Polyxena, visibly alarmed by the urgency of Zanar's words. "Perhaps it would be wise to listen to what he has to say...I believe we can safely release him, since he is unarmed and surrounded by soldiers."

Arsenio hesitated, concerned by the strange request. The prisoner appeared to possess some unexplained powers, considering the manner he used to invade the palace. Arsenio continued to be reluctant. However, he finally gave in to Polyxena's wishes, and ordered the guards to remove the restraints from the prisoner.

After regaining his freedom of movement, Lord Zanar reverted to his usual audacity and smiled while he made a show of rearranging his clothes. He then bowed with courtly manners and started to approach the Duchess with a confident stride.

Two palace guards grabbed him and held him back and compelled him to maintain a respectful distance. The guards released their hold, but flanked Zanar and stayed close.

"Very well," he finally said, "since I am forbidden to approach the Duchess, I will have to stretch my arm from this distance, in order to show her an item that I know will be of interest!"

Having garnered the attention he desired, Lord Zanar extended his right arm, as close as possible to the Duchess, flashing on his hand a splendid gold ring, prominently displayed on one of his fingers.

The magnificent jewel sparkled ominously in the torch light, while everyone in the room looked on.

"Do you recognize this ring, my lady?" he said with a triumphant and maleficent look. Polyxena stepped forward, and suddenly paled at the sight of the splendid gem.

"The Seal of Nemours! My father's ring. How did you get it?"

Lord Zanar remained silent for a few endless moments, savoring Polyxena's distress. Then, feigning sadness, at long last he responded.

"I have sad tidings for you my lady. The Duke of Nemours, your esteemed father, is not on his way home as you believe. He has been abducted by us, and is presently our prisoner."

Polyxena recoiled. "What have you done to my father? Is he hurt? Answer at once or you will pay with your life!"

"He is quite safe...At least for the moment," answered Zanar, disregarding the existing protocol and approaching the Duchess so that she could feel the warmth of his breath. She recoiled, and he continued in a softer voice.

"The safety of your father rests in your hands, my lady. Only you can save his life! At daybreak, if I don't safely exit from the castle in your company, the Duke of Nemours life will be forfeited!"

Polyxena was overwhelmed by dread and had difficulty catching her breath. Arsenio placed his arms around her and angrily responded, "You are a despicable man, and you must be mad if you think we will abide by your request...Your blackmail. I warn you! If any harm comes to the Duke of Nemours, you and your accomplices will forfeit your lives!"

Lord Zanar remained unmoved and responded in a curt, deliberate sound, "We are all prepared to die, if destiny wills it. However, I don't believe this is your decision to make, since your refusal to comply with our demands will condemn the Duchess's father to death, not your own!"

Polyxena was speechless. The terrifying choice seemed unreal. She was entrapped in a downward spiral by a destiny she was powerless to alter. The peaceful interlude she enjoyed since the birth of her son was now shattered. Her beloved father's life was in the balance, at the mercy of a mysterious enemy.

Arsenio took her aside to whisper, "You must be strong, Polyxena. There is nothing we can do to alter this tragic course. Our only solace is in the knowledge that the criminals who perpetrated such a despicable act will pay with their lives!"

"I cannot let my father die!"

"At this moment, we have no power to save him," said Arsenio with concern. "It is imperative that we don't give in to their demand. Not only your life, but also your honor would be in danger at the hands of these criminals. Please, you must remember that you are the Duchess of Lorengard-Lorraine…a position that holds great obligations. Your son and I love you and need you…you cannot follow a destructive path and forego your responsibilities."

Polyxena listened closely but did not look convinced.

"Your father would be the first to dissuade you from taking such a drastic step in order to save his life," Arsenio pleaded.

"But the choice remains mine...Please understand, Arsenio, I will not have another peaceful day in my life if I don't attempt to save my father's life."

"We don't even know if he is still alive," Arsenio exclaimed, simmering with fear and frustration in the face of Polyxena's determination. "He could have been victim of an ambush perpetrated by these intruders. Perhaps they killed him and took possession of the ring in order to blackmail you..."

"I refuse to believe my father is dead!" Polyxena answered with resolve. "These people appear to be fanatics who place little value to their lives, or else they follow some evil cult! They planned this act by kidnapping my father, in order to get to me. I don't know the reason why, but we have seen the lengths they will go to. I truly believe they will kill him if I fail to comply."

"Stop, Polyxena! Don't you understand the danger you face if you follow them? More than death awaits you in the ruthless hands of these dishonorable people!"

Polyxena remained unresponsive to Arsenio's fears. The young Duke was deeply distressed in the face of such reckless determination, and was compelled to take a drastic step in order to protect her life.

"I will not allow you go Polyxena. Your judgment is impaired by your sorrow, and because of it you are unable to make a rational decision. There are no guarantees that the Duke of Nemours will be saved by your sacrifice. We are dealing with dishonorable people, unworthy of trust!"

Arsenio was determined. The shocking demands from Lord Zanar had only strengthened his resolve. He suddenly turned to his head guard imparting a stern command, "The Duchess will not be allowed to leave the palace under any circumstances. She will be confined in the comfort of her rooms until further notice. This is my direct order to be implemented at once!"

He then moved closer to Polyxena, who stared at him in shocked disbelief. "Forgive me if you can," he whispered. "You are my wife and it's my duty to protect you against harm. I will make the decision in your place, and take upon myself the consequences for this action. If my command will result in the tragic death of your father, then let his blood fall upon my head, instead of yours!"

Polyxena was unable to reconcile with Arsenio's rationale. Her father's life lay in the balance, and saving his life at any cost was her primary concern. She moved away from Arsenio's arms and attempted to run out of the room, but Arsenio grabbed her arm to stop her.

All eyes in the room were focus on the royal couple. Their public discord was shocking, and no one present had ever witnessed such an open display of raw emotions, It was a shocking breach of etiquette in the repressed and honor-bound era of chivalry.

Taking advantage of the disruption in the room and the temporary distraction of the guards, Lord Zanar approached Arsenio and, with a flick of his wrist, tossed a silvery powder into the Duke's face.

Arsenio's vision instantly blurred. A paralyzing feeling overwhelmed his body. He stood motionless for a few seconds, then fell unconscious to the floor.

Lord Zanar was immediately seized by the palace guards and shackled as before, while Polyxena rushed to her husband's side. She placed her arms helplessly around him, looking on his face with great concern.

The court physician was immediately called to Arsenio's side, but upon examination he declared that the Duke appeared unharmed, but under some form of mysteriously caused trance or sleep. Apparently, he was one more victim of Zanar's mysterious potions.

The attack upon the Duke shed light on how the intruders were able to enter the castle with such ease. Polyxena's distress was eased by the sight of the nursery's attendants regaining consciousness and apparently unharmed by the spells.

The head guard moved aggressively to take control of the situation. He prepared to remove the prisoners from the nursery and place them in the castle's dungeons, awaiting interrogation and punishment for their crimes.

However, Polyxena, after been assured that Arsenio was not in any immediate danger, stopped the attending guards from following her husband's order. She was suddenly aware of being the person in charge while the Duke lay unconscious and unable to take control.

She addressed the head guard in a firm tone. "Guard! Position our best marksmen on the battlement of the castle, at once. They must be prepared for action and armed with longbows!"

A puzzled look flashed across the man's face. The command was to prepare a defense with the most powerful and deadly weapons they possessed. Longbows were capable of piercing armor from a great distance. The gravity of the situation loomed.

Polyxena continued, "At daybreak, the castle's doors will open and allow free passage to Lord Zanar and myself on horseback. Make certain that no harm comes to him, so long as he remains by my side! We will advance to the center of the plaza and remain in full view of the marksman positioned on the battlement of the castle. We will stop at the center of the square and wait for my father's release."

Polyxena took a deep breath. Her turmoil rose into rage at Lord Zanar's triumphant look.

"However," she continued, "only when my father is safely within the walls of the castle will the exchange take place. And then you will allow Lord Zanar to leave the confinement of the plaza, without being followed, undisturbed, and in my company!"

Polyxena stared hard at Lord Zanar. "He will have men waiting, no doubt, and you will also let them go with us. On the other hand, if any harm comes to my father before he reaches safety, or if anysigns of treachery are present, you will order the marksmen to shoot their arrows." She paused to let the gravity of her words sink in, and then added, "You are to aim to kill as fast as possible, with no regard for my life!"

"No, my lady!" objected the head guard. "We are sworn to protect your life with our own! We could never take your life...It would go against our honor and the code of chivalry!"

Polyxena did not falter. "This is my direct order, my lord, and you are compelled to obey it! The marksmen will shoot to kill if any sign of treachery is present and any harm befalls my father. You must listen to me...there is no other way to guarantee that Lord Zanar will not be able to use me as a human shield in order to escape."

An uneasy silence pervaded the area. She understood their distress, and how difficult it was for loyal guards to comply with such a drastic order. Her heart was moved by their loyalty, and she continued in a softer tone.

"Please understand that my command is dictated by the situation at hand and not my volition. I am prepared to face the possibility of death if destiny wills it. I gladly pardon the man who will shoot the fatal arrow and he will not suffer blame or consequences for it. All of you standing here are witness to my direct order and will honor my wishes!"

The head guard had no recourse but to obey. He lowered his head in consent.

Lord Zanar was released as requested. The enigmatic intruder appeared more subdued after witnessing Polyxena's courage and resolve in the face of danger. The young woman's intelligence and daring openly impressed him. He was not only attracted to her beauty, but even more so to her valor in the face of death. Those qualities held great appeal for him. He addressed her with a tone of respect for the first time.

"No harm will come to your father, my lady. I make this solemn pledge upon my honor."

Polyxena scoffed, "There is no honor in a man who threatens and blackmails innocent people! I abide by your wishes to save my father's life, but only you and I will leave the castle. Your accomplices will remain here!"

"It will be useless to hold them in captivity, my lady." Insisted Zanar. "They are sworn to secrecy and are prepared to die for our cause."

"Good. They can die here. Their lives will be spared only upon my safe return! You and I shall leave the castle unescorted…or we will not leave at all."

Polyxena stood tall before Zanar. In that moment, he understood the impossibility of bending her iron will. At last he lowered his head in acceptance. "As you wish your grace. My men will remain here and you and I will leave the castle at dawn, in exchange for your father's life."

An impending sense of doom overwhelmed her. The only option was to bide for time while hoping to unravel the dangerous web surrounding her. Until she learned the identity of her enemy, the fatal die had been cast. There was no way back. Once again, her fundamental nature was about to be put to the test.

✝✝✝

CHAPTER THREE

LORENGARD-LORRAINE

The cruel light of dawn appeared too soon. Polyxena began the morning as befitted the Duchess of Lorengard-Lorraine, dispatching her final orders. That done, she felt bitter tears when she prepared to say goodbye to Arsenio, who still lay unconscious under the spell of Zanar's powerful drug.

She caressed his handsome face and kissed his lips, then whispered into his ear, "Forgive me, my husband, for all the pain I will cause you with my actions, and I thank you for the gift of your love. I am compelled to follow this path. I leave our precious son in your care…I love you with all my heart Arsenio, and may the good Lord protect you!"

She took a deep breath and then retired to the privacy of her rooms to change into riding clothes for her journey to an unknown destiny. Ready then, she returned to the nursery and signaled the palace guards to open the doors.

As Duchess, she was immediately given free passage and for one sobering moment she acknowledged the pitfalls of absolute power. No one in the castle could question her judgment, even if her command could result in her death. With all the dignity she could muster, she exited the nursery, followed by Zanar and the palace guards.

The long walk toward the stables was somber and gloomy and an aura of anxiety was visible in the faces of all the people present. There was a feeling of doom as if the young Duchess was being escorted to her own funeral.

At the stable, two splendid stallions brimming with vitality awaited Polyxena and her abductor. Without delay, she mounted her horse and moved toward the exit of the castle, along with Lord Zanar.

They were given free passage out of the castle and entered the great plaza alone, while the escorting guards remained behind.

The Great plaza of Lorengard-Lorraine faced the imposing palace, and the gothic arches of the residence reflected its splendor in the crystal waters of a fountain that crowned the space.

The area was always busy around the clock, populated by honor guards and soldiers who swarmed the place with their colorful and imposing presence. However, on this morning the area was deserted by the Duchess's order. There was only stillness.

Dawn was already breaking, imbuing the sky with color while Polyxena guided Lord Zanar toward the middle point of the plaza. She reined her horse to a stop when she reached the spot where the exchange was to take place, then took a quick look to be certain they were positioned in clear sight of the marksmen. The battlements of the castle bristled with longbow archers.

Polyxena's anxiety was causing her fingers to tremble. In spite of her bravery, the ordeal was taking a heavy toll. It felt as if she had made a fatal mistake and thrust herself in a conflict she could not win.

They stood mounted in place, waiting for the release of the prisoner. Lord Zanar remained aloof, said nothing, and avoided eye contact. In this manner, the moments began to crawl past.

Time elapsed without no sign of the Duke of Nemours. The rising sun reflected ominously on the armor of the archers while they aimed their powerful longbows down upon them.

Polyxena felt herself beginning to panic, but made every effort to show no fear. Her hands became as cold as ice. Her breath felt sharp in her chest. If this was to be a trap, she would fight until she died, if only she could steady her hands and stand her ground.

Doubts plagued her. Could her father be already dead, as suggested by Arsenio? Did she place her life in jeopardy to no purpose? Was this another scheme concocted by some ghoulish entity bent on seizing the power of her throne?

Mercifully, muffled sounds rose out of the far background and grew louder near the far end of the plaza. In moments, three men appeared on horseback in the rising dawn. They rode slowly in her direction until Polyxena recognized her father. She nearly screamed with relief.

The Duke of Nemours, riding blindfolded, carried himself proud and defiant even though his hands were tied behind his back. Two armed men flanked him while his mount was guided toward Polyxena and Zanar.

The Duke was still unaware of her presence, but a moment later one of his guards removed the blindfold. For a few seconds he remained disoriented while he focused his eyes. When he finally recognized his daughter, alone there in the company of Zanar, he immediately understood the full measure of her sacrifice. Polyxena was the hostage now. She was the price for his freedom.

"Polyxena!" he cried out, but in same instant his horse was spurred by one of his escorts. He was still bound and could not stop his horse from taking them toward the castle.

"Father!" her response reverberated in the vast plaza. She followed her father's image until he reached safety. Part of her could still feel the reactions of a terrified little girl facing a monster alone. But she kept herself strong by pretending a strength she didn't really feel. She stood dignified, befitting the Duchess of Lorengard-Lorraine.

She signaled the marksman to lower their weapons and give Lord Zanar free passage out of the ducal square, with her in company. Without delay, she spurred her horse and they left the boundary of the plaza. Outside the grounds, as expected, they were joined by an imposing escort of Zanar's armed soldiers.

From the castle battlements, she was seen entering the sprawling countryside with the soldiers until they were all engulfed by a cloud of dust churned by their horses. They soon disappeared from sight, leaving behind only a somber silence.

Polyxena's departure left no one in charge. The Dukedom was in a state of alarm, since Arsenio was still unconscious and their Duchess had been abducted.

The Duke of Nemours was the only one available to take command in this state of emergency. As a seasoned man of arms, he took immediate control and demanded to be escorted to the bedchamber of the stricken Arsenio, who still lay unresponsive. Soon, as if Arsenio was somehow aware of the older man's presence, the young Duke began to regain consciousness.

Alexander Duke of Nemours waited anxiously while the doctor examined Arsenio to determine that he was out of danger from the mysterious drug. Slowly the young Duke opened his eyes and looked around, still in a daze. But at the sight of his father-in-law leaning over him with concern, Arsenio was jolted into reality. He pushed his physician aside, rose and staggered out of bed, oblivious to the doctor's objections.

"Where is Polyxena?" Arsenio cried in a raspy voice. "Where is my wife?" His words reverberated on the stone walls.

The Duke was moved by Arsenio's concern for his daughter and tried to soothe the younger man with hopeful words. "Be brave, my son, we must not give in to despair. The situation is not hopeless. We will find Polyxena. I swear it upon my honor!"

Arsenio responded with a weak smile, and remained silent while the older man helped him into a nearby chair. "I tried to stop her, my lord! I tried to protect her, but she refused to listen. She was so unyielding, determined," his voice broke as he continued. "And now she is gone..."

Alexander felt powerless, but placed his hands on Arsenio's shoulders. "I know you tried your best, my son, and no one questions your devotion. I am also aware of my daughter's nature. She cannot be easily controlled. But it is also her generosity of spirit that garnered your respect and made her the woman you love."

Arsenio bowed his head in tacit consent. The Duke continued, "However, despite Polyxena's recklessness in

53

following Lord Zanar on this tragic journey, she has left us a tangible way to find and rescue her; we are in possession of a powerful weapon that gives us hope!"

Arsenio stirred at the hopeful sound of those words. "What is it, my lord? How can we rescue Polyxena? Please don't keep me in suspense!"

Alexander lowered his voice and answered, "Several conspirators and followers of Lord Zanar are prisoners within these walls. I am certain they have knowledge of Polyxena's whereabouts and hold the key to the mystery of her abduction!"

Arsenio's excitement deflated. He shook his head, finding little comfort in the Duke's words. "We are dealing with fanatics my lord! Closed-minded individuals who are prepared to die for their evil cult. They are incapable of reasoning. How do you propose to break their silence?"

"I really don't know, Arsenio. But they are our only available link, if we hope to find Polyxena alive. We mustn't be discouraged. I am certain there is a way to break their silence and with resolve, we will find it!"

"Guards!" he called out. Two heavily armed soldiers suddenly appeared. "Place the prisoners in separate cells at once! Isolate them from one another. Be certain they are not allowed to communicate with anyone, under any circumstances!"

The guards departed the room while the Duke turned toward Arsenio to explain his course of action. "Listen well, my son. I believe our best course of action rests in putting one man against the other. We will instill the seed of doubt in them and cause them to believe that one of them has weakened and betrayed their oath. The prisoners will be under constant surveillance. We will discern which one is their weakest link and use him to break their silence!"

A shadow of hope brightened Arsenio's face. "Yes my lord, that might work. Your determination gives me hope that one of the prisoners will show us the way to Polyxena."

JOURNEY INTO DARKNESS

After Polyxena's daring abduction from the castle, Zanar and his followers sped from the Dukedom and into the sprawling hills of the countryside. They distanced themselves from Lorengard-Lorraine at a gallop and disappeared into the landscape.

The Duchess had been blindfolded, which intensified her sense of helplessness. Entrapped and terrified, she was at the mercy of a ruthless man and his fanatical followers of a powerful and mysterious enemy.

Her only solace rested in the knowledge that her sacrifice had not been in vain, and her father was alive and well, safe within the palace walls of Lorengard-Lorraine. The journey toward the unknown was long and torturous. Hours elapsed in total darkness behind her blindfold. No one spoke to her and the only sounds were the pounding of the horse's hooves and the cool wind howling around her.

Finally the arduous journey came to a sudden halt. She heard the sound of excited voices approaching in the distance, and their resonance became clearer while neared. She felt herself pulled down from her horse, and at long last the blindfold was removed from her face.

Slowly, as her eyesight became accustomed to the light, she saw a multitude of exotic looking men staring at her with wonder and curiosity. They communicated in a language unknown to her, and wore flowing, black robes cinched at the waist by crimson sashes.

They were in a sprawling compound, heavily guarded, with armed men everywhere. The whole place was nearly invisible to the outside world, surrounded by trees and heavy vegetation.

Polyxena was escorted toward a large tent in the center of the compound, then pushed through the entry flaps with no deference to her station.

At first glance, the interior of the pavilion appeared welcoming. The area was spacious and imbued in a soft, golden glow from brass chandeliers that dangled from the tent's frame. Luxurious Persian carpets covered the floor, and colorful pillows were scattered throughout. Small mahogany tables stood laden with fresh fruits, sweetmeats, and other exotic delicacies. The alluring aroma of myrrh permeated the air.

But the casual opulence of her host's environment only increased her sense of apprehension. One person's pleasure dome was another's gilded prison.

Lord Zanar followed the reticent girl into the tent and addressed her in his usual style, affecting an elegant manner tinged with sarcasm. "I hope you will be comfortable, you're Grace! I am aware the humble surroundings lack the luxuries a Duchess is accustomed to, but they will serve our purpose as a temporary shelter until we reach our final destination."

Polyxena noticed the wanton look in his eyes and remembered her husband's dire warning, that it was not merely her life, but also her honor was in danger at the hands of the abductors.

Lord Zanar smiled at her wariness. This young woman held a special lure over him. He was intensely attracted to her great beauty, and fascinated by her courage and her self-assurance. This lovely duchess was superior to any women he had ever known. He felt himself drawn to her irresistible sexual appeal.

Somehow, Lord Zanar found himself in the oddly intimidating position of wishing to find favor with this self-possessed woman. He clapped his hands and summoned the attendance of several women. At first glance the women's attire appeared strange to Polyxena; they were shrouded in black, with a dark veil that obscured their faces. Only their eyes showed.

The women bowed to Zanar, then surrounded Polyxena, moving like a flock of shadows. She was unaccustomed to women whose features were concealed, nevertheless, their presence felt reassuring. Anything was better than being left alone with Lord Zanar.

Zanar moved closer, speaking with a reassuring sound. "You have nothing to fear my lady, you are quite safe here. These women will assist and fulfill your every need. Their sole purpose is to make you comfortable and satisfy your desires."

The condescending words amplified her feelings of entrapment. They were becoming unbearable. She forced herself to glare at Zanar and answer him with defiance. "There is nothing here that I desire. I only wish to return to my husband and our child, and all the people we love."

Zanar stood for a moment, deciding, then threw a quick motion of command to the women. He bowed to Polyxena with more of his mock deference, then turned and left the tent.

The shrouded handmaidens moved away from Polyxena, to the far end of the tent. There they pulled back a silken drape to unveil an elegant, circular tub filled with soapy, scented water. The aroma washed over her with an inviting and seductive fragrance.

And still, instead of reassurance, this only increased the sense of being caught in a spider's web. Everything about this environment reinforced the message that this was a place and society dominated by men. Women toiled invisibly, shrouded by their clothes.

The handmaidens dropped the pretense of gentility, ignored her reticence, and forcefully removed the dusty travel clothes from her body. Polyxena was easily overpowered by their number and relented.

More strangeness: in spite of their aggressive conduct, the maidens showed deference to her modesty by shielding her nakedness with a silken wrap. They helped her into the warm and scented water of the tub.

Her trepidation dissipated in moments. She could not ignore the deep relief in the comfort of the liquid embrace. Her muscles were tense with stress and with the rigors of the arduous travel on horseback.

She gave in to the unexpected comfort of the bath and closed her eyes, breathing in the perfumed air. A numbing, sensual feeling began to flow throughout her being. Something in the exotic environment was working on her brain. It triggered a hypnotic state, and Polyxena's mind wondered in places far removed from somber reality.

She felt at peace while strange, visual images appeared before her eyes. Striking, multicolored lights opened her imagination to an alien world, and she was drawn in.

At some point, she felt herself helped out of the pool by the handmaidens, and while still in a half-stupor she felt a warm woolen towel being wrapped around her. Hands pushed her onto a nearby divan and massaged her body with perfumed oil. The women's experienced hands enhanced her relaxed state.

This done, Polyxena was helped to her feet and a bejeweled gown was draped on her body. It was made of a delicate and translucent fabric that did little to shield the perfection of her form. Finally, the women held before her a large, highly polished metal sheet that allowed Polyxena to view herself in this unfamiliar attire.

The sensual apparel, so obviously intended to arouse a man's desire, was a stark contrast to the fully covered bodies of the women attending her. She again felt the threat of the intoxicating surroundings.

She sensed the sexual aura put out by that satiny gown and its golden threads. Polyxena was as vulnerable as a child in this place where the mysterious maidens walked about the tent like gloomy shadows, silent and unable to protect her. Useless. They were as vulnerable as she was.

Polyxena again took refuge in her royal upbringing, which forbade outbursts or visual distress. She pulled herself to her full height and with a sharp gesture of the hand ordered the women to leave her presence. They bowed with deference and left the tent.

Finally alone, Polyxena paced the tent like a caged lioness, seeking answers that did not come. She was exhausted from the journey and emotionally drained. She needed sleep, but the risk in this place was too high. She concentrated on trying to stay awake and take some control over the dire situation. But it was soon apparent that she was far too tired to keep her eyes open. It was a pointless struggle. Finally, she relented to her need to sleep.

She piled several large pillows as a makeshift bed, and used a large woolen towel for a blanket. As soon as she lay down, she was overcome by exhaustion and fell fast asleep.

It felt as if her slumber lasted for about three seconds.

Polyxena was awakened by the strange sensation of someone's presence in the tent. She sat up, startled. The woolen towel fell to the carpet, revealing the splendor of Polyxena's body in the audacious gown, leaving her vulnerable in the inappropriate attire and facing an unwelcomed visitor. The mysterious Lord Zanar stared at her with eyes beset with desire.

"You are so beautiful my lady! So pleasing," he whispered while he dragged his bold stare across the curves of her body.

Polyxena retreated and reclaimed the woolen wrap from the carpet. She glanced around, checking for any route of escape, and realized there was none.

Lord Zanar only smiled. "You have no reason to fear, milady. You are quite safe here. I humbly regret having disturbed your sleep tonight. Why, I only wanted to make certain you were properly cared for and comfortable in your rest."

"Comfortable?" Polyxena parroted. "You are suggesting that there is comfort in a prison?" Her disdain colored her cheeks bright red.

"Calm yourself, my lady, your resentment is excessive. After all, you joined us of your own volition, disregarding your husband's request to remain in Lorengard-Lorraine!"

Polyxena was filled with rage. "You are a despicable, contemptible man who lacks honor! You kidnapped and threatened to kill my father, to make certain I would follow you on this tragic journey. You must have known that I would never allow you to take his life!"

Zanar was clearly amused by her helplessness and despair. "You are a foolish woman and your father is an old man who has lived his life, and because of his stubborn disregard of consequences, you are now our captive. You have foolishly sacrificed yourself for an unworthy person who cares more about his false honor than his own daughter!"

Polyxena glared at Zanar with contempt. "You have no understanding of honor or love. I am fortunate to be the daughter of such a chivalrous man; my regrettable circumstances are the result of your treachery alone! Besides, what vital information's did he refuse to give, that you now will demand of me?"

"You will be informed of that when I deem the circumstances to be right, and not before!"

Zanar drew closer to her as he spoke and she could feel the warmth of his breath and the aggressiveness of his muscular body against hers. She could feel how deeply he rejoiced in her helplessness and despair.

THE CRIMSON AMULET

She recoiled, but it was a futile effort. Zanar grabbed her wrists, pulled her toward him, and encircled her waist with the strength of his masculine arms. He felt the warmth of her sensual, seductive body, tantalizingly close to him. He felt the wild beating of her heart. His fingers trembled with uncontrolled passion, and he hungrily caressed her.

Beset with desire, he snatched away the obstruction of the woolen wrap and exposed her physical perfection. "There is no turning back, Polyxena," he murmured while passionately kissed her neck. "You belong to us and to the power of the Crimson Amulet. The decision to follow us was made of your own free will."

"Never! And you will never own me," she answered in defiance. But Zanar's strong, virile arms held her body in a such a powerful embrace that she was unable to get away.

Her revulsion only increased his excitement. He pressed his lips to her mouth and hungrily kissed her with such force that it took her breath away. She struggled to repel the violent sexual attack with all her might, and managed to free herself from his arms. But when she tried to run from the tent Zanar grabbed her again and held her with overwhelming strength. He slapped her face with such force that the blow propelled the girl to the floor.

"Coward!" she cried out. "You take advantage of a defenseless woman!" Polyxena glared with contempt, wiping her lips with the back of her hand to erase the distaste of his mouth.

Zanar was stunned and enraged, but at the same time he was fascinated by her daring. A woman of such independence and fighting spirit was a complete novelty to him, and every time she let her spirit flash he found it challenging and strangely attractive. He had always considered women inferior to men, subservient and to be used as sexual objects. Polyxena was different in so many ways. Her unique qualities enhanced his attraction and longing for her. His male ego was also deeply wounded by her rejection and he spoke to her with simmering anger.

"You are a captive, milady, there is no way out for you, and is useless to fight the inevitability of the situation. Sooner or later you <u>will</u> succumb to my pleasure. That is the only reality you possess, now!"

Polyxena turned away from him, trying to escape the somber reality and not give in to despair. However, Zanar surprised her by giving the appearance of being moved by her distress. His voice became softer while he helped her from the floor. He gently caressed her hair. "Perhaps if you stop this useless fighting and accept the inevitability of fate, you will be more at peace. You might even enjoy this interlude in your life if you bend your stubborn will. Why not accept your destiny?"

Zanar's face was very close as he spoke, and the allure of his dark, penetrating eyes was strong. He was confident in the power of his masculine appeal. Women had been always been available for his pleasure, and sometimes even grateful for his attention.

However, Polyxena's unique qualities gave her a special allure. He was not going to be satisfied to merely possess her body. There was no pleasure in the thought of forcing her to submit. Zanar wanted her to be receptive, most of all, while he held her in his arms.

He ran his lips along her neck and murmured, "Are you impervious to temptation, milady? Don't you long for the ecstasy of love? Or, do you fear the loss of honor if you give in to passion?"

Polyxena pushed him away with contempt."In such a case," she answered defiantly,"The loss of honor will not be mine."

Zanar was rattled now, and frustrated. His pride was deeply wounded and he felt diminished as a man to be unable to have her unless she was taken by force.

He drew her close to try again. "You belong to the Crimson Amulet, milady! Your defiance is useless. No one escapes its power!" He grabbed his shirt and tore away the front, unveiling his chest and the dreaded ivory skull hung around his neck. The rubies in the eye sockets sparkled in the candlelight with an ominous glare.

Polyxena recoiled from the symbol of death. "Why do you do this?" she cried. "You have taken me away from my family, my people, everything I love, what have I done to merit this?"

"The answer is obvious! You are the daughter of Templars, you are the scion of evildoers who ravaged my people and my land. And even so, I am not here to enact revenge. My quest is to bring you to the justice of the Crimson Amulet."

"Justice? You claim to follow orders from a mysterious enemy, but you are the only enemy I see! You used vile trickery to invade the sanctity of my home in the name of this evil cult and this idol that you worship!"

"I worship only Allah! However, I also respect and follow the justice of the Crimson Amulet, a most potent force. Therefore I am loyal to it. You, as a daughter of Templars, should know something about the meaning of honor!"

Polyxena realized she would be unable to puncture the barrier of Zanar's fanatical beliefs. She had no recourse but to continue to search for ways to control him. She tried a more deferential approach.

"Lord Zanar, if you are a man of honor, I beseech you to give me the gift of freedom. I beg of you in the name of the God you worship, be merciful, and you will be rewarded for your kindness. Please allow me to return to my home and the people I love!"

Lord Zanar listened to her pleas, unmoved. He caressed her flowing hair and replied, "This is your world now, Polyxena, right here. The people you love are no longer part of your life. You will never see them again! We are the only available reality, and you are powerless to alter the course of your life."

His voice became somber while he continued. "Think about it my lady, as I bid you goodbye. For when I return it will be in your best interest to be better predisposed to passion. Or be prepared for the consequences!"

With those words, Lord Zanar bowed curtly and left the tent to disappear in the surrounding darkness.

†††

CHAPTER FOUR

LORENGARD-LORRAINE
TURMOIL IN THE CASTLE

The Dukedom of Lorengard-Lorraine was thrown into turmoil at the news of their Duchess's abduction. Rumors flashed across the landscape and sorrow reigned, since the people had learned to love Polyxena for her kindness and generosity.

Arsenio and Alexander explored every means of finding her. All the intruders who had invaded his son's nursery were now in custody and under constant surveillance. Each man was kept in a separate cell, as requested by the temporary authority given to Alexander Duke of Nemours. After undergoing difficult interrogations, they remained unresponsive, almost listless, shrouded in a wall of silence. They spent most of their time crouched on their knees in prayer.

At the end of one more frustrating and unproductive day, Arsenio and his father-in law gathered for another meeting to explore new ideas and keep abreast of the situation.

"There is nothing new to report, my lord," said Arsenio with frustration. "After days of interrogations, not a clue from any of those men. They seem impervious to threats and unresponsive to pain, almost as if they were already dead!"

"Yes, we are dealing with unusual people, and they are fanatically dedicated to their cause." A look of determination flashed on his face. "But we are not giving up," he said angrily, "there must be a way to break the will of at least one of them!"

Arsenio shook his head. "There is something I don't understand, my lord: the reason why you and Polyxena were abducted. No money request has been made. Do you have any idea why this is being done?"

Alexander hesitated, then simply answered, "I have no idea, Arsenio, it's a mystery to me as well."

Arsenio was not satisfied. "What questions did they ask while you were held? They must have said something that could shed light on this."

Alexander appeared to become uneasy at this, enhancing Arsenio's concerns. "My lord, have I been kept in the dark about secrets concerning my wife? Is there something I don't know about this situation that has placed her life in peril? I believe I have a right to know, and it would give me some solace to understand the reason for this abduction!"

Alexander shook his head. "Be at peace, no secret has been kept from you, and whoever this enemy might be remains a mystery to me as well. However, I believe that somehow we will discover the answers to our questions in order to find Polyxena, and finally bring her home."

Arsenio was now embarrassed by his probing questions, which he deemed inappropriate and disrespectful. The Duke had proven himself to be noble and courageous.

"Forgive me, my lord," he said. "It is only my sorrow speaking. I do not wish to burden you at this difficult time."

The older man patted Arsenio's shoulders with fatherly affection. "I take no umbrage to the questions; you have the concerns of a loving husband. However, I promise if I learn of anything that might help Polyxena, you will know right away."

Arsenio finally donned his sword and said, "It may be futile, but I'm going down to the dungeons and once more to question the prisoners! I must do something to help her or I will go mad!"

Alexander followed Arsenio on the long walk to the dungeons. The trip was somber. Arsenio especially hated the dungeon; it was too close to the conditions of his own dismal days as a chained prisoner.

At the end of the long descent into the depths of the castle, they entered the area where the detainees were located. The cold stones were slick with the humidity that permeated the air, and coated with a foul sludge.

The royal pair was welcomed with deference by the attending guards and guided to the area where the prisoners were detained. The men occupied individual cells and were under constant surveillance to prevent suicide or any form of self-harm. As the only viable links to Polyxena, their safety was paramount to learning the identity of her abductor and returning her alive.

Great efforts were implemented in performing the individual interrogations, searching for that elusive weak link who would guide them to Polyxena. Unfortunately, the ploy had been a dismal failure so far.

Alexander called out to them, loud enough for his voice to echo on the stone walls. "Once again! We urge all of you to be reasonable and prevent dire consequences!"

He lowered his voice to a tone as cold as a blade. "This is your last chance to avoid trial by fire. Tell us who sent you here, and where to find my daughter?"

He had never seen anything like it. One of the prisoners glanced up at him for a moment, then turned away. The rest seemed unconcerned. They were completely detached.

Arsenio's frustration hit the breaking point. Grasping at straws, he ordered the guards to open the cell and give him access to the only prisoner who made any reaction to Alexander's threats.

He entered the cell, and looked down at the man. "What is your name?"

The prisoner lifted his eyes just long enough to reply, "Kusen el Assad." He appeared to be in his early thirties, slightly built. He remained defiant while Arsenio moved closer.

"Where have they taken my wife? Where is the Duchess of Lorengard-Lorraine? I order you to answer!"

He got only silence. The man turned his face away and stared at the back wall. The display of insolence robbed Arsenio of his remaining self-control. He grabbed Kusen and forced him to stand, and pulled so hard on Kusen's shirt that he ripped away the fabric.

And that's when he saw it, hanging around the prisoner's neck. The ivory skull of the Crimson Amulet.

"That symbol!" Arsenio exclaimed. "Misery and pain have touched everyone in this house since it appeared! I demand you answer me: where is my wife? Tell me or I will kill you with my bare hands!"

Arsenio proved it by seizing Kusen by the throat and choking him. "Tell me if you want to breathe!" Kusen was helpless against the power of Arsenio's rage and soon began to succumb and go limp.

Alexander rushed into the cell to restrain Arsenio, knowing full well that he was the only one there who dared to intervene against the young Duke. He threw his arms around Arsenio's shoulders, as if it was Arsenio he wanted to protect, not Kusen.

For Arsenio, the abrupt appearance of masculine energy that was protecting him, instead of opposing him, was enough to make him pause. He valued the older man's wisdom in a time of stress or danger and lessened the hold on the prisoner.

"Please my son!" he whispered into Arsenio's ear, so that not even Kusen could hear it.

"We must control our temper. Giving in to anger will not help our cause. These men will be punished for their crimes. We will make each one pay until it is no longer worth it to him to protect the information. But it will be done by men who can do such work as they would take apart a pig. He will not have the satisfaction of tormenting you."

Arsenio heard the truth of that and felt it in his chest while his heartbeat eased. "Thank you. Thank you, my lord. I fear that I could kill them all as easily as breathing."

Arsenio lowered his head. The Duke of Nemours placed a hand on his shoulder, sharing his sadness in that dismal cell.

Arsenio leaned toward the prisoner and ripped the Amulet from Kusen's neck. He screamed in defiance, but the young Duke pushed him to the side and walked out of the cell with Alexander.

They were both surprised by the unexpected emotional reaction from the Kusen over losing his amulet, and it gave them a hope of having some bargaining power over the prisoners.

Could the mysterious ivory skull be the key to the enigma of Polyxena's abduction? Alexander gently took the amulet from Arsenio's hand and turned back to approach Kusen once more. Terror flashed in Kusen's eyes as he stared at the ivory skull dangling from the Duke's hand. He stood still as if paralyzed with fear.

Alexander had already seen enough to know that he somehow held the upper hand in this moment. "Kusen! Do you want the Amulet?"

"Yes! Yes, my Lord! And may you be rewarded for your mercy!"

"You speak of mercy? Alexander snapped. "Where is your mercy for my daughter and her child?"

Kusen lowered his head.

"You show me mercy first! Tell me where they have taken her. Only then I will return the Crimson Amulet to you."

Kusen quickly shook his head. "I cannot answer! I do not know where they have taken the Duchess! We only obeyed orders and were never told."

"Very well, so be it. You have sealed your own fate. You and your cohorts will pay for your crimes in the most horrible way. Tomorrow at dawn, you will be placed upon the rack and learn of its nightmares. You will tell us where to find the Duchess or you will die in agony. All of you!"

Without another word, the Alexander left the cell with Arsenio for the second time. They kept on walking even after Kusen began to scream in wordless dread.

At dawn the next morning, Arsenio and Alexander met in the center hall of the palace and prepared to make their way back down to the dungeons, where the prisoners were being readied for their ordeal.

Such cruel procedures had been discontinued in Lorengard-Lorraine under the regime of Arsenio's father, Duke Edwards. For today the rack had to be hastily restored and readied for use.

Both Arsenio and Alexander feared a dire outcome, since they were dealing with fanatics who were avowed ready to die. Therefore they agreed that the only strategy available was to refuse to grant them the death they so desired by stopping short of lethal means. The art of the mission would be in making every moment of life too horrible to bear, without permitting them any release from unconsciousness or death. The prisoners, awake and alert, had to be able to appreciate what was being done to them and what would continue to be done to them until they could no longer endure.

Polyxena was the most important woman in the world for both of these powerful Dukes, and her life was riding on the outcome of today's cruel acts. So it would be, then.

"Have faith, Arsenio. We must be strong and believe we will be successful in breaking down the defenses of at least one of the prisoners. When we do, he will show us the way."

"I pray that you are right."

The two started toward the dungeons, but they were immediately stopped when the head guard rushed in. He gave a quick bow of deference to the royal pair and spoke in a voice tinged with panic.

"Your Grace! Please! Forgive the interruption! But Sire… Sire…The prisoners…The prisoners are dead, my lord."

"Dead?" Arsenio parroted in shock.

"We tried to awaken them this morning! Just as you said! But they were all dead."

Arsenio and Alexander both struggled to grasp what they were being told. Arsenio spoke first. "The prisoners were in individual cells, under constant scrutiny, on my orders. How can they all be dead? Speak! Tell me why you should not pay for your lack of supervision!"

Now Alexander found that the stress of this ordeal had finally broken his resolve. He sat down hard in a nearby chair and held his head between his hands.

"Heavenly father protect my daughter, Polyxena. Keep her safe. Please show us the way to find her."

Arsenio turned to the head guard. "How is this possible?"

The Head Guard answered, "My lord, none of us have any idea how the prisoners died. They were all under constant surveillance according to your orders, with no means to harm themselves. They went to sleep in the usual way. No one made any sounds during the night. This morning, they simply did not awaken and appeared to be dead. I knew that I had to come and tell you right away."

"Appeared to be dead?" A glimmer of hope sparked in Arsenio's eyes. "Then you are not certain? What if this is some diabolical trick? We witnessed the unexplained manner in which they entered the castle."

"Perhaps you are right, my lord," answered the guard, "but to be certain we summoned the court physician and he is currently examining the bodies."

"Well done," answered Arsenio. "Have the physician report to me at once."

"It will be done my lord!" The Head Guard bowed and hastily backed out of the room.

Arsenio and the Duke of Nemours were stunned by the news, unable to speak while they waited for the arrival of the court physician. Both men were alone with their racing thoughts. In just a few days, the lives of so many people had been drastically affected by the ominous appearance of Lord Zanar his men, and by the strange wickedness surrounding the Crimson Amulet. The sense of order and control in their lives had somehow been stolen.

Finally, the court physician appeared in the doorway, a man in his fifties with patrician features and an innate elegance to his stride. He stepped in and bowed to Duke Arsenio with flair. His manner was so dignified that it was impossible to guess if he had good news or bad.

Arsenio addressed him with urgency. "What news, physician? Are the prisoners truly dead?"

"Yes, your grace. All but one of them."

Arsenio unceremoniously grabbed the physician's hands. "Is he conscious, or, or, injured in any way?"

"No, my lord. He is not." The physician cleared his voice before continuing. "He was truly sleeping when they discovered the death of the other prisoners. The guards panicked and assumed they were all dead. He is the only one who was merely fast asleep!"

Arsenio felt the ray of hope grow stronger. He turned toward Alexander and noticed tears brimming in the elder gentleman's eyes and said. "The good Lord has not abandoned us. This is the miracle we were praying for! But We must be extremely careful in guarding the surviving prisoner. He is now the only person who can help us. His life must be protected at all cost."

Arsenio signaled to an attending guard to come forward. "Have the surviving prisoner physically restrained, with arms and legs securely fastened. Two armed guards will flank him in his cell at all times, and failure to implement my orders will be met with dire consequences."

Visibly intimidated, the guard quickly left the great hall.

Arsenio once more addressed the court physician. "My lord, are you certain the other prisoners are truly dead? I still have doubts, since these people possess strange and unknown powers. Perhaps they can simulate death."

"No, my lord." answered the physician with determination. "They are all truly dead. Their bodies have already begun to stiffen. They show no signs of injury, other than strange red markings on their tongues. It is not blood, but some kind of staining. It may have been caused by some form of poison unknown to us."

The court physician shook his head and continued, "I am truly mystified. We were certain that no poison was in their possession."

Alexander frowned. "I fail to understand how the prisoners committed mass suicide without the presence of poison. And why would only one survive? We must unveil this mystery!"

"I don't know if this will be helpful," answered the physician, "but I am told that the lone survivor is the prisoner you visited last night."

"Kusen!" exclaimed Arsenio.

"There must to be a connection," said Alexander.

Arsenio shook his head in frustration. "I have no idea how our presence could be connected with Kusen's survival. I remember the sound of his voice echoing as we walked away."

Alexander looked up with a flash in his eyes. "The amulet! Remember when you removed it from Kusen's neck?"

Arsenio swiftly walked toward a sculpted desk resting against a wall. He opened one of the drawers and removed a small jewel box containing the fatal object, still dangling from its broken chain.

He carefully deposited the talisman upon a silver tray and with care manipulated the ivory skull with the point of a knife, inspecting it thoroughly from all angles. The object appeared solid to the touch, with no secret openings or cavities that could conceal poison.

Arsenio and the Duke of Nemours were frustrated by the futility of their efforts, but continued to inspect the amulet. The rubies encased in the eye sockets sparkled in the torchlight, almost mocking him.

"There has to be a connection between this infernal object and the death of the prisoners." he exclaimed. "All those who died were wearing it around their necks. We should not have allowed them to keep them. Since we know that the only survivor wasn't wearing it, there has to be a connection!"

"I agree, my son," Alexander said. "However, you held the skull in your bare hands without consequences, if it is indeed poisonous and lethal, how did you survive?"

"True, but all the prisoners were wearing it around their necks, for an inordinate amount of time, without danger. The poison must be hidden somewhere within the skull, released in secret some way. I finally understand the reason why Kusen was so desperate when I removed it from his neck…he knew that if he survived, the specter of torture would be in his future.

Arsenio called out to an attending guard. "Go down to the dungeons accompanied by the court physician, remove the Amulet from one of the dead prisoners and be certain that you do not touch it with your bare hands. There might be hidden dangers in the ivory skull that could result in your death! Place the object in a suitable container and bring it to me as soon as possible."

The guard bowed deferentially and followed by the court physician he went out of the stately hall.

"I am certain there will be differences between Kusen's Amulet and the one that actually caused death."

"Good thinking, my son, I concur with you." Alexander patted him on the shoulders. "Your reasoning appears to be much clearer than mine under these difficult circumstances. And I am debating whether to burden you with information that has been kept from you."

Arsenio look at him with concern. "I feared there was something more, connected with Polyxena's abduction. Some mysterious reason that placed her in grave danger."

"I understand your frustration, and you were only left out of a matter of such importance for a vital purpose. I believe it is time for you to know. Before I disclose the information, you must understand the inherited danger in it."

"Whatever this secret might be, if it concerns Polyxena, I want to know in spite of any danger. Was she abducted because of it?"

Alexander sighed. "I am not certain, but there are things connected with her abduction that remain unclear to me, and they heighten my concerns about her safety. I will explain, but this knowledge will include you in a very dangerous situation that is connected to the honor and survival of the House of Nemours."

"I am honored my lord," answered Arsenio. "…and I will be worthy of your trust."

†††

CHAPTER FIVE

THE TEMPLAR'S TREASURE

"Arsenio," said Alexander. "I hereby introduce you to a distinguished ancestor of the House of Nemours. Over a hundred years ago, Wilfred the Valiant, Third Duke of Nemours, was a member of the Knights Templar. They are regarded by many as the greatest military order because of the role they played in liberating the Holy Land for Christianity. By others, they are despised as an invading force of infidels.

"The order was dissolved by King Philip IV of France, who was motivated by greed. Under his command, all known Templars were arrested on October 13, 1307, tortured, forced to give false confessions, and then burned at the stake. It was all done by the King for the purpose of confiscating their property.

"Wilfred the Valiant and a few of the other knights had suspected the King's treachery. They abandoned extensive properties in order to flee and protect the future of the order, hoping to enact revenge one day."

The Duke of Nemours cleared his throat. "I am also of the Order of the Knights Templar, and like them, I have sworn a holy oath to protect the Order. Despite the King's treachery, we have managed to survive. And that leads us to the secret.

"Destiny has placed upon the House of Nemours the awesome responsibility of guarding their legacy. It grants us power, but carries great danger. My trusted and loyal friend, the Count of Rozenberk, is also a Knight Templar and has knowledge of the secret. Recently Polyxena was included as well, just before her departure from Nemours.

"I have no doubt of your chivalry, Arsenio and I trust you with my life. However, since Polyxena is in grave danger with no certainty of safe return, it has become incumbent upon my honor to share this knowledge with you, in order to protect the legacy of the Knights Templar.

"A fabulous treasure was accumulated by the Templars as war plunder from the violent deaths of many innocent people. The greed of those Knights brought dishonor to the entire Order. The shame still remains."

"Then why was the treasure hidden in the castle of Nemours?"

"Wilfred the Valiant despised the dishonor brought to the order by those evil and misguided Templars. This great treasure is forever stained with the blood of murdered Christians, Jews, and Muslims. It brings shame to the proud name of the Knights Templar." The Duke of Nemours face hardened as he continued the tale.

"Violent conflicts exploded within the ranks of the Templars, who remained divided by good and evil, knight against knight, fighting to the death. Wilfred the Valiant was ultimately victorious. With the help of other righteous knights, he took possession of the war plunder and it was then that he had it secretly transported to the castle of Nemours. They built a new passage to secure and conceal the treasure. Wilfred ordered them to disguise the entrance to the treasure as his own tomb."

Arsenio struggled to picture what he was being told. "The treasure is hidden in Wilfred's tomb? Doesn't its presence bring inherited danger to the castle and to your Dukedom as well?"

"It does. I can only speculate on the reasons for choosing Nemours castle for the treasure's resting place. No record exists to explain it. Nonetheless, I believe the danger involved was the reason the castle was chosen. Perhaps Wilfred thought no one would believe he would be so bold as to place it in his own house!"

"That might be true." Arsenio smiled. "Wilfred must have been quite a rascal and with a sense of humor if that was his reasoning. On the other hand, he did place the Dukedom and his descendants in grave danger. No doubt there have been greedy and evil people on the hunt it for it. And members of your family are their obvious target!"

Alexander nodded. "Some of my gallant ancestors suffered torture and death because of that treasure."

"But Wilfred was not the only Knight connected with the riches, was he? What about the other Templars? How did they manage to keep the secret?"

"Wilfred and the Knights Templar swore a holy oath that none should seize or profit from the treasure and that they would only protect it and use it to aid the helpless against tyranny. They believed it was better for the treasure to be forever lost, rather than fall into the hands of evildoers."

"I understand now." Arsenio slowly nodded. "However, I don't see any purpose to such a great treasure. It apparently invites death and does little to benefit humanity."

"No, there are great benefits connected with the treasure! The secret was passed down with extreme care from father to son, or to any offspring deemed worthy of the knowledge. The person chosen as the new custodian has the power to decide how to share the knowledge and to dispense the wealth to the needy, but in quiet ways that can be kept secret.

"Throughout the decades, several tyrants have been toppled. Hundreds, perhaps thousands of people have been helped by that treasure! But none of them ever knew.

"The pitfall we guard against is the danger of becoming reckless with the dispensation of the wealth, to heed our natural impulse to aid larger groups of people. But that is precisely how we can attract undo attention and lose the treasure to greedy enemies. Our quest is to fulfill the wishes of the Templars by seeing to it that the treasure is used for the power of good and that means until the last piece of gold has been spent."

"I see now," answered Arsenio with a solemn face.

"Yes, you do. This source of danger is part of my heritage, and I constantly reconcile the need to help humanity with the need to exercise proper caution."

The Duke moved closer to Arsenio, placed his hand on his shoulder and spoke in a voice that was nearly a whisper.

"This is the reason that no one must know I am the one called the Unknown Templar. In that identity, I was able to dispense gold among the people and to pay for the mercenaries to help topple the regime of the Duke of Saxe-Hanover.

"But now I fear that our enemies could make the connection between the house of Nemours and the Templar's treasure. For safety reasons I believe it's best to let the people of Lorengard-Lorraine think that the true Unknown Templar is you! The proof will be that you miraculously returned from the shadows of death to enact revenge against his enemies."

Arsenio sat quietly for a long moment, then nodded. "My lord, I value and admire your quest in this matter of honor. I pledge my life to this end. And I pledge my allegiance to the protection of the Templars treasure!"

"Thank you Arsenio. Your alliance in this vital matter is invaluable. However, I must also ask you for a special promise…your word of honor that one day, if compelled by destiny, you will inform my grandson Alexander of the existence of the treasure. If I cannot be there to do it, then you must explain his responsibility as a member of the house of Nemours!"

"I swear it upon my honor. But what about Polyxena? We must be hopeful that she will soon be returned to us. Should it not be her place to inform our son of his noble heritage, rather than mine?"

The Duke of Nemours remained silent. A pained look flashed in his eyes.

"My lord," said Arsenio, "is there additional peril connected to Polyxena?"

"I have no evidence of that, it's just a feeling I have that she is in very grave danger. There is mysterious enemy out there, someone other than Lord Zanar, connected to the Crimson Amulet. And it is instrumental in her abduction, for some unknown reason."

"But why are you making this assumption, my lord? Did anything happen to justify this?"

"During my own abduction," answered the Duke. "I had the strong feeling that my daughter was truly the person they were after. I believe the reason I was held hostage was to abduct Polyxena, not to acquire knowledge of the treasure." The elder Duke paused for a brief moment and shook his head with obvious concern. "The situation is very strange indeed, since I was told that Lord Zanar is a direct descendant of Sheik Akbar-The Great, a legendary warrior and sworn enemy of the Knights Templar. His life's quest was to find the treasure and bring it back to his land and his people. Since I am the closest living relative of Wilfred the Valiant, I thought it was odd that my abductors seemed more interested in my daughter than me."

"Do you know of anyone among them who wishes her harm?"

"I know of no enemy, Arsenio. She lived a very sheltered life in Nemours and is loved by all the people who know her. However, I suspect there is something nefarious going on that is connected to the Crimson Amulet and the safety of my daughter. During my abduction I noticed all the people involved wore the Amulet around their necks. It appears to be some kind of a cult, considering the mysterious way your castle was invaded and the deaths of the prisoners."

"But why?" Arsenio snapped in frustration. "There has to be a reason for this."

"True, we are dealing with a ruthless adversary. By all accounts, whoever it is has great knowledge of powerful magic unknown to us. This person may come from a different land and culture, perhaps a doctor or even an alchemist."

Arsenio paced the hall feeling overwhelmed. Alexander was moved by his sorrow and placed an arm around his shoulders. "Have courage that all is not lost, despite our concerns. One of the prisoners is still alive and we have possession of Kusen's amulet. Somehow, we will discover the way to save Polyxena."

Arsenio nodded. "May our heavenly father heed your words, my lord, and bring my wife back to all who love her!"

THE MESMERIZING SOLITUDE

Weeks elapsed after Polyxena's abduction and she found loneliness to be the most difficult ordeal of her captivity. The solitude in her gilded prison was devastating. She needed to communicate with someone, anyone, to maintain mental balance and a sense of reality.

The only physical presence was provided by the handmaidens, who brought food and attended to her comforts with perfumed baths and lavish clothes. But they continued to be silent shadows, hidden in thick veils and dark garments.

In spite of her isolation, she was always dressed in revealing clothes that offended her modesty and enhanced her fear of violation. She suspected that someone was lurking in the shadows, perhaps a voyeur who enjoyed spying on young women, scantily dressed, using her as a tool to satisfy his lustful obsession. The aura of mystery was enhanced by the delicate aroma which infused the tent and seemed to possess a mind-altering power that made her feel disoriented.

During her baths, the aromatic scent seemed to intensify, possibly enhanced through the steamy waters. She felt overwhelming warmth through her limbs and a desire to be held in a passionate embrace. She fought the disturbing effects of the drug and the conflicting desire of being physically possessed, while fearing the inability to control her emotions and the loss of her honor.

She realized that she needed to get away from the mesmerizing environment of the tent. The maidens had disappeared after placing bountiful amounts of delectable food on silver trays. She swallowed a few bites without tasting it, in hopes of regaining some strength.

Holding her breath, she carefully parted a small portion of the heavy fabric that obstructed the entrance, then pushed her head through the opening to look outside. She winced at the bright morning sunlight and was surprised by the chill in the air.

The glance outside made her feel overwhelmed and claustrophobic in the controlled environment. She looked around and realized that no guards were near the entrance. She wrapped herself in a woolen towel that had been used to dry her after her bath. The fabric was still moist, but it would at least give her some protection.

She sneaked outside and scouted the area, hoping to find some possible avenue of escape. It was still early in the morning and only a few people were visible in the distance. She noticed some women attending to their work and a few guards sitting around a fire. But her gaze stopped on a multitude of horses gathered in a makeshift corral on the far end of the compound. Fortunately, it was located at some distance from the guards.

All the guards were involved in conversation and no one appeared to be aware of her presence. The wonderful possibility of escape filled her mind.

But the cold morning air made her shiver under the damp towel, and she realized how unsuitable and awkward it would be to attempt an escape on horseback in that ridiculous garment. Her delicate, jeweled sandals were also unsuitable for out-of-doors use and were easily damaged by the rough terrain, exposing her bare skin to the stark environment.

Only warm clothes and real shoes could protect her against the harsh elements, but she was unsure on how to get them. Food, water and a sword were also essential.

In desperation, she dared to sneak to the opposite side of the encampment and approach the horse corral. The animals stood without saddles and reins. Tempting, but still, without clothing, supplies, or proper horse tack, her chances for survival would be extremely poor.

She began to shiver uncontrollably, plagued by the terrifying thought of being recaptured and forced back into the imprisonment of the dreaded tent.

Just then the chilled silence was broken by the sound of horns announcing the arrival of a group of men on horseback. They made a confident entrance and quickly approached the guards at the fire. The guards welcomed them and helped them unload the carcass of a doe and a large assortment of game animals and birds.

Polyxena gently moved into the small herd of horses. A beautiful black stallion caught her eyes, glistening in the sun and brimming with life—it reminded her of her favorite steed, Hildebrandt back in Nemours. The purebred Friesian was a prized gift from her father. She remembered the many wonderful hours spent galloping in the verdant hills of the Dukedom in his company. Surprisingly, as she approached the splendid steed he welcomed Polyxena like an old friend and allowed her to caressed his restless head and proud, shiny mane.

After the pleasant interlude, she continued to carefully watch out for anyone who might become aware of her presence in the corral. Her thought process was still labored, under the after effects of the drugged bath air.

In the distance, she noticed that one of the hunters had tossed aside his woolen cape and left it resting on the ground, close to their fire. A mantle like that could protect her during a horseback journey in frigid air. But to get it, she had to leave the protection of the corral.

She gathered her courage and began to move away from the corral, but determination could do nothing to prevent her muscles from shivering violently in the cold while she edged toward the fire. Mere walking was barely possible and she nearly fell several times. The moisture in the damp woolen towel began to freeze and cause it to stiffen while she struggled over the frozen terrain in her sandaled feet.

Desperation drove her. She advanced toward the woolen cape, now only partially shielded from sight. She moved slowly to minimize the crackling noises of frozen twigs and leaves that snapped beneath her flat sandals.

She did not move carefully enough. A bolt of pain shot up her right legs as a jagged piece of wood pierced the edge of her foot. An involuntary gasp erupted from her throat and attracted the attention of one of the guards.

She stood helpless and terrified. Frightening images flashed in her mind and she envisioned herself being dragged back to the tent. She remained frozen with fear on the sterile ground a voice behind her cut through the air, cold as an iron blade. She turned suddenly and Lord Zanar appeared as a malevolent vision standing tall and menacing in front of her.

"You cannot escape, my lovely Duchess, without proper assistance. You are free to go, if that is your wish. However, a cruel and certain death awaits you out there and you know it!"

Zanar continued with evident satisfaction. "I am by nature magnanimous, Polyxena, and I value you too much to allow the woodlands to entrap you in their deadly embrace. I would have come to your aid despite your recklessness behavior."

Polyxena struggled to regain some focus and motivation. She took a deep breath to slow the pounding of her heart, but said nothing to him. Meanwhile, the black stallion that was left unattended at the edge of the encampment moved slowly toward her, as if waiting for her join him in a wonderful gallop in the forbidden forest.

Zanar noticed the horse and was amused. "You made a friend, my lady. That is strange indeed, since he is a hostile beast who doesn't give his affection readily…I will make you a present of him, if that is what you like?"

Polyxena looked up, and through the veil of tears was able to see the beautiful stallion in front of her. She was so grateful to him, it was almost as if her beloved Hildebrandt had come back to life and was comforting her distress with his presence.

Polyxena's will to survive began to take hold. It was clear that Zanar was in full control, at least for the moment. The sound of his voice returned a sense of reality and pushed the fog of the tent farther from her senses.

Polyxena took a step and gasped in pain from the injury on her foot.

"You are hurt!" he exclaimed, and in spite of her reluctance he investigated the injury, managing to admire her legs at the same time. He caressed her skin, touching her ankle with obvious desire and ignoring Polyxena's displeasure.

"There is a bad cut under your foot," he finally said with concern. "It's dirty and filled with splinters from walking with unsuitable shoes on the rough terrain. You better not stand on it. I will carry you back to the tent and have the injury attended to at once."

Without waiting for an answer, Lord Zanar picked up Polyxena with amazing ease and held her in a tight, sensual Embrace. She could hear the accelerated beating of his heart while resting her head on his chest. After all the stress endured she was unwilling to continue her struggle. Then a strange calm took over her in the comfort and warmth of his arms, as he took her back to the tent.

UNRAVELING AN ENIGMA

Meanwhile, in the castle of Lorengard-Lorraine, Arsenio and Alexander waited for one of the guards to retrieve an amulet from a prisoner. Arsenio stepped to a sculpted ebony chest and removed the ill-fated gift to baby Alexander. He opened the jewel box containing the Crimson Amulet and studied the sculpted ivory skull and the brilliance of the ruby eyes. This amulet was much larger than the diminutive versions worn by the prisoners, more lifelike and ominous. But the examination did not reveal any secret openings that might shed light to the unsettling mystery.

Finally the court physician reappeared in the archway of the stately hall, followed closely by a guard carrying a small version of the infamous ivory skull.

Arsenio eagerly placed the little skull in a silver tray on a desk by a window. The location was ideal because of the bright morning light. He scrutinized it from all angles, maneuvering it with the help of the sharp point of a dagger. He and Alexander both looked for any hidden mechanism that could activate an opening, but this effort was also fruitless.

"Perhaps, your grace," said the physician, "we would get better results by examining the amulet with the touch of the hand. The ivory skull could be manipulated with greater accuracy and if there is some hidden opening it might be easier to find it. However, we must be cautious in touching an object that could prove to be fatal."

"I will do it," replied the Duke of Nemours. "I do not fear possible death from the amulet if can be helpful in saving my daughter."

"No, my lord!" said Arsenio. "Polyxena is my wife, and it is my place to do it."

"I believe there is a solution," interjected the court physician. "While gloves would interfere with the sensitivity of touch, we could use a delicate fabric instead, and still retain enough sensitivity to examine the amulet."

While speaking, the physician removed a pure white linen handkerchief from his pocket. The delicate fabric appeared dense enough to shield the hand for possible danger and yet soft enough to allow a thorough exploration through the power of touch.

Arsenio took possession of the handkerchief and placed the amulet on it. He began manipulating the small object, exploring with care even the smallest indentations. The procedure didn't seem to pose any danger and after another fruitless examination, he replaced the amulet on the silver tray, then dropped the fabric next to the amulet.

In that moment, all eyes were drawn by tiny red stains marring the white handkerchief. He carefully opened the small piece of fabric. The stains were small but clearly visible, as if the ivory skull had released some fresh blood on the delicate fabric.

Alexander, Arsenio, and the physician were equally confounded. The younger Duke pointed to the eye-sockets of the amulet. "Look at the skull, those are not rubies in the eye cavities, it is only red pigmentation! Please bring over Kusen's amulet for comparison."

Under the window's morning light, the tiny jewels in the eye-sockets of Kusen's amulet sparkled sinisterly.

"Could the rubies be the actual poison that killed the prisoners?" Arsenio finally said. "Bring over the original

Crimson Amulet given as a gift to my son…I would like to try an experiment!"

Arsenio took possession of a sharp dagger and pressed the metal point carefully against the ruby eyes of the gift. The jewels remained intact and unaffected, sparkling in the sunlight. He rubbed the surface of the stones with the handkerchief, but no staining was released. The young duke repeated the procedure on Kusen's amulet, placing the point of the dagger against the much smaller jewels in the eye cavities. This time, under the pressure, the tiny jewels crumbled to the metal touch into a red translucent powder. The powder stained the handkerchief with spots the color of blood.

"This is the poison used for the suicides!" said Arsenio triumphantly.

"Yes, your grace," responded the physician. "There is no doubt about it!" "This explains why the dead had red stains on their tongues; it must be a powerful poison that kills instantly and without apparent discomfort. Our secretive enemy must be someone with considerable knowledge of chemistry. Most likely an alchemist!"

"I believe we have made an important discovery," said Alexander. "It is time to face Kusen. Perhaps he will be more disposed to help us find Polyxena, now."

"I agree," answered Arsenio. "Although I fear he will not be amenable to help us. He knows that his life is valuable, since he is the only one able to give us information about Polyxena. We cannot use torture. He might die in the process and take from us the only person able to help find her."

"But I am also concerned," said Alexander, "that it will be very difficult to garner any news from the man. He is obviously a fanatic who fears the wrath of his cult more than death. We must remember that all the prisoners were on a suicide mission! Perhaps it would be best if I interrogate the prisoner first. I believe the Crimson Amulet will prove itself useful in breaking Kusen's defenses."

Arsenio let out a deep breath and nodded. "I value your judgment. We will try this your way."

Alexander placed his arm around Arsenio's shoulder and without delay ushered him out the room, followed by the court physician.

Finally, the threesome reached the dungeons, traveling down the winding stairwell into the depths beneath the palace.

At Kusen's cell, they found the man curled on the floor, ignoring the small cot against the barren wall. He didn't move a muscle and also ignored their presence.

"Kusen!" said the Duke, "It is important that we discuss the penetration into the palace, and the resulting abduction of the Duchess. We are willing to forgive your participation in this dishonorable act and allow you to regain your freedom without punishment. If you will help us find the Duchess…"

Silence was the only response.

"You are aware that we could use different methods to induce your cooperation. We do not relish imposing torture. But we will make an exception for you, if you will not help us."

Kusen continued to ignore the Duke, and remained almost lifeless on the floor. Alexander approached him and leaned close to be certain his face was visible to him.

"Here is your crimson amulet!" He showed him the ivory skull in the palm of his hand. "We took the precaution of removing all the poison encased in the eye sockets. This dreaded symbol of death will no longer be able to kill anyone!"

Kusen stirred at this and he looked up to meet Alexander's determined gaze. "Have mercy, my lord," he whispered. "Please return the amulet to me. Since is no longer dangerous, it should hold no special value to you!"

"Perhaps," answered the Duke. "However, it is valuable to you, and considering your lack of cooperation I see no reason why you should be rewarded."

The Muslim lowered his eyes and said no more.

"Kusen, you should be grateful to the Duke of Lorengard-Lorraine, who saved you from certain death by removing that fatal amulet from your neck. He stopped you from following your foolish cohorts to their grave."

Only more silence followed.

"Very well, if that is the way you want it, so be it! You will be placed on the rack until you will tell us all you know about the Duchess!" Alexander threw a worried glanced at Arsenio.

He knew that there was nothing left but torture to convince the fanatical Kusen and bend his will.

But again, the prisoner remained unresponsive, as if rejoicing in their helplessness. This sent Alexander into an open rage.

"By God! I will destroy this evil symbol of death! I'll crush it in front of your eyes! Guards! Bring forth a hammer!"

This at last bore fruit. Kusen lifted himself to a sitting position with a wild look of despair.

Arsenio and the Duke of Nemours followed his every move and played their only available hand. Alexander placed the tiny amulet on the floor in clear view of Kusen, who now appeared overwhelmed with fear.

A guard soon arrived brandishing a hammer and prepared to smash the tiny object upon order. But a blood curdling scream erupted from Kusen's throat. He lunged forward, trying to cover it with his body. He was restrained by the guard and forced to retreat to the back of the cell, where he fell to his knees, shaking in terror.

The Duke of Nemours was relieved to find a weakness in the fanatic's armor. He retrieved the amulet from the floor and addressed the prisoner with determination. "Why should we abide by your wishes? You have been an obstinate man who refuses to help us find the Duchess?"

"My lord! The abduction of the Duchess was not of my making! I was simply obeying orders. Upon my honor!"

"You have no honor!" Alexander snapped. "You were a willing accomplice in this tragedy. You violated this house with trickery, in order to abduct my daughter. No mercy to the likes of you!" The Duke shouted to the guard, "Destroy the amulet!"

"No, lord!" screamed Kusen. "You will condemn me to eternal damnation! Please! Have mercy!"

The man remained silent and terrified, a victim of his own fanatical superstitions. For the first time, after all the uncertainty, Arsenio and the Duke of Nemours, felt a sense of hope, that they finally had the upper hand.

†††

CHAPTER SIX

A MOMENT OF ECSTASY

Zanar entered the tent with his usual assurance, looking around with inquisitive eyes. He ignored Polyxena, as if she were suddenly invisible. Zanar's presence and striking good looks were evident in a white silk shirt with flowing sleeves and an open collar that showcased his sculpted chest. A red sash emphasized his narrow waist.

He remained silent and paced the area restlessly as if in deep thought, then finally approached a copper container and swiftly removed the cover. A sweet, pungent aroma permeated the tent. He took several deep breaths with apparent pleasure, allowing his nostrils to savor the fumes before sitting down on a plush mound of pillows by the far wall of the tent. His eyes remained closed and he soon appeared to fall into a deep slumber.

Polyxena also felt herself being affected by the fumes. They seemed to convey a mind-altering energy. It felt dangerously enticing and seductive. She became lightheaded, engulfed in a mélange of sensual and sexual impulses. Her limbs where overrun by tingling sensations. She felt herself yearning to be possessed in a passionate embrace.

The unsettling impulses frightened her. She felt a strange compulsion to caress her own silky skin and trace the contour of her curvaceous body. She enjoyed the soft roundness of her breasts, barely shielded by a translucent veil designed for lustful pleasures. Her feelings of fear and desire left her confused and vulnerable. Her attempts to remain strong were not enough. Her willpower dissolved like salt in warm water.

The dignified Duchess of Lorengard-Lorraine was reduced to a lustful girl incapable of tempering her deepest passions and desires, regardless of the danger.

Without being able to explain herself, she craved Zanar's manly arms. The sexual aura inside the tent captivated her. She yearned for the warmth of his body against hers.

At the same time, she was torn by a desperate desire to run away from this strange, lustful longing. Her own condition was baffling to her. She struggled to hold onto any sense of reality at all and not to give in to her basest instincts.

But the resonance of soft, enticing music echoed in the tent. Lord Zanar awakened and lifted himself into a sitting position, gazing at Polyxena with smoldering desire. The young duchess was nearly paralyzed by the intensity of his stare. It seemed to invade her with sexual hunger. She could not find the will to stop them.

Zanar abruptly stood up, aware of the power of his masculine appeal, and smiled while he pushed back the open collar on his shirt to expose more of his masculine chest.

Her arousal intensified and her skin felt the warmth of his body dangerously and invitingly close. She tried in vain to find strength to hang onto reality—in spite of the mind-altering effects of the mysterious potion and the overwhelming attraction it was causing her to feel for her captor.

She closed her eyes as he approached and without meaning to see it, envisioned his arms encircling her waist and holding her in a powerful embrace. Her state of fear blended with intense desire. Ecstasy and terror overwhelmed her.

Zanar longed to put his arm around her and hold her forcefully in an ardent embrace, to finally dominate the unreachable Duchess he had coveted for so long. But he also relished her vulnerability and felt a perverse desire to rebuff and debase her. That urge was stronger than any other. It felt good to push her away, as good as punching a man in the stomach.

Polyxena fell on her knees, relieved to have been somehow spared from the consequences of her weakened condition. She could not explain her inability to control lustful desires for a cruel stranger, in what she perceived to be an amoral and reprehensible act of lust. However, she also felt the blow of the rejection by the sadistic and unpredictable Lord Zanar.

He returned to the soft pleasure of the mounds of pillows, then clapped his hands twice. In immediate response, the shrouded handmaidens appeared and formed a circle in the middle of the tent.

Hidden musicians began to play and the women initiated a graceful dance, gyrating with agility even in their cumbersome attire. Polyxena stared in amazement when they removed their burdensome cocoons, reveling young girls in a state of semi-nudity. They continue their dance, moving their slender bodies in sensual, provocative moves that intensified as the music became louder, almost frenzied.

Polyxena felt herself once more overwhelmed by the seductive environment. She was mesmerized by the sensual movements of the maiden's bodies, who danced without modesty or restraint. Finally, as if exhausted by the pace of the dance, they fell collectively on the floor, panting as if in a collective orgasm. After a brief pause they slithered gracefully across the floor of the tent and encircled Lord Zanar in a voluptuous, communal embrace.

He responded to the sexual overture by caressing their bodies and feeling the softness of their breasts. He grabbed one

107

of the maidens by the hair and she responded by pressing her full, ripe lips against his mouth with unbridled passion.

Polyxena had difficulty catching her breath. Zanar was showing contempt for her by exposing her to such a sordid spectacle. Even in her altered state of mind she felt disgusted by his display. The usually modest maidens showed expertise in sexual pleasures as they surrounded him and opened their bodies to sexual practices Polyxena had never witnessed.

Some of the young women were light-skinned with red and blond hair, obviously of European descent, perhaps kidnap victims who had been turned into sex slaves for the pleasure of Zanar and his men. Others shared his smoky features.

The orgiastic scene intensified, accompanied by the raptures sound of the music and the frenzied women. Polyxena was nearly paralyzed by the scene—the sweet aroma that permeated the tent diminished her inhibition and self-control. The sexual practices appeared violent and perverse to her. There in the entrapment of the tent she was exposed to all the decadence and raw excitement of unknown sexual games.

She was repelled and yet fatally attracted to it. Her limbs burned with urgency. The unrestrained sexual pleasure played out in front of her was invasive and infectious at the same time.

Finally, Lord Zanar grew tired of the games and pushed the young maidens away. He stood up tall, proud, and abruptly ended the impromptu performance with a gesture. The maidens disappeared as quietly as they had made their entrance, leaving Zanar and Polyxena alone.

He stared with intense desire at Polyxena's loveliness. His sculpted muscles were dampened by the heat of passion and glistened in the torch lights. She was overwhelmed by the sight and drawn in by the sexual aura he exuded.

He came to her and his arms hungrily encircled her waist in a passionate embrace. Their lips met in a volatile, deep kiss that took her breath away.

It was an ecstatic moment. Chills of pleasure went through her. But the interlude was brought to a surprise halt by Zanar. He once again found himself reluctant to fulfill his sexual desires because of her obvious fear of him. This was like nothing he had ever experienced.

With Polyxena, he felt something that was more than mere lust. He felt a romantic connection and an overpowering need to be desired by her, a sentiment he had never experienced. He looked with longing into her splendid green eyes and felt diminished by the sight, overcome by her beauty. She ought to have been his conquest, that day. But Polyxena had won a special place in his heart. An extraordinary aura was present in her.

Zanar was excited by her responsiveness, yet he knew it was artificially manifested in her with one of his potions.

He now wanted more than a forced sexual encounter from Polyxena. With unusual restraint, he caressed her lovingly and allowed the simmering passion to burn within him. He placed her gently on a mounds of pillows, gazing at the curves of her body. He kissed her lips with more restraint than before, but she remained under the spell he had placed upon her and responded with abandonment, throwing her silky arms around him with such ardor that the closeness of her body scorched him like a raging fire.

Her lips melted with his in a passionate kiss that became longer, deeper, in a moment of ecstasy and intensity such as Zanar had never experienced. He felt her trembling in his arms, and reveled in the warmth of her body.

Despite her manufactured willingness, Zanar was unable to think of her as a sex toy any longer. Under the spell of the drug, her desire was suddenly unacceptable to him. He wanted to truly possess her, not a shadow of her.

He gently caressed and kissed her and whispered her name with passion, "Polyxena, I want you, I desire your love!" And then he spoke the word that seldom left his lips: "…Please."

Polyxena felt the touch of his hand, caressing her body with gentleness, and in that mesmerizing moment, she was home again in the loving arms of her husband.

"Arsenio," she whispered. "Arsenio, my love…"

Her words flashed in Zanar's mind like a bolt of lightning.

Jealousy was the only emotion at his command in that moment. His monumental ego had been crushed by three simple words. He had allowed himself to be vulnerable and this is what it got him. He despised himself for allowing such weakness. He pushed Polyxena brutally away and slapped her across the face.

The cruelty of the attack worked in her favor—it mercifully snapped her awake her from the drug's spell. She saw the danger clearly when Zanar sneered at her.

"Arsenio is lost to you forever, my lady! I am the only reality you possess and I hold the balance of your wretched life in my hands. You will pay for your disrespect and I will bend your haughty nature to my desires!"

Polyxena remained silent, shaken and confused by the suddenness of his anger. However, with clarity returning, she felt grateful to have been spared. She gathered the scant robe around her and tried to shield her nakedness from his fiery eyes.

"You should not bother, my lady," said Lord Zanar. "I do not want you anymore! You are a beautiful statue that gives pleasure to the eye, but is cold and lifeless!"

Without further ado, he stormed out the tent, leaving Polyxena alone and traumatized.

The young duchess was badly shaken, scalded by the idea of what she had almost done. "Arsenio," she murmured under her breath. "Please help me. Please help me somehow."

THE LONELY SEARCH

Arsenio, Duke of Lorengard-Lorraine, and Alexander, Duke of Nemours, were heartened by Kusen's reaction to their threats

111

against his personal crimson amulet. They moved toward the door while the prisoner followed them with a wild look in his face.

"Why are you leaving, my lord?" he said. "Please, return the amulet to me." Kusen's helpless plea resonated in the stone walls. The two kept walking.

"I will help you!" he finally shouted. "I will help you! Please don't leave! Come back!"

For a long while there was no answer to Kusen's plea, and panic began to overtake him. Finally, Arsenio and Alexander reappeared by the cell door.

"It is time to stop playing these useless games!" Arsenio told him. "We are wasting time and the Duchess's life is in the balance. Where have they taken her?"

"I will have to guide you," responded Kusen, relieved by their presence, "you will never be able to find her without me!"

"Then I will give the necessary orders," Arsenio replied. "I will have the guards prepared in short order and we will leave as soon as possible!"

"No, my lord," said Kusen. "I will show the way to only one person. If an army of soldiers follows us, we will be spotted immediately and the Duchess will be lost forever!"

"I do not believe you!" responded Arsenio. "This is a vile trick to escape, and we will not fall for it!"

"I am not lying my lord! Believe me, your castle is under surveillance and an army of soldiers will be spotted immediately!"

"Perhaps, he is right, Arsenio. Said the Duke of Nemours. "An army is easily spotted."

"But we cannot trust him. And if he escapes, we have no one to show us the way. What if some of his cohorts are hiding in the surroundings and he leads us into a trap?"

"I will not betray you," cried Kusen. "I give you my word that I will guide you safely to the Duchess!"

"Your promises are meaningless!" answered Alexander. "You have no honor and are not to be trusted!" He turned to Arsenio. "However, there might be a way to guarantee that he does not betray us!"

"How my lord?" Arsenio asked.

The Duke guided Arsenio outside the cell before he told him, "The Crimson Amulet! That symbol of death is the only hope we have in our possession to guarantee his loyalty."

Inside the cell, Kusen panicked and fell on his knees pleading for clemency. "My noble lords, you hold in your hands the key to my eternal life!"

The Duke of Nemours reentered and smiled. "Your words are meaningless to me. However, you are the only available person to show us the way to the Duchess. Because of that we may be willing to compromise."

"Then you will return the Crimson Amulet to me?"

"Not so fast," the Duke of Nemours replied. "We will return the Amulet on one condition...you will show us the way, without trickery...and my daughter is found alive! Then, and only then!"

"You do not trust me, but how do I know you will keep your word?" Kusen huffed.

"That is my offer. I swear it upon my honor, as a Knight, that if my daughter will be returned unharmed you will not suffer any consequences for your conspiracy in the abduction! You know I live by the code of honor. Unlike you, my words can be trusted."

The Duke of Nemours faced Kusen proudly as he spoke, and the man appeared intimidated by his presence. "The Duke of Lorengard-Lorraine will be the only person to leave the palace in your company. However, your amulet will remain in my possession as a necessary precaution."

His voice became more threatening, "Be warned, if any harm befalls the Duke or the Duchess, I will personally destroy it and your soul, just as you describe...will be forever lost!"

Kusen lowered his head in tacit consent.

Alexander and Arsenio immediately left the dungeons after instructing the guards on the final preparations for Arsenio's departure with Kusen. A heavy silence burdened the two men as they reached the great hall of the palace. They each felt overwhelmed by the slim possibility of finding Polyxena alive.

"I fear that without the necessary protection of guards to facilitate the search, the possibility of finding my daughter alive becomes even more remote," said Alexander. "Besides, the surrounding forests are very dangerous and foreboding, they will leave you at the mercy of Kusen for guidance and safety. And in case you need to escape, how will you find your way back from the unforgiving labyrinth of the forests?"

"We have no other choice. I believe Kusen's warning that the castle is under surveillance. A large presence of guards could sound an alarm and cost Polyxena her life. I will try to leave some markings on the way, unbeknownst to Kusen in order to facilitate the pathway for soldiers to follow. I may also need it for guidance on the way back."

"I pray it's not too late." Alexander shook his head. "You are taking a terrible chance in following Kusen, in what could very well be a wild goose chase. You could lose your life to no purpose if Polyxena is already dead." The Duke sighed bitterly with those words.

Arsenio shook his head. "It is no more than Polyxena did for me, my lord. I intend to go through with it, regardless of the consequences."

The elder Duke was deeply moved by Arsenio's courage and chivalry and shook his hand proudly. "Then may the good lord protect you in all your endeavors. You are truly worthy of my daughter's love!"

Suddenly, the voice of the court chamberlain resonated in the vast hall. "Your grace, Monsieur Berthold Ballon wishes an immediate audience with you."

"The innkeeper?" answered Arsenio. "If he must."

The chamberlain stepped aside and Monsieur Ballon made his entrance, impaired by considerable weight and elaborate attire. His breath was labored from the long walk throughout the winding staircases. His chubby legs were encased in uncomfortable, but elegant leather boots, while a flowing mantle that nearly reached the floor made his gait a bit unsteady.

He bowed with all the grace he could muster, from within the splendor of his highly ornate garments.

"Monsieur Ballon," Arsenio said, "we are honored by the presence of one of the most loyal citizens of the Dukedom."

"You are kind, my Duke…and I will not delay revealing my purpose. I came to extend the lease on my vineyards, but instead, I have a proposition."

"Then I hope it will be brief, my friend. I am afraid we are short of time here."

"I will come to the point. I have been informed by the head guard that you will be leaving at sundown with the surviving prisoner, without the safety of your normal escort?"

"That is true my friend, unfortunately the present circumstances dictate as much."

"I came on other business, but it is of no matter, today. Instead I wish to offer my help in this regard."

"How do you propose to be of help, Monsieur?" asked Alexander.

"If the Duke enters the forest without a proper escort, he will be blindly following a dangerous man who cannot be trusted, a man who was instrumental in the abduction of our Duchess!"

"We are aware of the inherited danger," answered Arsenio. "Unfortunately we have no choice in the matter, if we ever hope to find the Duchess alive we must abide by the existing circumstances!"

"Then I propose to follow you instead of the usual guards! You see? I will not raise suspicions with my presence! I am well known and familiar with the surrounding forests. I have traveled through them many times to purchase my wine in neighboring vineyards."

"It would be too dangerous," said Alexander. "You should know that we believe the palace may be under surveillance from our enemies. By getting involved, you risk your life!"

"Then I will leave from my own inn, instead of the palace! Before sundown! Who would take notice of this overweight man, who looks so little like a soldier?"

"You are too humble my friend," Arsenio told him. "You carry the heart of a lion. I value your generosity and true friendship."

The Duke of Nemours approached Berthold and placed his hand on his shoulder. "You must understand," he said. "that in order to be helpful in this dangerous endeavor, it is imperative that you appear to all as nothing more than an innkeeper fulfilling chores for his inn, not an aristocrat in disguise. Wear casual clothes and place a sharp blade at your side."

Berthold nodded his consent, but he was clearly taken aback at the realization that he was truly going to partake in a dangerous mission that could cost his life. Despite such fears, he maintained his determination. "Before nightfall," he told them. "I will exit from the Inn in my usual wine cart and since these outings to the surrounding vineyards are commonplace, no one will pay attention.

"I will leave at the east end of the Dukedom, since it is close to the palace. I will enter the forest from that direction and hide in the shadows, waiting for the arrival of his Grace, Arsenio Duke of Lorengard-Lorraine and your prisoner. After they pass, I shall follow at a discreet distance, leaving necessary markings on the way in order for the palace guards to follow."

"Excellent Berthold." Arsenio exclaimed. "I believe your plan is good and you could be of considerable help to our cause. Remember, one thing remains certain; if they suspect you are connected with us, you could forfeit your life."

"I know my lord," was Berthold's somber reply. "But the life of an innkeeper has little excitement. I have reached the age where I need a sense of purpose. If I am killed, my principal regret will be to face the good Lord in my humble traveling attire."

The Duke of Nemours and Arsenio glanced at each other in amusement. Berthold was a generous, heroic man and yet in his eyes he required ostentatious clothing to bolster his cringing self esteem.

Arsenio remained pensive for a brief moment than walked toward his sword at the far end of the stately hall. He removed the long blade from his scabbard and invited Berthold to come forward and kneel in front of him.

"Monsieur Ballon, because of your services, courage, and selfless devotion to the state, we are rewarding you with the honorary title of Knight of the Realm, Baronet of the vineyard of Ruhann Sensere and tributary land. The proprieties and title will be yours throughout your life and continued in perpetuity through your heirs!"

Arsenio touched Berthold's shoulders with the tip of his sword, saying, "I dub you Sir Berthold Ballon, Knight of the realm and defender of the people. Rise, Sir Berthold!"

The humble innkeeper was so shocked and overwhelmed by the tribute that for a long moment was unable to speak. "I am truly a Knight?" he whispered. "How can this be possible? I only came today seeking to extend the lease upon my vineyards."

"You now own them," Arsenio proudly replied. "You are truly worthy, my friend. You have nobility of spirit."

Berthold's eyes brimmed tears of joy and for a brief moment he forgot his grievances and fears, rejoicing in his new found status. He was a Knight of the Realm, a title impossible for a man such as him. Despite his considerable weight, Berthold felt like he was floating.

"Congratulations, Sir Berthold!" Alexander smiled. "A well deserved Knighthood for a true patriot!"

"Take your sword, Sir Knight." Arsenio placed the heavy weapon in Berthold's hands.

But the cold impact with the heavy blade brutally awakened the genial innkeeper from his reverie. The mighty sword was far too long for Berthold's shorter frame. He stumbled around the room, trying to find balance with the weapon.

Alexander stopped him and suggested that perhaps a shorter sword would be better suited to his needs.

"If good fortune is on our side," Alexander told him. "You should not be subjected to armed combat. Remember, your task is to make certain we know the location and direction that will be taken by him and the necessity of leaving proper markings for our armed guards to eventually follow. That is all."

"We must make haste," interrupted Arsenio. "There are only a few hours until sundown and there is still much to do. I believe it would be helpful to send Sir Berthold to the head guard, who will properly attire him and give him some basic technique in the use of arms."

Berthold bowed his head in consent, trying to muster his courage and face the situation for which he had recklessly volunteered.

AN UNLIKELY HERO

They chose the most advantageous place in the forest for Berthold wait to rendezvous with the Duke and his traveling companion. He was warned again to make certain Kusen remained oblivious of his presence unaware of being followed.

In spite of his fears, Berthold used the remaining hours to become a little more adept in the use of arms. He finally managed, after great efforts, to hold the sword steadily in his hand, instead of dropping the weapon on the floor.

Once Berthold returned to his Inn, he busily readied himself for the journey. He had the necessary provisions at hand for the excursion. All of it was stacked on his dependable wine cart and pulled by his hardworking Normandy horse, Catherina.

He reluctantly removed his flashy and luxurious garments, and with great care placed them in a cedar trunk in his modest bedchamber. He felt himself overwhelmed by a sense of doom as he enclosed them in the trunk; as if he were saying good bye to an old friend he feared he would never see again.

He looked around the room wistfully. The Inn was his own little world, humble, but the only place where he truly felt safe. Now he was a Knight of the Realm, it was ironic that he was compelled to pass himself off on this mission as nothing more than a simple innkeeper.

He placed a woolen mantle on his shoulders, and walked his rotund body out to the stable, where his beloved Catherina was enjoying a dinner of freshly cut hay. The gentle animal welcomed him with a soft neigh and had already eaten enough that she allowed the host to attach her to the wine cart without reticence.

He offered her a few lumps of sugar as a treat and placed before a bucket of water before her so she could drink well before the long journey ahead.

And with that, he was finally on his way, shivering from the cold and the fear of the unknown. The streets were mostly empty except for a few children playing on the cobblestones and screaming at the tops of their lungs. Their sharp voices resonated in Berthold's distressed mind. Finally, he reached the edge of the Dukedom and urged Catherina into the greenery of the surrounding forest.

The road was one he had taken many times, on his way to the nearby vineyards to purchase wine for his Inn. Those outings were always pleasant. For this excursion, however, he was filled with apprehension. His overworked imagination envisioned enemies lurking everywhere, ready to strike a fatal blow.

He wrapped the woolen cape tightly around his limbs, attempting to stifle his shivering, and despite the chilly air, pearls of sweat surfaced on his brow. In Berthold's imagination, the late afternoon sun rays cast ominous shadows on the landscape that appeared to conceal grotesque enemies, ready to strike. He grabbed the handle of his sword, mostly to relieve his feeling of helplessness. The feel of the weapon diminished some of his torment.

He arrived safely at the conveyed spot where he was to discretely wait for the Duke and Kusen. The location was shielded by thick vegetation that easily concealed his presence and the wine cart.

After looking around to make certain he was safe and alone, he stepped out of the cart and guided Catherina farther into the greenery. He patted the animal's proud mane and encircled his arms around her neck, taking comfort in the warmth of her body.

He removed some more brown sugar lumps from a small pouch and held them before the horse's mouth as a special treat. Catherina crunched and swallowed the treat with relish. Berthold decided that some sustenance for himself at that stressful moment would also be good and swallowed a handful of the horse's intended sugar lumps.

Dusk approached. Berthold knew that the Duke and Kusen would soon leave the palace, shielded by the gloom.

There was no way back. The die had been cast, in Berthold's mind the irony of it all was that the success of the mission actually depended upon him and his incapable hands. The thought was distressing. He feared his own ineptitude, and that because of his incompetence, the life of the Duchess could be lost.

"Dear Lord," he finally said, in desperate search for help and relying on the power of prayer. "Give me guidance I beg of you, and please give me strength!" But at that moment, Berthold's words died in his throat. The sound of approaching horses rumbled through the forest.

The sounds came from the wrong direction and therefore could not be the Duke and Kusen arriving prematurely. "Then who is coming my way?" Berthold asked, trembling like a leaf. The sound was growing closer and definitely coming in his direction.

With is heart pounding, he hid behind a tree and waited. In moments, a black stallion became visible to Berthold, then a second horse appeared spurred on by an armed soldier shrouded in a dark mantle. The horses came to a sudden halt as the mysterious man noticed Berthold, who was only partially hidden by the tree because of his robust size. The rider quickly dismounted the horse with great agility.

"Sir Berthold!" he called. "Sir Berthold Ballon!"Finally two hands reached through the greenery concealing Berthold and grabbed him by the shoulders. "Sir Berthold, it's me, Roland, head of the castle guard!"

Berthold was embarrassed by his cowardice. "Roland? Why are you here? I heard the sound of horses coming from a different direction than the chosen pathway in the forest and I feared I was under attack from our enemies."

"I am sorry for your distress, Sir Berthold, but I dismounted my horse as a friendly gesture, since no foe would give up the great advantage of being on horseback!"

The innkeeper was further humiliated by Roland's logic and by his ineptitude in the face of danger. He straightened his body and rearranged his attire, trying to regain his dignity.

"Then you must be here for an important reason, since your presence might endanger our quest."

"Quite right. We do not wish to tempt fate. However, I was very careful and entered the forest in an area far removed from the castle to avoid undesired encounters. I am here to bring to you the horse you will require for your travel!"

For the first time Berthold noticed the presence of a second horse accompanying Roland. The splendid animal was the color of night and stood bristling with energy.

"A horse for me? For what purpose? I already have a horse, my faithful and dependable Catherina."

Roland smiled, slightly amused. "The Duke thought it would be wise to have available a steed who could move at a faster pace and for a longer time. In case there was a need."

"But I am not an experienced horseman. I will surely fall off and break my neck. Please thank the Duke in my name, but the only steed I will travel with is my Catherina!"

Berthold was not willing to compromise—the fear of being alone was devastating. Catherina was much more than a horse to him, he considered her a trusted companion and he counted on her presence to face the difficulty of the mission.

Despite Berthold's categorical refusal, Roland didn't seem to be discouraged. With great tact, he addressed the frightened man with soothing words. "The Duke understands your affection and loyalty for your horse. But my lord, you must remember that you are a Knight of the Realm and defender of the people and this exalted title calls upon you to ride an animal worthy of your rank. It is my pleasure to introduce you to Rasham, a purebred Arabian. He is gifted with great speed and will carry you with ease. He is docile to the touch and responds to commands with intelligence!"

He clapped his hands and Rasham immediately approached him and the host. Berthold, still intimidated, but deeply impressed by the sight of the splendid animal. Rasham was truly an impressive horse, worthy to carry the noblest of Knights.

"But what will happen to Catherina, my faithful horse?" He asked. "I cannot abandon her!"

"Have no fear, Sir Knight, your horse Catherina will be an honored guest in the palace stables and will receive the very best of care."

The reassurance broke through Berthold's misgivings. He was pleased to know that his beloved Catherina would be housed among the Duke's horses. Such an honor made his fateful Normandy horse into an aristocratic thoroughbred.

"Convey my thanks to the Duke for being so generous! I am truly grateful. However, there is an area of contention, since I don't understand the reason why I was kept in the dark about the change of horses for the journey. Your arrival was unexpected and caused me considerable stress and unnecessary concerns."

"You needed to be seen riding your wine cart pulled by your own horse, as usual, to avoid attracting unwanted attention. I believe it was wisely decided to deliver the horse to you in the woodland without bringing attention to it and raising unnecessary suspicions. This horse is fully saddled and prepared for the journey. He carries proper provisions, food, water, and even added weapons in case there should be a need."

Roland removed a metal flask from the saddle of the horse, and showed it to Berthold. "This flask contains a red dye which is water resistant and can be utilized in leaving markings on the way; a brush is also included to facilitate your efforts as you follow the Duke. The markings will be vital for guidance to us and bring the necessary aid at the proper time."

"I will do my best," answered Berthold somberly. "With a bit of luck and the help of the Lord, my efforts will bear fruit. And despite my limited abilities in the use of arms, I hope to be of help."

Roland regarded him with genuine esteem. "We are all grateful for your courage in volunteering in such a difficult and dangerous mission. The Duke informed me that he will also make every effort to leave markings on the road, whenever possible, without alerting his traveling companion of his actions."

Despite his fears, Berthold was aware of the importance of the mission. His resigned state of mind gave him a sense of peace. He finally lowered his head in consent and addressed Roland like a man reconciled to a cruel fate.

"I will abide by the Duke's wishes and ride the new horse as requested." He approached Catherina, placed his arms around her neck, and gently caressed her mane.

Catherina was his old devoted friend and in case of his death he felt proud to reward her loyalty and afford the horse's waning years a comfortable life in the stable of the ducal palace.

As a final good bye and last gesture of affection, he retrieved the sack containing the lumps of sugar and handed them to Roland. "Please, my lord, make certain that my Catherina gets her daily dose of sugar treats, which she is used of getting from me. It will be a way to make her feel comfortable and at home in alien surroundings; this is my only request in case I will not be able to return."

The head guard was moved by the sight of the rotund, eccentric little man and by the loyalty and affection he displayed for his Duchess and his beloved horse.

He addressed the innkeeper with sincere respect. "Be at peace Sir Berthold. Have no concern for the welfare of your horse. She will be cared for as you have requested, and will get daily exercise in the vast grounds surrounding the palace. All necessary efforts will be made to help her maintain the best of health until your return. Now take your helmet; it is necessary for you to wear it as a vital protection against possible enemies." He looked the innkeeper up and down and added, "or a fall from your horse."

He handed Berthold a shiny helmet crowned by an imposing, pointy top that was as sharp as an arrow. He took the helmet uneasily. It was a bit small for his large head and he struggled to force it onto his scalp.

"The helmet is too snug for my head! I prefer not to wear it, my lord...please return it to the Duke with my compliments, and inform him that I favor traveling without it."

"I am sorry, Sir Knight," answered Roland. "This one was the best available."

"I prefer not to wear it," insisted Berthold.

Roland was forced once more to rely on flattery. "My lord, Duke of Lorengard-Lorraine wished that a noble Knight and warrior such as you should wear the proper gear, in case of battle."

"A warrior?" Berthold mumbled softly. "Very well! I will abide by the Duke's wishes." He forced the helmet onto his head.

Roland bowed to Berthold, then mounted his horse and grabbed Catherina's reins. She obediently followed and they disappeared into the greenery, leaving the wine cart behind.

Now Berthold felt completely alone. The sounds of the forest were becoming muted while the last glimmers of sun rays were swallowed. An aura of gloom and solitude descended.

Soon, the unsettling silence was broken by sounds of approaching horses. "The Duke is coming!" Berthold breathlessly said as he hastened toward his new mount. He grabbed Rasham's reins and clumsily managed to mount the horse. Fortunately the animal was truly docile and responsive to the touch. He spurred Rasham forward, looking for an advantageous position among the greenery to get a better view and make certain it was indeed the Duke and Kusen arriving on the faithful journey.

Berthold held his breath as he waited for the riders to get closer. Upon first sight, it was difficult to distinguish their identities. Long mantles and hoods covered most of their bodies, and in the fading light he struggled to see their faces. Suddenly, one of the men pushed back the hood away from his head and in the remaining glimmers of light he was able to recognize Arsenio.

The Duke had wisely decided to give Kusen the leading position, in order to remain out of sight from him while he gave necessary guidance to inexperienced innkeeper. Arsenio noticed Berthold and motioned with his hand not to rush or follow them too closely.

With the pathway through the forest familiar to Berthold, he felt confident he could follow the Duke at a discrete distance without being noticed or losing sight of them. He was relieved to know that the Duke was going to help him by also leaving markers on the way. Berthold would reinforce them with red dye and add his own.

Within moments, Arsenio and Kusen had disappeared from sight, swallowed by the surrounding trees and darkness. Berthold could still hear the horse's hooves hitting the pathway, so he didn't move to follow them until there was silence.

Then, gathering all the courage he could muster, he spurred his new mount Rasham after them. The unlikely Knight was on his way, in spite of his fears, and going forward to challenge the unknown.

CHAPTER SEVEN

THE ELUSIVE ENEMY

Difficult days elapsed in the confinement of the tent. The isolation instilled a sense of doom in Polyxena. Throughout that time, Zanar was nowhere to be seen. The maidens barely entered the tent other than to bring sustenance.

She was being punished by her volatile captor and her only solace was her ability to think with a clear head. Zanar had stopped lacing the perfumed waters of her daily baths with that ungodly potion, whatever it might be. For that much, at least, she was grateful. She washed herself in a small basin of tepid water using a coarse piece of soap. The enticing see-through gowns were replaced by a simple woolen caftan and matching slippers. She was far more comfortable in the modest caftan and in the warmth of the woolen cloth. These changes were an improvement, if only for the torment of dread.

The clarity of mind was a mixed blessing. She regained the ability to see her situation as it truly was, but this left her with the equally clear challenge of doing something about it.

Her concentration was continually broken by thoughts of her husband and child. She missed them with an ache that resonated in her bones. Her choice to follow Zanar haunted her in those hours, along with the pain of knowing how awful her choice must have been for Arsenio and her father. Still, she took consolation in knowing that no other choice was available. She could never allow her father to die without making every effort to intervene. Her life of privilege did not blind her to the fact that life was cruel and harsh for everyone. But the uncertainty of her destiny and the anguish of her captivity made her fear that this challenge was too daunting.

And now, in this moment, she felt tired. With plenty of time to sleep and no way to rest, she spent most of her time walking aimlessly in her gilded prison, waiting for sheer exhaustion to relax her enough to allow asleep. She ate the dates and drank the water provided to her, with the intention of keeping up her strength until she could find a way out. Only after she exhausted herself with pacing was she mercifully able to feel drowsy. She

133

gathered a few soft pillows scattered about the tent's floor and laid on them with great relish.

Hours melted away while she slept. However, the apparent peace of the scene was only more of Zanar's crafted illusions. He watched her from hiding to take voyeuristic pleasure in her private moments. On this night, not long after she fell asleep, her breathing slowed to the point that he became alarmed.

He glided into the tent and knelt by her side to be certain she was all right. But the closeness of his face and the warmth of his breath stirred Polyxena from her slumber. She recoiled, startled by his presence.

"Calm yourself my lady!" Zanar purred and hastened to offer her a cup of water. "You were sleeping so quietly, hardly breathing, I wanted to make certain that you were in good health."

Polyxena drank a small sip of water. "I thank you for your concern, my lord. It is always pleasing to know that someone cares for you."

Her remark disturbed him. He considered caring to be a sign of weakness in a man, and didn't want Polyxena to believe that he was emotionally involved with her. This would expose his weakness to her, and he was still angry and offended by her rebuff over his overture. He had no desire to show signs of affection to a woman who injured his pride, no matter that she did so in a moment of distress.

His answer was curt, "You are valuable propriety my lady. Your presence is essential to our final destinations. Caring had nothing to do with it."

Polyxena looked straight into his eyes, but spoke in a soft voice. "I know you are in a position of power, my lord and I have no recourse other than rely on your kindness. My only request is that you show some leniency and lessen the difficulty of my situation. I have been taken away from my family, my people and all that I love and value in life, and I still don't know the reasons why and for what purpose. Our paths have never crossed before that fatal night in the castle and I have never harmed you in any way. It is puzzling for me to see the magnitude of your contempt."

"Puzzling? You are the daughter of a Templar and he is the enemy of my people. The Knights Templars ravaged and pillaged my home land...the hatred and mistrust we have for each other is without end. Need I say more?"

Polyxena shook her head. "I was born a daughter of Templar, as you were born a son of Islam. Neither of us had any choice in the matter. It was destiny."

"Words. Such empty words you have spoken my lady. The stain of guilt is part of your heritage. It requires the blood of vengeance!"

The captive duchess remained stoic, pretending to be untouched by intimidation. "But for what purpose do you hold me hostage? Mere revenge? Revenge for memories that have no part of me in them?

She leveled her gaze at him and spoke in a low, even tone. "Make an end to the indignity of my abduction, then. Kill me. Let my blood slake your thirst for vengeance!"

Zanar was impressed with her in spite of his cynicism. Every time he was with her, she displayed herself as the most remarkable woman he had ever met. Even in the modest woolen caftan, she was as resplendent as ever. Her innate nobility remained untarnished by her captivity.

Nonetheless, Zanar had an image to sustain and it mattered more than she did. "We will decide when it is your time to die. And it's useless to hide behind your veneer of defiance. You are going to share your secrets with us before exhaling your final breath. You may be certain of that."

"What secrets?" Polyxena challenged.

"No denials, my lady! I am not fooled by the look of innocence in those beautiful eyes. Where is the Templar's treasure? You must return it to the fatherland if we are ever to have peace between our people! I have pledged my life to that quest and now your life is wagered on it, as well!"

Polyxena continued to appear unmoved. "I must concede that I have heard rumors of a fabulous treasure brought back from the Holy land. However, there is no proof that the story is real, since it could be the fruit of someone's imagination. For over a century, there have been endless searches for the elusive riches…And yet no evidence validates the story. I believe it is a myth, and that your treasure hunt will be fruitless. And for this, I was abducted? Solely based on the fact that my father was a Knight Templar? I have no information about any supposed treasure."

"Your father is much more than just a Templar, my lady! He is the direct descendent of Wilfred the Valiant, the known leader of the Knights who pillaged the Holy land during the crusades. They stole unimaginable treasures!"

"I have known about my ancestor Wilfred of Nemours all of my life and about his participation in the holy wars. However, any connection he might have had with the Templar's treasure was never an issue discussed by my father, which leads me to believe that this story is a myth and nothing more!"

"According to the legend," she continued. "many Knights were involved in taking possession of the spoils of war, and with such wealth, greed was certainly a factor. And if greedy, then they certainly divided the riches among themselves, instead of hiding the treasure for posterity. What greedy person loves posterity that much? Do greedy people want to benefit posterity more than themselves? Do they love posterity more than their own families? I think not. And this is in the remote possibility that any such treasure ever existed! If it did, it is long since gone."

"You weave a pretty story," Zanar sneered. "But there is proof that the treasure exists. And as for the people involved, including your distinguished ancestor, they were a gaggle of religious fanatics. In their fanaticism, they believed that the riches were evil because they were tainted by blood…As if there are riches anywhere untainted by blood. Such treasure would never be used for their own gain. Not because they were noble, but because they were afraid!"

Polyxena swallowed hard. Zanar's words were close to the truth.

"It is true that no actual proof exists to connect Wilfred with the treasure, but he must have had knowledge of what happened to it. And most likely, he was instrumental in choosing the hiding place, since he was the knight in charge. I believe the treasure is part of the legacy of the house of Nemours and his descendents. Therefore, Wilfred the Valiant would never have taken that secret to the grave; he hoped instead that posterity would benefit from it, innocent of the blood behind it. That is the main reason you are here, my lady and why we are eager to talk to you."

"If finding the treasure is the reason for my abduction, I think it is highly suspect that you released my father so readily. He is the Duke of Nemours and a Knight Templar and I am only his daughter. In the age of chivalry very little is shared with females…If knowledge of a treasure truly exists, only a son who carries the family name would be so privileged as to know of it."

"Ah, but you are not the usual female, my lady! I was privileged to observe your dexterity in the use of arms and since I have never witnessed such ability in a woman. I assume you have been trained in a skill reserved for Knights and gentlemen of high rank. You are also the only child of the Duke of Nemours. Who else can carry the knowledge of the treasure forward, but you? I believe he trained you in the use of arms to make you worthy of such knowledge."

"So you released him? You are certain that he possesses the secret of the Templars' treasure, and you let him go?"

"Your father was stubbornly prepared to die before giving up any information. You are here because we believe you will more readily yield your secrets!"

Polyxena slowly shook her head. "Perhaps I am not my father's equal in the face of danger. However, you are mistaken in assuming I was trained in the use of arms to be a worthy recipient of family secrets. In reality is connected with the Count of Rozenberk, a Knight Templar and my father's most loyal friend, who taught me fighting skills because he thought that I had an aptitude for it.

"While I was growing up, my father was compelled to be away from home at the head of his army for many years. During that difficult time, my guardian became concerned for my safety. He encouraged me to become adept in self defense. That is the true reason for my aptitude in the use of arms, not to guard family secrets...Besides, I do not believe that my father has knowledge of the treasure because the subject was never brought up in my presence. As you say, I am the only living heir of the house of Nemours and thus I would have been taken into his confidence if such knowledge existed. My lord, I cannot reveal information I do not possess.

"Great efforts went into my abduction and your life was placed in grave peril, along with your men. Why make such an effort on the remote possibility that I had knowledge of the treasure? There has to be another reason. I am in the dark about the identity of my adversary and the uncertainty I face every day torments me. Please my lord, have some compassion and tell me, who is my enemy?"

Her splendid green eyes gazed at Zanar with a hypnotic stare. He could inhale the fragrance of her hair and feel the warmth of her body, disturbingly close. Her caftan did little to shield her sensual curves. She was helpless and available to him and yet her aura of dignity was somehow intimidating. It created a barrier between them.

Polyxena was aware of the power of her beauty over Zanar and realized it was likely to be her only asset there. She noticed his demeanor changing in response to her behavior. His tone of anger lessened and he became a bit more composed.

"I cannot tell you, Polyxena. It is not for me to say. You will find out in due time. However, if I were you, I would not be so eager to reach that final destination, which could bring dire consequences. You should be grateful for my generosity and the comforts you have been afforded here!"

"Comforts?" said Polyxena, unable to control her displeasure. "This is a gilded prison that offers little joy…I have no desire to extend my stay, even facing the possibility of greater danger or even death! I deem anything preferable to this!"

"There is little gratitude in you, my lady. You have enjoyed many comforts, considering that you are a prisoner. And yet, you would rather face the unknown, even the possibility of death, rather than relax your ridiculous code of honor and simply share this place with me?"

"Perhaps my assessment of the situation is a bit harsh," she said soothingly. "But you must understand my plight and my desire to be free. I yearn freedom with every fiber of my being."

"You will never be free!" exclaimed Zanar. "Not as long as you are enslaved by your sense of morality and tradition." He lowered his voice to a seductive tone. "Lower your defenses and allow your true passionate feelings to surface. You could find the wonder of ecstasy in my arms, my lady, and pleasure you never experienced before!"

Zanar strong arms encircled her waist. She felt helplessly entrapped, but also feared that an open rejection could have devastating consequences. The warmth of his breath was dangerously close to her mouth. His hands caressed the contour of her body without restraint. She attempted to turn her head away while he ran his lips along her neck.

Polyxena attempted to twist free of his aggression, but he held her so tightly she was unable to move while he pressed his body tightly against hers.

Zanar forced his lips upon hers with such a smoldering, passionate kiss that the force of it took her breath away. She struggled while their bodies melted together and she could feel the strength of his aggressive touch burning against her skin. The deep, penetrating kiss was so invasive that she had the terrifying feeling of choking, as she fought desperately to push him away and regain her breath.

Zanar was not going to get the same response from her that his drugs elicited. She was fully aware. As the Duchess of Lorengard-Lorraine, her lofty title was closely connected to the concepts of dignity and self-respect. However, in the grim truth of her imprisonment, she was just like the maidens—a helpless sex slave to be used at will for the pleasure of men. She continued the struggle to protect herself against violation.

The attraction she felt for Zanar under the effect of the powerful potion was nonexistent without them. Despite his sexual appeal and good looks, he was now simply a dangerous man groping her body without restraint or respect.

During the struggle, Polyxena's caftan ripped open. Her rounded breasts were exposed to Zanar's predatory stare. The struggle intensified and became increasingly violent, while Polyxena attempted to resist his increasingly brutal attack.

Zanar seemed to enjoy the fierce sexual encounter, disregarding her horror and disgust.

During the uneven struggle, she felt the hard edge of a metal object and noticed a small dagger tucked into the sash around Zanar's waist. She twisted her body until her hand could reach it. An instant later, the sharp blade gashed his arm.

Zanar cried out and released his hold and Polyxena instantly moved away from him, brandishing the knife. He grabbed his wounded arm, which was spewing blood, and wrapped a silken scarf around the gash as a tourniquet. All the while, he glared at Polyxena in outrage.

"Wretched woman!" he cried out. "What do you think you can accomplish with a knife? You have no place to go and your belligerence will not free you!"

"Perhaps not, my lord," she answered while she tried to rearrange her torn clothes. "But at least I was able to stop your debasing aggression, by inflicting a flesh wound with your dagger!"

"A scratch, you fool!" Zanar responded. "You will pay dearly for your hostility and because of this foolishness you will deserve all the woes that will befall you!"

Zanar approached Polyxena again, but she swiftly moved away, wielding the dagger at him. He laughed at her combative stance.

"I am always amazed by your boldness, my lady. And while I am aware of your prowess in the use of arms, I doubt you will be able to accomplish much with that small dagger against my scimitar and the armed men surrounding the tent. Put down your weapon and cease your foolish behavior. It will not save you or open the doors to freedom!"

Polyxena remained silent. Her cheeks were flushed and her hair disheveled, and still she presented such an image of beauty and pride that she took Zanar's breath away.

He had disdain for his weakness and attraction to the Duchess, but her chivalry in the face of danger only heightened the burning desire he had for her. However, her rejection wounded his pride so badly that he continued taunting Polyxena with a barrage of threats.

"What are you trying to do, my lady, forestall the inevitable? You will soon be a captive in my arms, since this little interruption only heightened the desire and hunger I have for you. Besides, you cannot deny the awakening of your lustful nature."

Zanar drew closer to Polyxena while speaking those passionate words. She recoiled.

"Stand back!" she cried, pointing the dagger at Zanar. "If you move forward I will inflict more than a scratch upon your body. I warn you, my lord, do not tempt fate!"

"When will you cease your foolish behavior?" Zanar raged. "It is very unwise in the face of danger! This is a place filled with lustful men and I am your only protector against them!"

Polyxena did not believe Zanar would go so far as to subject her to the horror of mass rape. However, there was no way to be certain of the behavior of this unpredictable and volatile man. And in spite of her fears, she continued to appear brave, standing tall with her usual regal bearing.

"This is your last chance," Zanar finally said. "Give me the dagger at once, or you shall suffer fierce consequences!"

"Your vile threats do not intimidate me! Nor will they bend me to your will!"

"You must be delusional! Have you not heard me? Your life is hanging by a thread!"

"I thought I was considered a prize captive?" Polyxena taunted him, seemingly impervious to his treats. "I am certain that the powerful enemy who ordered my abduction will not be pleased with my premature death, since I suspect that I am to appear in person and not only as a corpse?"

"How dare you challenge my authority? I am in control here, and no one who wishes to live another day dares to show me disrespect. I have been far too magnanimous and it is time for you to learn who is in charge here."

"I suppose abusing a defenseless woman in this way makes you feel strong and powerful," she replied with contempt. "I feel sorry for your misguided behavior. You are a week, vile man, and I have no respect for such a person…Only pity."

Zanar was astounded by Polyxena's boldness. His cheeks flushed. "Very well, my lady, if this is your answer…you will suffer the consequences of your foolish behavior. Guards!" Responding immediately to the command, several guards pushed into the tent, brandishing their arms.

Zanar pointed to Polyxena. "Seize her!"

"Stand back!" she cried out to the men, and without warning she turned the weapon around, pointing the dagger against her chest. "One more step and I will plunge this knife into my heart. Your hostage will be delivered to my secret enemy as a corpse!"

Zanar regarded Polyxena with amazement while she stood erect, proud, holding the dagger firmly in her hands. He signaled the guards to stop.

"You are a foolish woman. I doubt you truly intend to end your life, but I am not willing to take the chance with your unpredictable behavior. Besides, if you intend to go through with it, you will destroy a precious life in the flower of youth for no purpose. You have been given choices, but spurned them without regard."

Polyxena answered with sadness, but the sound of her voice remained strong and determined, "I have not been given choices, only demands! It is not my wish to die. However, the dishonor I have been offered is worse than death! I will not be defiled! I only hope that my people will not be ashamed in the manner of my death."

While speaking those uncompromising words, Polyxena placed both hands around the handle of the dagger and lifted the weapon above her head, preparing to plunge the fatal knife in her breast.

"Stop Polyxena!" Lord Zanar screamed. He paused, then lowered his voice, "I do not wish for you to die. I am sure we can find a way that is less drastic and a better understanding between us."

"What understanding? You have made it quite clear that there is no hope for me, since I have been threatened with violence and dishonor. Death is my only salvation!"

Lord Zanar was disturbed by Polyxena's response. He surprised her by lowering his voice and taking on a softer tone, "My retort was driven by anger. I never intended to have you defiled by my men, I only wished to crush your haughty spirit. I give you my word of honor, that if you give up your weapon, no harm will come to you!"

"Honor? You have no honor my lord and you have proved it by your actions. I see no hope, because your words cannot be trusted. I will not give up my weapon. It is my only way to freedom and death is my salvation."

"No, Polyxena," insisted Zanar. "I grant that you might not have cause to trust me, but I swear upon the sacred name of Allah that no harm will come to you. However, I cannot be held responsible for what will happen to you once we will reach the final destination and I will deliver you as my hostage. I have my orders and I intend to follow them. It is my duty and a matter of honor. You are someone who understands the meaning of honor."

Polyxena remained silent. His words seemed truthful but the dagger was still the only bargaining power she possessed.

"I do not trust you, my lord! It is a sad reality to live in uncertainty and terror. I am a captive and the possibility of violent death looms over me anyway. I prefer to end all if I must, of my own volition!"

"There is always hope with life, Polyxena," insisted Zanar. "I do not promise you freedom. However, I give you my assurance that you will have nothing to fear from me or my men. Give me the dagger, Polyxena. Trust me this once and I promise not to disappoint you!"

He continued to advance toward her while he spoke, "Give me the dagger." He moved closer. Then his strong hands encircled her wrists and he snatched the dagger from her hands.

She closed her eyes in silent prayer, vulnerable and terrified. With no more defense, her only hope was that Zanar would keep his word instead of seeking revenge.

Zanar clapped his hands. She felt immense relief when the handmaidens appeared in response and the menacing guards disappeared from sight. "Prepare Her Grace for a journey on horseback, bring forth her traveling clothes and proper nourishment for the impending travel. Make certain she will be ready within two hours."

Polyxena was glad to leave the nightmarish entrapment of the tent, regardless of the whatever dangers awaited her elsewhere. She looked at Zanar with gratitude, but he appeared angry and remained stern and remote, refusing to make eye contact. Instead he bowed politely and walked out of the tent.

When silence returned and she had time to think, it occurred to her that dusk was approaching, a strange time to travel on horseback. Nonetheless, she was eager to leave, and began to feel hopeful that this could be the reprieve she was hoping for, and that with a bit of luck she might find a way to escape.

Soon an abundant meal was brought in for her. She ate with gusto to replenish her strength—spiced meats, stuffed dates, a profusion of fresh fruits and a lavish assortment of sweets. She even drank a glass of wine, and enjoyed the relaxing warmth the ruby liquid imparted.

Soon the maidens returned with her traveling clothes, and she wondered at the unfamiliar attire. The garments included long, loose fitting pants of heavy woolen cloth. The ensemble was black in color topped by a short cassock and a leather vest with ankle boots. The flowing cloak was fur lined and a fur hat completed the apparel. A wide leather belt held a scabbard with a shiny sword. She was surprised by the presence of the weapon, but assumed that in the wilderness it was a necessary protection.

When she was fully dressed, a makeshift mirror was placed in front of her and she looked with wonder at her reflection in the exotic garments, and marveled on how comfortable and warm they felt against her skin.

Soon Lord Zanar reappeared outside the tent on horseback. He was wearing traveling clothes. There was a great allure in the handsome man sitting proudly upon his steed, wrapped in a flowing mantle. He remained somber, but his face brightened at the sight of Polyxena, so fetchingly attired.

Zanar held another horse by the reins. Like his own mount, this black stallion was fully saddled and carried a large amount of provisions, food, and water for the challenging ride through the wilderness. A thick rope and bow and arrows were also included. She recognized the horse as the black Friesian she briefly befriended in her escape attempt.

The usual escort was missing, and Polyxena was relieved that they would be traveling alone. Perhaps she would find a way to escape.

Zanar dismounted with agility and brought the black stallion forward, toward Polyxena.

"I am sure the presence of this horse will please you my lady, since you became such good friends in a short time. it was surprising, since he is actually a very stubborn animal who doesn't respond well to command."

"Perhaps he needs a little kindness," Polyxena answered, caressing the proud head of the beautiful animal. "It will be like traveling with an old friend. He looks so much like Hildebrandt, my former mount, that I almost believe he has come back to life."

"Hildebrandt!" she called out. The stallion surprised them both by responding to the name as if it was his own.

"Amazing!" exclaimed Zanar openly amused. "Your Hildebrandt has returned and he is yours as long as you want him. Now we must make haste, my lady. Sundown is approaching. It will take at least an hour before our first stop at a safe house."

"Will we be traveling toward or against the sun?" asked Polyxena.

"It is futile to ask such probing questions, my lady. You will never find your way out of the forest, without my help.
We will be traveling north-east."

Zanar extended his arm to Polyxena and helped her mount the horse while lightening appeared in the distance. Threatening clouds mixed with the brilliance of the sunset.

A shadow of storm is brewing, she thought. *May the good lord guide my steps and help my quest to find the way home!*

Following Zanar, Polyxena spurred her horse to a faster gallop, and they soon disappeared in the surrounding greenery.

✝✝✝

CHAPTER EIGHT

THE CRIMSON TRAIL

Sir Berthold continued undaunted, following Arsenio and Kusen at a discrete distance. It was a moonlit night and he was able to see them clearly enough in spite of the gloom and the thick vegetation. He held on for dear life to his horse, which was moving much too swiftly for him. The mysterious sounds of the forest made him uneasy. He had the unsettling feeling of being surrounded by monstrous, powerful enemies in every direction. Despite the chill in the air, he was thoroughly covered with sweat. Nevertheless, his promotion to Knight gave him strength he would not ordinarily possess. Steely determination spurred him on, regardless of his fears.

The pathway in the woodland was rocky and uneven, but he was familiar with it, having journeyed through it many times on the way to the surrounding vineyard. But he had never attempted the journey in the dark of night. Now the region seemed alien to him. Berthold wondered if they were going to stop somewhere to spend the night, or continue to travel forward through the menacing darkness.

He was aware of some rocky formations further ahead in the forest, and wondered if Kusen knew of them as well. Natural caves were present in the rocks and could make a handy shelter for weary travelers.

He hoped the Duke and Kusen would perhaps take advantage of the rudimentary shelter. At last, with great relief, Berthold saw that the men were slowing their pace, obviously looking for a place to stop for the night. The two men had found shelter in one of the caves in a rocky hillside.

He secured his horse to a nearby tree and found a suitable cave of his own, which offered some protection from the elements. He even managed to start a small fire in order to keep warm in the frigid environment and ate a little food before lying down for the night.

Thoroughly exhausted, he laid down on a blanket and closed his eyes, hoping to find some respite from the stressful occurrences of the day. But disturbing thoughts continued to plague his mind and enhance his fears.

Was Kusen truly showing Arsenio the way? Or was he merely stalling for time to save himself, and perhaps lure the Duke into a deadly trap? The premise was too unsettling and he tried to dismiss it from his mind, enough to allow him a few hours of sleep.

Nearby, Arsenio and Kusen were also ready to get some rest for the night. Both were unaware of Berthold's proximity. The Duke could only hope that the innkeeper was following them in spite of his fears, and that he was somewhere in the vicinity.

Arsenio had embarked on the journey with a good measure of skepticism about this plan as the only available way to find Polyxena alive. He willingly placed his life in danger to that end, despite also harboring little faith in the trustworthiness of Kusen. He kept his sword readily available.

Throughout their trip so far, Kusen had been morose and uncommunicative. He continually looked around to make certain they were not being followed.

Arsenio tried to engage him in conversation several times, but found it impossible to connect in a dialogue with the man.

"Are you going to tell me where we are going now, Kusen? Or are you backing away from your promise of being helpful? I suggest you remain true to your word to avoid dire consequences. Since you have proven to be untrustworthy, you cannot expect me to follow you blindly, without even the slightest clue of what direction we are taking."

Kusen reluctantly responded. "I want to make certain we are not being followed by anyone, because it could prove fatal to me in more ways than one. I also fear betrayal by you, despite your assurances and I am concerned that this area will soon be swarmed by your soldiers."

"I gave you my word," insisted Arsenio. "My guards are not following us."

In the age of chivalry, a nobleman's word could not be bantered around casually and had to be respected at all cost. Arsenio was comforted by the thought that Berthold was not a member of his guard, and thus he was speaking the truth.

Kusen relented. "We will be going to a nearby village, located three or four hours from here, depending upon the traveling conditions and the weather."

"Is my wife there?"

"No your grace, it will only be a stopover, the final destination is still far away."

"At least tell me if we going to travel toward the mountains or following the seashore."

"It isn't necessary for you to know." Kusen snapped. "You must trust me and my guidance without question, understanding that I cannot guarantee the Duchess is still alive at this point. I will bring you to the place where I believe she is being held…and that is all I can do."

Arsenio was shaken by the words. The possibility of Polyxena's death was devastating. "We better get some sleep now, and have an early start in the morning. If we did not need to rest the animals, I would insist that we press on through the night."

Kusen nodded and the men finally managed to find sleep and rest in spite of the rugged terrain beneath them.

After a few hours of uneasy slumber on the harsh, rocky ground, the Duke woke feeling somewhat refreshed. It was still quite early and pre dawn darkness reigned. Kusen was still fast asleep, so Arsenio decided to allow him a little more rest and wait for dawn. Only then did he unceremoniously awaken Kusen, eager to get under way. They shared some food and a little water, tended to the animals, then mounted their steeds and spurred them to a fast pace.

Nearby, Berthold was awakened by the sound of the departing horses. Caught off guard by the early departure, he quickly collected his belongings, waddled over to his horse, mounted, and spurred him on in pursuit. The Duke and Kusen were already a considerable distance from him, barely visible in the soft morning light. In spite of his fears of falling, he spurred Rasham forward at a greater speed, bouncing in the saddle.

The unlikely Knight was disheveled from the force of the wind and his heart beat wildly from the excitement of the chase. Nevertheless, he ignored his fears and pressed onward. The splendid animal soon closed the distance to the Duke and

Kusen, and the chase continued uninterrupted for a couple of long hours.

Soon the landscape before them began to change. The verdant vegetation became more sporadic while the terrain became rocky, almost barren. Still, although the sun was now well into the sky, the horizon showed no sign of a village. Arsenio again became concerned that Kusen might be taking him on a wild goose chase. He flanked Kusen's horse and asked him in a strong voice.

"Where are we going? I see no sign of a village anywhere, how long more to reach our destination?"

"Not much farther, my lord," Kusen answered, pointing his finger toward a large hill rising prominently ahead. "Just over that hill, there will be a ravine with a deep narrow passage. The village is on the other side of the mound."

For Arsenio, the idea of entering a gorge with his treacherous guide seemed dangerous and he feared entering an ambush or a trap. He rested his hand on the pommel of his sword.

Berthold was now so close to the other two men that he slowed the pace of his horse. He had been faithfully leaving visible marks on the road, as requested, to allow the Duke's army to follow them.

They were now traveling over territory unfamiliar to Berthold—vast extensions of land he never traveled. His anxiety was becoming even more acute over the possibility of losing sight of the men and getting lost in the vast wilderness. He also feared that a strong rainfall could remove the red stains he was leaving for guidance. His timid nature conjured up dire scenarios that kept him on edge.

He saw Duke Arsenio and Kusen approaching a narrow ravine barely visible in the distance, and quickly lost sight of them. It was as if they had been swallowed by the landscape. The sudden disappearance rattled him, and after a few unsettling moments, he decided to come out of hiding and follow them into the gorge.

The ravine was shadowy and treacherous, with uneven and rocky terrain and side walls laden with loose stones that could be easily dislodged. He was greatly relieved by the sight of the Duke and Kusen making their way up ahead.

The silence was only broken from time to time by falling rocks, making the passageway even more dangerous. He was grateful that the Duke and Kusen slowed their pace in order to avoid causing a rock slide.

He stopped for a while to allow a bit more distance from the two men. The gorge passageway was narrow and of considerable height. Cave-like formations were everywhere, creating echoes and amplifying sounds. Berthold decided that it would be wise to follow the Duke on foot. He secured Rasham on a nearby tree and continued walking on foot, taking great care to remain hidden.

Venturing forward at a slow pace, Arsenio and Kusen finally reached the end of the gorge and were suddenly embraced by sunshine so bright that it momentarily blinded them. When their sight cleared, a beautiful waterfall came into view, flowing into a river surrounded by lush greenery and flowers.

Arsenio was stunned by the amazing sight, a special oasis so different from the barren area just on the other side of the hill. In addition to the beautiful scenery, a few mud huts were present in the area. He assumed it was the village Kusen told him about.

The inhabitants appeared to be mostly women who busily attended to their chores, while children played throughout the area. Domestic animals walked freely around the pastoral setting. The only men present appeared to be of an older generation and Arsenio wondered if the younger males were hunting or engaged in warlike activities away from home. There was no visible presence of guards or weapons. Arsenio was cheered that at least they were not entering a military compound.

Kusen appeared familiar with the place and spurred his horse forward toward a little whitewashed hut on the far end of the village. An old gentleman sat out in front, resting in the sunshine. He was startled by Kusen's sudden appearance but then appeared pleased and welcomed him with a friendly smile.

Kusen dismounted the horse and bowed in deference. The man called out loudly and in response an elderly woman came rushing out the door with obvious excitement.

She was dressed in a traditional white abaya, with a multicolored hijab covering her head. Arsenio noticed a look of affection in her eyes when she looked at Kusen, but she remained at a respectful distance, deferential to the men. Kusen greeted her politely and bowed. The Duke assumed that he was in the presence of Kusen's parents and that the whitewashed hut was his home.

The woman entered the humble hut and returned carrying a large terracotta cup filled to the brim with goat's milk. Kusen drank the white nectar so quickly that some spilled from the sides of his mouth. He then engaged the couple in a lively conversation, using a language alien to Arsenio, who remained silent and uneasy, confused by the rude reception—he had been virtually ignored by the elderly couple.

He assumed that Kusen informed his parents of the situation at hand and most likely suggested that they ignore the Duke and consider him an unwelcome guest. Although he was unable to understand the conversation, he heard the name Sulimah mentioned several times, but it was difficult to understand if that person was well liked or not, although Kusen seemed more animated at the sound of the name.

Arsenio wondered who she was and how she was related to Kusen. As the conversation continued, it became animated at times. It seemed strange to Arsenio that it was conducted outdoors and that Kusen was not invited to enter the house.

Finally, the perplexing conversation came to an end. Kusen appeared eager to leave after he bowed once more to the couple and signaled the Duke to follow him.

They soon arrived at a more attractive whitewashed hut, with small windows decorated with blooming flower pots. The area around the hut was pristine and was obviously being cared for by loving hands. A small vegetable garden was strategically located near the river.

After securing the horses, Kusen invited the Duke to enter the shelter. The interior was comprised of a fairly large room, modestly furnished, but clean and inviting. The rough floor was partially covered with colorful carpets and scattered pillows. Cooking utensils were carefully placed on a corner of the room by a wood burning fireplace and the shiny copper pots hanging on the wall were the only touch of class to the humble abode.

There was also a separate room, shielded by a colorful drape and perhaps used as a sleeping area. "You can set yourself here for the night, my lord." said Kusen, pointing to a carpeted area with some scattered pillows resting against a wall near the fireplace.

Arsenio had noticed that the man's demeanor had changed considerably since he entered the village. He appeared far more confident and at ease than before. Kusen approached a large container filled with water and washed his face and hands before sitting down on a nearby pillow, then encouraged the Duke to do the same.

They appeared to be alone, but Arsenio had the strange feeling that someone else was in the house, and that for some unknown reason, the individual chose to remain hidden.

To break the uncomfortable silence, he addressed Kusen, "Those people you were speaking to before, are they your parents?"

"Yes," Kusen replied in a distracted manner. It was obvious to Arsenio that something was troubling the man, but he decided to remain silent. He needed Kusen's help to find Polyxena, and despite his waning patience he had little recourse but tolerate Kusen's unpleasant personality.

Finally Kusen decided to break the silence and clapped his hands sharply and called out, "Sulimah."

In immediate response the curtain separating the room moved suddenly to the side and a woman appeared, covered from head to toe in a traditional burka. Only the brightness of her eyes was visible. Still, it was evident that the attire shielded a very young woman.

The Duke jumped to his feet and adhering to his chivalrous nature in the presence of a woman, greeted the mysterious lady with a respectful bow. Kusen also stood up and approached her, but his demeanor was quite different from Arsenio. He appeared to be unfriendly almost hostile.

Sulimah recoiled.

"My Lord, this is my wife, Sulimah. It will be her responsibility to make you comfortable in our home."

The Duke smiled and bowed again in greeting and in closer proximity he was able to see the color of her eyes, which were dark and striking. She gazed at the tall, handsome Prince and appeared particularly interested in the golden color of Arsenio's hair which was a rare sight among her people.

The gracious manners of the Prince were also something she was not accustomed to. She stood silent, fascinated by the unexpected guest, almost in awe of him.

Her admiration did not escape Kusen's eyes. He was angered by the sight and rudely pushed Sulimah toward the back wall, causing her to stumble.

Arsenio was appalled by the crude behavior, but prudently remained silent and decided not to interfere. He did not want to inflame the volatile situation.

Kusen barked some orders to his wife, who hastened to obey instructions and brought forth refreshments. She approached the fireplace and speedily filled a large tray with an enticing assortment of sweet meats, dried fruits, and two cups of goat's milk.

Sulimah's distress was evident. She appeared unsteady on her feet while attending to her chores and when she tried to carry the cumbersome tray laden with food, the tray proved too heavy for her petite frame. Her movements were so impaired by the cumbersome burka that she stumbled forward, nearly spilling the contents of the large tray.

Arsenio jumped to his feet and steadied Sulimah by the shoulders, preventing her from dropping the tray and falling over. The young woman quickly regained her balance, but Arsenio noticed the terror in her eyes—he felt a flash of confusion. He realized that it was considered a grave breach of etiquette according to the laws of Islam to touch a woman outside one's family and that this applied in the strongest terms to an infidel. But he assumed that such a thing as keeping someone from falling would be exempt. In the next instant he realized that he was mistaken about that.

A scream of anger filled the room. Kusen yanked a small dagger from his waist and pointed it toward the Duke, swinging it like a man possessed. Arsenio quickly sidestepped the attack and managed to grab a couple of pillows from the floor to shield against the dagger. The Duke was an experienced fighter and managed to keep Kusen at bay, relying on his agility and cool head in the face of danger.

Arsenio finally managed to restrain the man by grabbing the wrist holding the knife, and pushed him back against the wall. Kusen continued to fight and the two men fell together to the ground. They rolled on the floor while Arsenio struggled to remove the dagger from his hand. The deadly assault continued under the terrified eyes of Sulimah, huddled against the back wall during the scuffle. At last, with a well-placed punch, the Duke was able to knock Kusen out and recover the knife.

It was now obvious that Arsenio was dealing with an unstable and violent fanatic. This created deep concerns, since he had no recourse but to accept Kusen's behavior.

Remaining under the same roof, with Kusen's wife in such close proximity, made the situation highly volatile. But it was imperative to get along with him on some level in spite of all the difficulties.

There was little time to contemplate a plan. Kusen began to awaken. Sulimah hurried forward with a vessel filled with water and prepared to pour some of the cool liquid on his face.

Arsenio stopped her, and motioned with urgency for her to leave the room and stay out of sight, since their presence together might increase Kusen's rage. The girl understood Arsenio's concerns and immediately responded by disappearing from sight. Arsenio bound Kusen wrists with an available piece of rope before pouring the cold water on his face.

Kusen opened his eyes and for a brief moment was still disoriented, but as soon as clarity returned, he attempted to resume his attack. When he realized that he was restrained, his wild eyes filled with rage, making the quest to pacify him very challenging.

"Calm down, Kusen." said the Duke in a firm voice. "I meant no disrespect, I was only trying to stop the food tray from spilling over and help your wife regain her balance. I did not want one of my hosts to be injured."

"You touched her!" Kusen answered foaming at the mouth. "Your unclean, infidel hand, touched my wife. I should kill you with my bare hands for such an act."

"It was an accident and I am not familiar with your customs," insisted Arsenio, trying to pacify his rage. "I give you my word of honor that this is true and promise never to touch your wife again."

"Not if you care to live another day. And I swear that if you don't honor your word, I will kill you like the infidel dog you are."

"I have given you my word. That should be enough." Arsenio, struggled to control his temper. "I suggest you stop this vile verbal attack. It was your idea to bring me into your house; I would prefer to sleep outside, rather than be subjected to your temper."

"You must remain here," growled Kusen. "My father, who is in charge of the village, refuses to have an infidel among our people. I managed to convince him to allow you to stay here for a couple of days, before we leave for the final destination…but only if you remain in the house and you are not to be seen by anyone."

"Then why don't we just go away right now?" Arsenio asked, thoroughly frustrated. "I do not wish to remain here another moment. Finding my wife is my only concern."

"We will remain here." Kusen harshly repeated. "I also have a wife and I desire to spend time with her before the journey, since my survival remains in question and the shadow of death is in my path. We will depart when I say and not before."

Without waiting for a reply, Kusen got a challenging look in his eyes and placed his wrists before Arsenio, signaling him to remove the restraining rope.

The Duke understood that he had no other choice at the moment. In truth, he was the one whose hands were bound. Reluctantly, he consented to the demand and untied the rope. The men finally sat down by the fireplace and managed to eat some of the food prepared by Sulimah. She silently reentered the house and sat hidden in a far corner.

For a few moments, peace reigned in Kusen's abode while the two men ate. Then Kusen stood up and strode to Sulimah, holding out an empty cup. "Is this all you have to offer me, woman," he asked in a cold voice. "goat's milk? There is no reason to guess, since you know what I really like." While speaking, Kusen grabbed Sulimah by an arm and pushed her violently forward, toward the entrance door, telling her, "Bring it at once."

He threw the cup against the white washed walls. It broke in pieces and a terrified Sulimah rushed from the house in response to the command and the anger behind it.

She soon returned with a goat's skin filled with wine, which had been cooling in the frigid outdoors. Arsenio realized the container had been placed out there to avoid having wine in the house, since consuming alcohol is discouraged by Islam.

Kusen grabbed the bulging skin from Sulimah's hands and drank with voracious gusto, slopping the wine onto his clothing. Arsenio found the scene disgusting, but neither he nor Sulimah dared to interrupt him.

Kusen became quickly inebriated and soon staggered throughout the room. Arsenio was surprised by the man's unrestrained consumption of wine, which Kusen always refused to consume while prisoner in the Ducal palace. He was proving to be a strange combination of fanaticism, violence and overindulgence.

Sulimah was clearly terrified of her drunken husband. She looked pitifully toward Arsenio for comfort and protection that he could not offer.

He was troubled by the terrible situation, since his chivalrous nature prompted him to act in defense of a woman. However, Sulimah was Kusen's wife and regardless of the distaste he felt for the man's aggressive behavior, he knew he was not permitted to interfere.

Arsenio was debating whether his sense of honor should trump common sense while the drink fest continued. Next Kusen focused on another desire and his bloodshot eyes gazed at Sulimah with lust. The young woman recoiled toward the back wall when he approached her, her distress visible even through the cumbersome burka.

Kusen grabbed his young wife by the waist, easily lifting her off the floor. Arsenio heard a desperate gasp emerging from Sulimah as she was forcefully carried to the back room.

The Duke's resolve was truly challenged, but it was clear that even the most well-meaning interference could devastate his quest to find Polyxena. He understood the challenge and difficulties in dealing with people of a different culture with different religious beliefs, and interfering with a couple who was married according to the laws of Islam was particularly inadvisable. The quandary truly paralyzed him as he sat on the floor, feeling overwhelmed and distraught.

The aggressive sexual act unfolded almost immediately in the tiny back room, shielded from Arsenio's sight by the flimsy curtain, which swayed ominously during the desperate struggle in that confined area.

Kusen's sounds of passion were loud and clearly audible, coupled with Sulima's sobs of pain and fear. Arsenio found it appalling to be the unwilling witness to the brutal sexual encounter between a frightened young bride and her domineering, sadistic husband. He was certain she had endured sexual aggressions many times before and it seemed certain that she loathed and despised her husband for treating her this way.

Out of sight from Arsenio, in the small bed chamber shielded only by a colorful drape, Sulimah lay stripped of the burka and all her clothing. Her drunken husband had finally satisfied his lust and released his powerful grip on her.

She rolled onto her side and tears streamed from her eyes. Sulimah was truly a child bride, between fourteen and fifteen years in age as far as she knew, and her frail body had not quite developed to full bloom. Her lovely, oval face was highlighted by large eyes framed by thick, curved eyelashes and arching brows. Long, raven hair crowned her features with beauty. She was more an adolescent than a full grown woman, and yet an aura of maturity and intelligence radiated from her that contrasted with her youthful appearance.

Her penetrating eyes focused on her husband, to make certain he was fast asleep and unable to inflict any more distress for the moment. Kusen was overcome by the wine and appeared to have fallen into a deep slumber. He began to snore.

Very carefully, trying not to awaken Kusen, she gathered her clothes and dressed herself, and within a few minutes she was again shrouded in the weighty burka. The cumbersome garment gave her a sense of comfort, as if it could protect her from abuse.

She carefully moved the drapes to the side and peered into the main room through the reddish light from the burning embers of the fireplace. She saw that Arsenio was also asleep, resting on some scattered pillows on the far corner.

The young Duke presented a very different image than her husband, with his aristocratic features and tall, well-built body. He wore clothing of an elegance and refinement that she had never seen. She moved closer to Arsenio and knelt by his side, gazing with wonder at the handsome stranger who had shown her such respect and kindness. There was a special attraction to the golden, blond hair that framed his face and shimmered like precious metal by the light of the fireplace.

His benevolent presence in her humble home was truly a miraculous gift. She felt a compulsion to touch him and be certain he was real.

Unable to control her desire, she gently touched one of the Duke's hair locks, murmuring in spite of herself, "It looks like gold…"

Arsenio was startled by the sound. He immediately sat up, fearing treachery, and grabbed the sword at his side. He was surprised to see Sulimah hovering over him. He moved the weapon and hid it underneath his body.

"What are you doing here?" he whispered. "It is dangerous and unwise to be in my company with your jealous husband nearby."

"I only wish to thank you for your kindness toward me, my lord. I have come to express to you that it is my honor to have you as a guest in our home."

"I thank you." Arsenio frowned. "But it is still not advisable for you to be here."

"He is sound asleep from the heavy drinking, I am certain he will not wake up for many hours, my lord."

"Regardless, it is not advisable to tempt fate. I think you better return to your bed chamber until your husband awakens."

"I am afraid of him, my lord. And there is no one here who can help me."

"I am pained by your sorrow, I wish I could be helpful, please believe me. Still I am not in the position to do that. I am in desperate need of your husband's help and can't afford to antagonize him. Have you no family or friends to aid you?"

"No one, my lord. Kusen owns me now. He brought me here some time ago, taking me away from places and people I knew and loved...I am alone."

"I am sorry, my lady, however, I believe your husband is a dangerous man. You must not antagonize him, I beseech you. Return to your room."

Arsenio spoke to her as gently as possible, but his voice was firm. Sulimah remained reluctant, fascinated by the handsome stranger who expressed concern and kindness toward her. The presence of the nobleman and his compassion and understanding toward her was exciting.

Kusen began to snore in the next room. He was fast asleep. They were safe enough for the moment.

"What is your name, my lord?" she quietly asked. "You must be a very important person from a distinguished family. It is apparent by your gracious manners and the elegance of your demeanor."

"My dear Sulimah, if I may be permitted to call you by your name, I am not an important person at the moment. I even lack the power to protect my wife. However, I do hold a position of great responsibility. I am Arsenio, Duke of Lorengard-Lorraine."

"You are a Duke?" interrupted Sulimah, deeply impressed. "Such a great honor for my house." She bowed with deference to Arsenio and fiercely whispered, "It is truly a miracle that you are here. Allah has answered my plea, sending a golden prince to deliver me from my oppression."

Arsenio was startled by the speed with which the situation was becoming dangerous and complicated. Sulimah saw a savior in him, but she had a jealous husband who was volatile and violent by nature.

He tried again. "I am not your savior, Sulimah. Much as I might wish to be. My wife has been abducted from our home, and your husband is the only person with knowledge of her whereabouts. I fear treachery from him, but I am compelled by a cruel destiny to follow his guidance, to find my wife."

"I am saddened by your misfortune, my lord. I hope that a kinder destiny will help you find your wife."

"Then my lady, please go back to your bed chamber, if you wish to be of help. Your husband must not see us together when he awakens, or I fear he will never show me the way to find her."

"But my lord, he is an evil man," insisted Sulimah. "Kusen took me away from my family when I was only nine years of age. He first noticed me while I was playing with friends and he was instantly attracted. He ignored my aversion and fear of him

173

and approached my parents to request me as his bride. They turned him down, not only out of intense dislike for him, but also because he is of a different Islamic faction. Much blood and hatred exists between our two peoples. There is a deep distrust of one another. My parents would never agree to such an arrangement. It would be like sending their daughter off to live with the devil.

"Since my parents would not consent to our marriage, he abducted me. I was taken far away. I was disgraced, violated, and had no other recourse but to marry him. I endure violence and cruelty. He considers me nothing but a possession. We traveled to many distant places because his family also objected when he took me for a bride. We were not allowed to enter his parent's house. He joined several religious groups, trying to find a mission in life and to belong somewhere, but he became an outcast because of his marriage to the daughter of enemies.

"He is not a true man of God. He is cruel and vindictive. I know he will never let me go, as long as he lives. And as you see, he drinks without regard to religious teaching."

Sulimah was suddenly started at the sight of a corpulent male face in the window. She jumped to her feet and was about to cry out in fear, when Arsenio signaled her to be silent. He recognized the face of his jovial inn keeper, Berthold.

Arsenio motioned for him to get down and stay out of sight. "There is no danger, my lady, no reason to fear. He is a friend, and poses no peril to you. He follows me as a precaution, to protect me from unforeseen threats."

Sulimah took a sharp breath. "Your friend is in grave danger, my lord. The people around here are not hospitable to strangers, especially infidels. He may be safe for the moment, but he must not let his presence be discovered."

"I know, Sulimah. He was unwise to venture into the village, but it was out of concern for my welfare."

"Then I will help you." Sulimah beamed. "Because I believe that you are a good and chivalrous man. But we must act before Kusen awakens."

"How do you propose to be of help?"

"There is an abandoned shack. It is only a short distance from here, if you follow the river banks moving south. The area is shielded by trees. No one ever goes there. It would be a good shelter for your friend. I can provide food and water for him and for his horse, until you are ready to leave again for your journey."

"I thank you, Sulimah. But we must act immediately. If Kusen awakens it will be disastrous and you will have placed your life in danger to no purpose."

Without delay, she wrapped around her shoulders a mantle and slipped out of the house. She ran on her toes until she soon joined Berthold, anxiously waiting there on Arsenio's command. She kept running and signaled him to follow her.

They were soon hurrying along the edge of the river, their bodies barely visible in the pale moonlight. A minute more, and they had disappeared into the darkness.

†††

CHAPTER NINE

IN THE PRESENCE OF ENEMIES

Berthold hurried through the darkened forest on his way to a shelter in the company of the brave Sulimah. He did not know her story yet, but whatever it was, she was surely placing her life in grave danger to help Arsenio and himself.

When they reached the spot, Sulimah cautioned Berthold to remain hidden in the shelter. She also volunteered to bring food and water for him and the horse for as long as needed. Most important to Sir Berthold was Sulimah's promise to inform him as soon as the Duke and Kusen were ready to leave so that he could follow them at the right distance.

Berthold found the wooden walls of the abandoned shack to be solid and inviting, offering a perfect shelter from the harsh environment. Sulimah described how she used it to protect the potted plants for her garden during cold weather.

He lit the oil lamp and got a better view of his surroundings, if not his guide, who remained shielded by a traditional burka. She pointed to some wood stacked against the wall and gestured for him to bring some to the fireplace.

Before leaving, she started the fire for him. It would have been too much for him to accomplish. He was still shivering with cold and fatigue.

He bowed in gratitude to Sulimah and escorted her to the door. He then stood in the doorway and watched her go, shivering the whole time, until he could no longer see her.

Later, Berthold thought it over while he relaxed in the safety of the shelter. The squalid room in that abandoned shack was more than enough. She was like a special angel who had delivered him to safety. He went to his horse, Rasham, who stood restlessly shaking his head and tossing his mane. Berthold was comforted by Rasham's presence and took relief in the warmth of his body. The horse was his only friend during this lonely travel, someone he could trust even during terrifying gallops across the countryside.

He tied Rasham where he could easily graze and the horse gladly consumed the available hay. Berthold then retired to the fireplace, near exhaustion. He took relief from the warmth there and the red-amber firelight.

He managed to get steady enough to eat some of his food and drink from his flask and to keep it all down. He then placed a blanket on the floor and lay down, knowing he needed to rest. But his mind wandered and slumber eluded him.

Sulimah soon returned to her house and put Arsenio's mind at ease, explaining that Berthold was safe for the moment in the abandoned shack. Kusen still slept soundly after his heavy consumption of wine. His loud snoring was a welcome sound to both Arsenio and Sulimah.

Arsenio remained concerned for her safety. She was far too eager to help in spite of personal danger. She seemed infatuated, and he was anxious about the necessity of having to rely on her help.

It was not his nature to place a woman's life in peril for personal reasons. The desperate quest to find Polyxena dictated the events, however, and he had to pursue every avenue for help.

"From my heart, Sulimah. I thank you. May God reward your kindness."

"I am so glad to help in any way I can." She quickly moved closer and gently touched his arm with a delicate hand.

Arsenio recoiled, knowing well the deadly risk in the slightest casual touch from a Muslim woman with a violent husband. He still had no idea what she looked like under the cumbersome burka, but he saw the sensual desire burning in her eyes. Intuition told him that her loneliness and fear explained this sudden attachment to a stranger who had only showed her common courtesy.

If she actually believed he was a gift from Allah, that further complicated everything. Clearly, it was necessary to stay away from her as much as possible, not only for his benefit, but Sulimah's safety as well.

"Please, my lady. I entreat you to return by your husband's side. When he awakens, he must find you next to him."

"But my lord, Kusen is fast asleep and gives no signs of waking. I wish to spend a few more moments in your company. Your presence helps me to feel less afraid…I had lost hope and even feared that Allah had abandoned me. From the first moment I saw your face, I knew you were a blessed person sent to me by God."

Arsenio saw that it was impossible to reason with this girl, whose belief in miracles was likely born in the emptiness and torment of her life. Her delusional state gave her a sense of excitement and a whiff of joy.

He thought it best to change the subject. "Why are you living alone with him in this house, Sulimah, when Kusen's parents live nearby?"

"It is as they wish it. I am not allowed to enter their house. As I told you, I am considered the daughter of enemies. They only relented enough to permit me to live in their village and receive necessary food and protection until Kusen returned from his many jaunts and missions."

Sulimah took a breath, then went on, "I don't want to be here. But I have no place to go. And so I remain here with my in-laws and suffer their coldness. I have learned to grow my own food, so as not to be a burden and give them cause to dislike me even more. I wish to be as independent as possible and spend my time growing flowers and herbs, but I have no friends here. They all regard me with suspicion. My garden and flowers are the only company I possess until my husband returns. But the truth is that the abuse he inflicts is worse than the loneliness. At times it seems that death is my only salvation."

Arsenio was moved by her words and could not avoid feeling the pain radiating from her. She was trapped in a terrible situation.

"I understand your sorrow, Sulimah, and I wish with all my heart to have the power to help you. But I have no way to control destiny, and right now my only aim is to pacify Kusen and hope he will honor his word and show me the way to my wife. My sole aim is to bring her home to our family; only then can I turn to other things."

"You love your wife very much, my lord?"

"Yes. I cannot imagine life without her loving presence."

"How fortunate she is, to be so loved by someone as wonderful as you."

"She is not fortunate, my lady. Tragedy and pain have followed her for most of her life. Right now, she is in grave danger because of her determination to save her father."

He gave her a direct look and added, "You have my word of honor, when I return to my home and I can once more be the Duke of Lorengard-Lorraine, I will find some way to come to your aid, in gratitude for your help and friendship."

"Thank you, my lord," Sulimah exclaimed. "You see? You have been sent by God. I promise to follow your counsel and I will make a greater effort to pacify Kusen, as you desire."

She smiled and reluctantly turned toward the colorful drape. Her heart was in turmoil. She despised lying next to Kusen and feeling him touch her body. She fought her revulsion to survive their sexual encounters, because Kusen was a very lustful man and his desire was even stronger than his raging hatred for her. She was certain that deep inside, he was perfectly aware of her contempt.

She endured the wine on his breath. Sometimes he kissed her with such hunger that he made it hard for her to breathe. He never failed to invade her body with violence, disregarding her pain with deliberate cruelty.

He aspired to fill her body with sons and see his posterity secured. Also, in that way, he could truly possess her for all time.

His efforts were in vain. She remained barren. And although he and his family considered her to be less of a woman because of it, he couldn't get her out of his blood. He frequently burned with desire at the mere sight of her.

Sulimah felt blessed for being unable to conceive. How could she want Kusen's children? Her hatred for him ran too deep. She also knew his parents would take any child away from her to be raised according to their rules.

Just before entering the small bed chamber where Kusen slept off his wine, Sulimah whispered, "I will lie down next to him, my golden Prince. I will make believe his touch is welcome. I will endure this out of love for you."

She disappeared behind the curtain. Her words had been spoken too softly for Arsenio too hear. While he did not make them out, he caught her tone of voice and thought it was probably better that way.

Several hours later, Arsenio was awakened by the sound of giggling from the adjacent room, and then sounds of passionate lovemaking. The tryst sounded less violent than before and apparently the gallant Sulimah was feigning desire for Kusen's overtures.

Time moved slowly and the sexual encounter dragged on. Finally, there was stillness, and then the sounds of a conversation—while he couldn't understand what they were saying it was obvious that the lovemaking had ended.

He hoped they would soon come out of the room, for Sulimah's sake as well as his own. He was eager for the embarrassing situation to come to an end.

At long last, the couple made their exit from the bed chamber and emerged into the main room. Arsenio made believe he was still sleeping to make the situation easier.

Kusen approached the seemingly sleeping Duke and shook him to wake him up while Sulimah remained at a distance by the exit door.

Arsenio opened his eyes as if waking from a sound sleep.

Kusen spoke in a stern voice, "We are going out for a while, my lord. I warn you to remain in the house until our return. If not, you will be in grave peril. I am certain you will be able to take care of yourself without Sulimah's help." He smiled too widely at that. "There is plenty of food…goat's milk, bread and fruits. Fresh water is in the container by the window."

"I will remain here as you request, Kusen, and I am grateful for the hospitality. But when are we leaving? Time is of the essence."

"I will inform you when the time is right. Not before."

Arsenio grabbed his arm, frustrated by his insolence. "I warn you, Kusen, I can no longer tolerate this stalling. I need an answer."

Kusen pushed his arm away. "It will be soon. I promise. But on my terms, and not yours."

The Muslim grabbed Sulimah by the hand and left the room with haste, slamming the door behind them. Arsenio felt helpless and frustrated. He was beginning to lose faith in Kusen's ability or willingness to help him. The man was a true enigma and his unstable nature made him impossible to understand.

On the positive side, he had to assume that Kusen would not bring him under the same roof with his wife, if he had no intention of keeping his word. Still the man's mood swings were a deep concern.

Arsenio also feared Sulimah's obvious infatuation, along with Kusen's resentful nature. If his jealousy raged, the man would surely enact revenge by refusing to help him.

Arsenio decided to be patient for a little while longer. He had noticed that Kusen seemed more relaxed, almost happy, since Sulimah altered her behavior and became more loving and eager to please him. He was so elated over her receptiveness that he never questioned the amazing transformation.

In the past, their sexual encounters had been nothing more than a violent struggle to satisfy the sadistic side of his nature. Now, however, his lust appeared to have been deeply satisfied, and for the time being, he seemed content.

Several long hours elapsed since Kusen and Sulimah had left the house. Arsenio could only wait. The situation was becoming unbearable. Time moved slowly and still there was no trace of them. Arsenio fought despair. His blood boiled to leave that place despite Kusen's dire warnings. He also wondered what happened to Berthold. With the innkeeper in close proximity, he was also in the path of grave danger.

The Duke's greater fear was not dying. He was prepared to sacrifice his life to find Polyxena. Right or wrong, he lived his life according to the code of chivalry and was repelled by the thought of hiding from mysterious enemies who remain invisible and out of reach.

Finally, his determination could take no more waiting. He decided that if Kusen and Sulimah failed to return, he would steal out of the house regardless of the danger.

Berthold also felt distressed, hidden in the desolate shack by the river with no comfort from his loneliness but the company of loyal Rasham. Sulimah had not returned as she had promised, and although he had food and water of his own, he was all the more concerned for the safety of the Duke. Things were not right.

He made preliminary plans, mostly to offset the panic that he could feel creeping through himself. If they did not show up by the evening, then protected by the gloom, he would attempt to reach Kusen's house and carefully spy through the windows, and carry out his duty to make certain the Duke was alive and well.

Kusen and Sulimah finally returned to the house after many painful hours. Arsenio was relieved, but prudently decided not to ask questions, hoping the man would volunteer some information—but, he was greeted by a gloomy silence.

Sulimah ignored Arsenio and instead placed food and fresh water by the fireplace for Kusen, then offered him some wine. She gently touched his arm with a sensual invitation before disappearing behind the colorful curtain.

He gulped the ruby liquid while his eyes burned with desire and he gazed toward the hidden room. He already envisioned Sulimah's slender body, free from the bondage of the burka. The prelude to passion was apparent in his eyes.

Duke Arsenio withdrew into the shadows, to remove himself as much as possible for what was about to take place in such close proximity. Kusen ignored him and continued drinking wine with abandonment. Finally satisfied, he followed after Sulimah into the bedchamber.

For a long while, there was only silence behind the drape. Arsenio assumed he was either too tired or too drunk for bed sport and had perhaps fallen asleep. He was pleased for Sulimah's sake, and for the first time in the difficult day he began to feel a little more relaxed and at peace. He lay down by the fireplace, finding comfort in the warmth of the burning embers. His eyelids grew heavy. He closed his eyes and finally fell asleep.

For a brief time there was only silence in the small house. Then a shadow appeared in one of the windows and the eyes of an intruder gazed in. Berthold who had decided to investigate was greatly relieved to see Arsenio well and alive.

He decided to remain a little while longer, protected by the shadows of darkness, then return to the shack by the river.

He continued focusing on the interior of the house until he became almost hypnotized by the sight. His eyes stared intensely on the flames of the fireplace, and little by little be began to feel tired and lethargic. Berthold's eyelids became heavy and he rested his head on the rough window sill, until he fell asleep in spite of the cold.

He thus did not see the female inside the house while she emerged from behind the colorful curtain and approached the sleeping Arsenio on the floor. She wore a traditional robe, but her face was visible while she gracefully kneeled by the Duke.

For a few seconds she remained still, admiring his handsome features. Then she touched his shoulder gently to awaken him. Arsenio opened his eyes and was startled by the sight of the lovely young woman leaning over him. He had never seen Sulimah without the burka and was confused for the moment.

By the light of the fireplace, her eyes sparkled in the contour of her face, and her arched brows suggested a strong, determined nature. Her youthful face was framed by raven black hair that extended below her waistline and her golden skin was enhanced by the glow from the fireplace.

She addressed him gently, "Do not be distressed, my lord, it is I, Sulimah. I thought this would be the proper time for you to see my face and to know who I really am. I believe it is the right thing to do. Because you are a special man. An honorable man. Sent by God…"

The Duke was stunned by her irrational words. He glanced around to make certain they were alone. "Sulimah. What are you doing here and where is Kusen?"

"He is sleeping soundly, do not be concerned, my lord. There is no danger, I assure you." She attempted to caress his hair, but Arsenio recoiled.

"Sulimah, I demand that you to return to your husband's side at once. You are placing us in grave danger."

She ignored his words, smiling. "I have something of great importance to tell you, information that I know will give you great comfort. I also believe this is the proper time to show you my face."

"You must leave at once," Arsenio interrupted, pushing her gently but firmly away.

"No, my lord," she insisted. "You must listen to what I have to say."

But the words died in her throat while a scream of rage resonated in the room, loud enough to awaken the sleeping Berthold from his slumber in his spot outside the window. He peered inside and watched helpless while Kusen entered the room like a man possessed and before anyone could react, pushed Sulimah violently to the side. Arsenio was still crouched on the floor when Kusen struck him with such a powerful kick to the throat that it left him choking and gasping for air.

Berthold saw Sulimah's brave attempts to help Arsenio and pull her husband from him, but she was repelled by her maniacal husband, who continued to have a strangle hold on the Duke's neck.

Berthold was desperate, filled with dread. "What can I do?" he whispered in prayer. "Dear Lord please help me." Without help, the Duke would be dead.

Finally, determination prevailed over panic. He grabbed the handle of his sword and hurled his considerable body weight against the door. He crashed into the room brandishing the weapon and screaming at the top of his lungs.

The force of his charge propelled him toward the opposite wall, which he struck at full force with his prominent belly and bounced backward into the middle of the room. This startled Kusen enough to release the pressure on the Duke's throat while he lunged for Arsenio's sword on the floor. He seized the weapon and initiated a fierce attack against his intruder.

Berthold screamed in fear, swinging his weapon with both hands to keep his enemy at bay, while Sulimah dragged Arsenio toward the open door, hoping the cold air would revive him.

"My Lord in heaven," Berthold cried out. "Please help me."

And in that moment he stumbled on a piece of broken crockery and fell forward, striking the tip of his bladed helmet on the wall and pushing it down over his eyes. He bent forward, trying to pull it back up and ran in panic, hoping to make it to the door. Suddenly he felt a powerful bang on top of his head as his body was abruptly stopped by the pointed metal spire which had became infixed somewhere.

A bloodcurdling, agonizing scream resonated in the room, which enhanced Berthold's feelings of helplessness and dread. He was almost paralyzed with fear, as the room appeared to be swinging around him. The trauma of the moment was so debilitating. He was resigned and actually waited for the fatal strike of Kusen's sword.

A long moment went by and only a gloomy silence reigned in the room. The stillness was so complete, that after so much action it was almost unnerving. Finally, Sulimah's voice broke the quiet. It sounded to Berthold like it was coming from very far away, almost under water.

"My lord, are you all right?"

Berthold felt her gentle hand touch his shoulder. It was very strange. Why had Kusen spared his life?

He tried to move, but his head was still entrapped in the helmet and aching from the impact. With care, he freed himself and a limp body fell to the floor, splashing Berthold with blood.

It was Kusen. The sharp point of the helmet was still imbedded in his stomach.

The reluctant innkeeper-knight managed to lift his hefty body to a more dignified position, while also scooting away from Kusen's bloody remains.

Sulimah shook with emotion, but still managed to bring some water to Berthold and refresh the unlikely hero. He regained some of his clarity. "Where is the Duke, my lady? Please tell me, is he still alive?"

She managed to smile and point to the spot where Arsenio crouched outside the door of the house. He was still working at recovering his breath.

For Berthold, the sight of his Duke alive was a soothing tonic. He stood on unsteady legs and approached Arsenio, eager to offer help.

Sulimah remained inside. She was deeply shaken, despite the hatred she had for her husband and all of the abuses she endured throughout the years, there was no rejoicing in her heart.

She took a clean sheet and delicately placed the cloth upon Kusen's body, then stood before him in silent prayer according to the teachings of Islam.

Outside the door of the house, Arsenio was finally breathing with ease. He shunned helpful hands and stood up.

Berthold was embarrassed by his disheveled condition, and tried to rearrange his clothes to some degree of decorum. He bowed to the Duke. "God be praised for your safety, my lord."

"Thank you, Sir Berthold." Arsenio patted him on the back. "I owe you my life and I am indebted to your loyalty."

Despite the Duke's kind words, Berthold felt embarrassed by his overgrown body and his lack of fighting skills. "Please forgive me for my ineptitudes in combat, my lord."

"What? My friend, you have the heart of a lion." Arsenio laughed. "No one could have done more to help. You acted bravely without regard for your own safety. You are a true knight...I am forever in your debt."

"A true knight?" For a moment, Berthold forgot all his grievances and envisioned himself as the brilliant knight in shining armor such as he had only dreamed about before.

When Arsenio glanced at Kusen's body on the floor, the reality of the moment set in. Dread filled him. He turned to Sulimah and saw the young woman acknowledge his worst fears with her eyes. The only pathway to his wife was lost to him.

Arsenio lowered his head. This new pain nearly took his breath away once again. With no one else to show the way, only a miracle could prevent Polyxena from being forever lost.

"I am so sorry, my Lord," Berthold attempted to say. "It was an accident caused by my clumsiness and lack of skill in swordplay. I was forced to intervene."

"I know, my friend," Arsenio sadly replied. "I know that without your valiant intervention we would all be dead." The Duke patted Berthold's fleshy shoulder. "It's no one's fault, only a cruel destiny that has taken my wife away to some mysterious location and kept her out of my reach." He clenched his fists.

"How can I help her now? She has disappeared without a trace, and there is no one left to show me the way. I have lost my wife."

Arsenio pounded his fists against the cold plaster of the wall. At first he was unable to hear the soft voice of Sulimah when she tried to attract his attention. So she nearly shouted, "But I know the way, my lord. Please hear what I am saying, I know the way."

The words broke through the barrier and Arsenio turned to her in wonder. "You know the way, my lady?"

Disregarding etiquette, he grabbed Sulimah by the shoulders. "Did I hear you right? You know the way?

"Not where she is at this hour. But I know where they are going to take her…"

"Sulimah. Why did you not tell me this before? Why leave me in the dark for so long?"

"I didn't know it before this day, my lord, or I would have told you. Kusen confided in me when we went out together on this faithful day. I tried to tell you this very night, my lord, this was the news I spoke of. But we were interrupted by Kusen.

"He was in an unusual mood and took me for a walk to a wine shelter he conceals in the forest. He was in a talkative mood and confessed to me that he hated you and his decision was to never show you the way to your wife. He planned to kill you instead. I didn't know what to do, or how to stop him. I decided to play to his weaknesses. His lust for wine. His desire for me…"

Sulimah blushed violently and turned her eyes away. Arsenio stared back at her in surprise.

She went on, "I let him make love to me despite my revulsion, to gain his trust. To find out where they took your wife, so I could help you escape the village. Once the wine worked its magic, he told me where they planned to take her."

Arsenio exhaled hard. "I am grateful, Sulimah. And I am forever in your debt for your help."

Sulimah's lovely face flushed at such approval from the Duke.

"The place he told you about, is it far?"

"Yes, it is at a great distance. Three or four days on horseback. However, it will be easy to find, without fear of getting lost. We simply follow the river all the way to the destination."

"Is the place familiar to you?"

"It is close to the village where I was born. As a child, I could see it from afar, shrouded in the mist and clouds, always appearing so foreboding and majestic. I remember how it sparked our imaginations and our curiosity because of its mysterious aura."

"Do you know anyone there?"

"No, my lord. My parents ordered me to stay away. Grave danger was said to greet trespassers. I don't believe anybody in the village really knew the place…they speculated, but stayed away. There were rumors about a mysterious sorcerer or demon monster occupying the place, something with great powers. It demands solitude and dispenses death to anyone who dares to approach."

Arsenio recalled the mysterious circumstances surrounding Polyxena's abduction. He was unwilling to dismiss Sulimah's accounting as fantasy. "Do you believe that this sorcerer or demon or this monster somehow ordered the abduction of my wife?"

"Kusen only told me where your wife would be taken, nothing more. I truly believe he was in the dark about the abduction itself…he only took part because it was a cause for martyrdom."

Sulimah took a deep breath, overwhelmed by bitter recollections. "As long as I can remember, Kusen aspired to become a martyr, aiming to regain favor from Allah, which he thought he had somehow lost. Disowned because of his marriage to me, he convinced himself that I had bewitched him. He was certain that martyrdom would bring honor to his family. This would be his revenge upon me…for bewitching him."

"I am sorry to hear these things, Sulimah. But we can be thankful that they mean nothing to you, anymore. They are the memories of a bad dream…and now it is gone."

Arsenio addressed both Berthold and Sulimah, "We have to leave as soon as possible. But first we must bury Kusen. If his body is found prematurely they may follow us before we can distance ourselves from here."

"Thank you for your kindness," Sulimah said. "Despite his evil nature Kusen, was my husband and a Muslim. I know he sinned in the eyes of Allah, but because of my own transgressions I hope to make some atonement to God by preparing him for burial according to our faith."

"Of course my lady," concurred Arsenio. "We will abide by your wishes. If you will prepare his body for burial, Berthold and I will dig the grave by the river's edge."

Arsenio moved toward the exit followed by Berthold. He turned toward Sulimah. "We will locate a suitable spot for the burial as soon as possible and immediately following the ceremony we will gather our horses and be on our way. You will ride Kusen's mount, Sulimah, and with a little bit of good fortune we will be long gone before sunrise." With that, he and Berthold left her to the lonely task.

Alone now in silence with the cooling corpse of the only man she had ever known outside her birth family, Sulimah was powerless against a torrent of guilt and sadness. She had no idea how she could have made things turn out better than this, but the weight of it lay heavily upon her.

All of her hatred for the man who abducted her in childhood and then spent years subjecting her to heavy sexual abuse receded. With Kusen dead, his final judgment would come from Allah.

A strange coincidence that her husband's greatest wish to become a martyr had come true. He died fighting an infidel, an enemy of Islam, sword at hand. Sulimah prayed that Allah in his infinite mercy might open the heavenly gates of Jannah and forgive Kusen's transgressions, granting him eternal peace.

With her hands shaking but full of determination, Sulimah managed to wash and anoint his body, following the tradition of her faith as closely as possible. She tried to clean blood stains from the floor, but the floorboards retained a clear outline of the body. She slid a small carpet over the area.

She left the body in the torn and bloodstained clothing of his death, befitting a martyr, and placed his Quran under his head, before finishing the ritual by wrapping his body in a clean white sheet.

"Goodbye Kusen," she finally said aloud. "I forgive you for your failings and I pray that merciful Allah will grant you peace, and allow you to enter the peace of Jannah."

Time left her no more chance to grieve. It was her hour of escape from the village that had been her virtual prison for so long. There, she was trapped with an abusive husband and a village that treated her with contempt. As a Muslim woman she felt guilty for her own transgression through her feelings of attraction to an infidel. She hoped that despite the rigidity of the Muslim religion, Kusen might be forgiven by Allah and she might be forgiven as well.

When Arsenio and Berthold returned, they moved Kusen's body to the grave site and placed the body facing Mecca. They filled the grave and concealed it with stones and grassy patches of earth.

Now with Kusen finally resting under the ground, the trio quickly gathered food, water, weapons, ropes, and warm blankets. Sulimah put on the traditional burka, covering herself head to toe. She was comforted by the anonymity of the garment. It not only made her hard to identify, it helped her conceal her conflicting sense of relief and dread.

She realized that her attraction to the handsome duke had triggered the fatal conflict. Her consolation was that there could never have been a happy ending to her old life. Sooner or later, her violent and unbalanced husband would have killed her.

Arsenio was the one person who showed her kindness and respect since she had been abducted as a child. She felt exhilarated, in spite of her fears at the prospect of a new life ahead.

Arsenio sensed her distress while he watched her mount her horse. He smiled and reached over to gently squeeze her hand in an effort to comfort her. He hoped that would not prove too much for her gentle nature and overwhelm her ability to help him find Polyxena, while he and Berthold mounted their steeds and the group moved forward.

Arsenio noticed that Sulimah did not look back while they rode away. He flanked her mount and spoke quietly to her, "Do not worry Sulimah…you are safe now and under our protection. I pledge my life to that end. It will be our responsibility to help you in every way we can, as long as we travel together on this difficult road."

When they were far enough from the village, they spurred their horses to a faster pace and took up a brisk trot that the horses could maintain for miles without slowing.

"You have much to look forward in life, Sulimah," he called over to her. "You can go back to your family. Since your old village is close to where they have taken my wife, we can escort you all the way there."

"My lord, I can not go back." she exclaimed. "I don't know if my parents are alive…and they would not welcome me, because of my marriage to Kusen. In their eyes I am a fallen woman who brought shame to the family. There is only contempt in the Muslim world for someone who walks on the side of infidels."

Sulimah lowered her head. Even the heavy burka could not conceal her distress. "I belong to no one and I am lost in the midst of two different worlds that each judge me harshly."

"You judge yourself too severely, my lady," objected Arsenio. "This is the beginning of a new life for you." He looked at Sulimah with a comforting smile. "Know that you have a home, if you wish, in the Dukedom of Lorengard-Lorraine. You will be welcomed and respected as a member of my own family...and you are free to keep your faith."

"But, my Lord, why won't the citizens hate me? I was the wife of the man who kidnapped their Duchess."

Arsenio smiled at that. "On the contrary, you will be loved and admired by my people as the savior of their Duchess...And I know Polyxena will extend her sisterly affection to you."

He addressed Berthold with the full dignity and commanding tone of a Duke imparting a special order, "Sir Berthold, it is my express desire that after we reach the location where my wife has been taken prisoner, you will go on to Lorengard-Lorraine and inform the Duke of Nemours of the success of our mission. You will give them the geographic position of the enemy for a possible assault by the army on their camp...Sulimah will accompany you. And under my direct order, she is to be welcomed in Lorengard-Lorraine, with all the respect and deference due to a member of my own family."

Berthold bowed in response to the young Duke's command.

Arsenio continued, "The Dukedom will be her permanent residence, if she wishes. She will be the recipient of a dowry of fifty gold florins per month and the bequest will continue indefinitely throughout her life time, even if I do not return. Upon your arrival, all this will be stipulated in writing and placed in the hands of the Duke of Nemours."

Sulimah was thoroughly overwhelmed. She had never experienced kindness from anyone and yet here it was coming from an infidel she had been warned to revile.

At that moment, the heavy burka felt excessive, almost claustrophobic. Following a strong impulse, she removed it and allowed her lovely face to be visible, crowned by her lustrous and long raven hair. Under the burka she was dressed in the traditional traveling clothes of her people, warm and modestly made, suiting the humble station of her life. The garment was made of woven wool, held at the waist by a makeshift belt of rope.

Her slender figure and rounded breasts shaped the fabric into a charming image. Arsenio and Berthold were struck by her boldness in casting off the traditional garment, and then struck again by her loveliness.

Sulimah blushed under the admiring glances of the men. "I thank you my lord, for your kindness. And may the blessings of Allah be upon you for your generosity. I pledge to you my loyalty and my life in your quest to find the Duchess."

Arsenio bowed his head in approval.

Sulimah smiled, still under the allure of her youthful infatuation. Without further delay, she signaled the men to follow her and spurred her mount into a brisk gallop toward the edge of the river. Arsenio and Berthold engaged their steeds to match her pace and in a short time all three were swallowed by the darkness.

†††

CHAPTER TEN

UNVEILING AN ENIGMA

Polyxena remained unaware of the evolving circumstances and of Arsenio's efforts to find her. She only knew that her fate was uncertain. Despite her trepidation, she was relieved to at least to be on her way. She hoped this leg of the journey would present some opportunity for escape.

She found herself relishing the cold air while they cantered their mounts through the shoreline forest. Her beautiful steed resembled her beloved horse, Hildebrandt, and was a familiar comfort. She thrilled to the invigorating embrace of the wind and closed her eyes, and for a few moments the power of motion made her dare to feel the possibility of freedom once again.

Thunder rolled in the distance and brought her back to the moment. They were traveling at a late hour and in uncertain weather. It was dangerous to be entrapped by a storm while surrounded by trees. She rode close to Lord Zanar, but he communicated his displeasure.

"We must move faster," he finally said. "A dangerous storm is brewing and lightning has already begun to flash in the sky. There is a house not far away, where we will be safe. We should try to get there before the downpour begins."

They raised their pace to a gallop, but the rain began to fall with real force, accompanied by strong gusts of wind. The downpour impaired their vision and it was quickly evident that they were at the mercy of the storm. The house he sought was not yet within sight, and the ground was already so saturated by water that it took on the appearance of a lake.

Thunder and lightning quickly filled the sky, frightening the horses. Polyxena and Zanar were both experienced riders, but the spooked animals bucked at every thunderbolt. The journey became increasingly dangerous.

Torrential rain now included icy wind. It forced the travelers to slow their pace in order to navigate the uneven terrain.

"We must stop, my lord!" shouted Polyxena over the turbulence. "We can't continue to move forward...I believe it would be wise to secure our horses to some solid trees."

"No! We must go forward a while longer. The safe house is at the other side of the ravine ahead. I got a glimpse of it when the sky lit up just now. Keep close control of your mount and follow me."

The ground was so slippery that the horses had difficulty keeping their footing. Being a huntress and an exceptional horsewoman, she was able to keep her mount more stable than Zanar's horse. The animal was nearly in a frenzy and added additional danger to the moment.

"Please, my lord, it is unwise to continue following this dangerous course. We must reach higher ground. Do you see that small hill ahead topped by a plateau? It would be an ideal location to avoid deadly mud slides. If we remain here, we are in danger of being drowned or washed away."

"No, Polyxena," answered Zanar sharply. "This is the closest way to the safe house. We will be distancing ourselves from our destination by climbing that hill. The horses are already worn out from combating the storm. Let us not waste time…Follow me!"

Lord Zanar spurred his mount forward and disregarded the conditions of the road. They followed along an incline while treacherous mud slid down the slope past them. She was amazed by Zanar's recklessness. He appeared oblivious to the danger.

Hildebrandt, that splendid Friesian horse, took courage from Polyxena's sure touch and continued to brave the dangerous ground with resolve.

Zanar forged ahead, ignoring Polyxena mainly as a matter of manly pride. His mount continued to buck violently and he struggled to remain in the saddle.

Polyxena was angry and frustrated by such reckless stubbornness. She knew that Zanar was only ignoring her advice because she was a woman. It was galling that his foolish male pride was more important to him than safety.

Forward movement was becoming extremely difficult—time appeared to stand still while she attempted to make small gains in the unfriendly terrain. She avoided looking down when a terrifying precipice loomed before her eyes. A deep and flooded gorge ran parallel to her pathway, much too close for comfort.

Disaster arrived when the gale force winds snatched a waterlogged branch from a nearby tree and whipped it through the air. Zanar and his horse were directly its path and the heavy limb struck him with such force that it propelled his body from the animal. He landed in the cascading mud near the edge of the precipice.

Polyxena was helpless to intervene while the forces of gravity and the cascading mud dragged him toward the edge of the gorge. Lord Zanar grabbed at anything he could reach, trying to slow himself down and forestall the fatal plunge. But the ground was smoothed over by the slimy mud and his battered and bloody hands were unable to hold onto anything until he finally grabbed onto the same large branch that knocked him from his horse.

The limb caught in some of the heavy brush sprouting from the rocky terrain and altered Zanar's direction of fall so that he landed instead on a small plateau on the steep incline. But he bounced off and was catapulted into a large mud pit. The mud engulfed him with the deadly embrace of quicksand.

He was now imprisoned in the thick mud at the center of the deadly pit, with no ability to move or reach out to the solid edges. He began to sink, still clutching the big tree branch, which by now was sinking with him.

Additional mud continued to slide in from the incline. The deadly pit continued to fill, covering Zanar from above while he continued to sink, trapped and helpless.

Even from a distance, Polyxena saw the terror in Lord Zanar's eyes. He continued to sink helplessly while holding onto the tree branch that did little to hold him up.

She jumped off of Hildebrand and accosted Zanar's mount, which had loyally remained close by. Both of these animals would be vital to the travelers, if they ever hoped to survive and find a way out the mighty forest.

She secured the horse to a nearby tree before removing a long rope coiled at the side of the saddle. The rope was strong and appeared long enough to reach him, if he didn't sink too quickly. She tied one end of the rope to the pommel on Hildebrandt's saddle, and the opposite end around her waist.

"Try not to move." she shouted to Zanar. "You will only sink faster." Then she slid carefully down the incline, holding the rope with both hands. The route going down was laborious in spite of her athletic ability. Mud continued sliding down the incline, coupled with the rocks being dislodged by the heavy rain.

Her safety depended on Hildebrandt's steadiness and his hold on the rope. The ground where the horse stood was quickly eroding away, and parts were already collapsing toward the cliff. If the mount lost lose his footing they could both plunge to their death. However, the splendid steed remained proud and steady, holding Polyxena like a mighty rock.

Polyxena tried to place her feet in any available protrusions in the rough terrain of the incline, moving carefully and clinging to the rope. Meanwhile, Lord Zanar continued sinking in the mud pit and little time was left to save him.

Finally, Polyxena reached the little plateau on the incline and stepped onto solid ground and since time was of the essence, she immediately advanced toward the area were Zanar languished. The ground was uneven and treacherous, made sleek by the flowing mud. To her dismay, she reached the end of the rope. It was not long enough to reach him in the center of the pool. There was nothing within reach for her to use in extending her reach close enough to him.

She kept looking around while she struggled to catch her breath, searching for anything she could use to help them. She moaned in frustration. The only person who knew the way out of the lush green prison was this evil man, now trapped and sinking in tons of mud and debris. He would soon be buried alive.

The only option was to use herself as a conduit to reach him. She looked up at the only friend she had at that moment, trying to gain some strength from Hildebrand's comforting presence. The faithful Friesian, whose black and shiny pelt blended with the darkness, stood tall atop of the incline like a guardian angel with his long flowing mane blowing in the wind. The faithful animal gazed intently on Polyxena, waiting for some sign or for a command to follow.

Despite the fact that he was a remarkable horse, intelligent and receptive, she wondered if he would instinctively know what to do, and move back far enough to save their lives. The uncertainty left her with the terrifying thought of being buried alive in the mud for her trouble.

Now the sky opened again with torrential a rain that fell with relentless power. The winds surged again to gale force and made visibility almost nothing. The violence of the storm swelled to the point that she lost sight of Zanar.

Polyxena feared the worst, that the cascading waters had dragged Zanar under the surface and to his death. A scream of anguish erupted from her throat. Her fighting spirit was all but driven out of her.

She heard her horse whinny in the distance. She looked up and with great relief saw her beloved Hildebrandt safely on the summit of the incline, bold and resolute despite the wild weather. He stood fixed in place despite the thunder, with his intelligent eyes focused on Polyxena, waiting for some kind of a signal or command.

The sight of the splendid horse invigorated her like a magic tonic. She reclaimed enough of her strength to rise to her feet and struggled her way back toward the mud pit with a renewed sense hope and determination to find Zanar, if he was still alive.

She struggled to see, until a powerful bolt of lightning lit up the sky, revealing Lord Zanar, with his head and shoulders barely visible in the surrounding debris.

He was not moving, and she wondered if he was already dead and she was only viewing his lifeless body. But when she heard him cough and gasp for air, she was reassured that he still lived.

She called to him to have faith and hold on a little longer while she attempted his rescue. The first problem was that he still remained entrenched in the middle of the pool, at too great a distance from her.

She fastened the rope tightly and securely around her waist, then with deliberate steps, began to enter into the mud pit, moving slowly toward Zanar. But there was a deep incline inside the pit, and the depth increased as she moved forward. But from where she stood, the rope would still not allow her to reach him. She could feel that if she advanced further, she would lose contact with stable ground.

But now the mud was rising around Zanar's neck. It was apparent that both of their lives depended on the ability and intelligence of a horse, who although being an extraordinary mount, might or might not know what to do for them.

"Help me, Polyxena!" Zanar cried out. She was startled, and spun to face the doomed man. She could sense the intensity of his anguish at that instant and it made her feel a sudden compulsion to help him.

Disregarding consequences and guided only by her heroic disposition, she pushed her body forward into the thick muck, losing contact with the ground. With a last Herculean effort, she lunged forward and managed to grab Zanar's wrist just as his shoulders and head began to disappear into the pit.

Zanar was momentarily lifted by Polyxena's grip and he was able to breathe a few gulps of air. However, she was now helplessly encased in the deadly mud herself, with no possibility of returning to safety on her own.

Suspended and imprisoned in the thick mud, she called out, "Hildebrandt...Move back. Back...Back up now."

The mud continued to relentlessly swallow her. She pulled on to the rope secured around her waist, but her arms felt nearly paralyzed. Her strength was so depleted she could barely move at all.

Lord Zanar was coming in and out of consciousness while she continued hold onto his wrist. The thought of being buried alive was more terrifying than anything she had ever experienced, not even during battle. She wanted so much to go on living, and to enjoy the gift of love that Destiny had provided to her a second time.

"Arsenio, my love…" she whispered as his beloved image, flashed before her eyes, while salty tears flowed down her face.

"Alexander, my beloved child, my dear father and all those I love, goodbye…May you never know the manner of my death."

A painful sob erupted in her throat, but Polyxena experienced a surprising clarity in that terrifying moment. Instead of going farther downward, she suddenly, miraculously, felt herself pulled from the pit with a steady force. It felt almost like levitation, being suspended into air.

Was she dreaming? Her hand remained instinctively clasped around Zanar's wrist while her body was liberated from the stranglehold of the mud, pulling him with her.

The feeling of freedom was exhilaration such as she had never known. All her grievances seemed to disappear, giving place to a sense of rebirth, with the sight of her faithful Hildebrandt receding slowly, steadily pulling her out of the mud pit and back into life.

Polyxena felt as if she must be dreaming. She crawled to the edge of the pit and climbed to her knees, then pulled Zanar out, both of them gasping for air. She removed the rope from her waist and wrapped it around Zanar, then signaled Hildebrandt to move backwards, hoping he would not cause the man additional injuries.

Again the amazing animal responded perfectly and thanks to his effort, Zanar was finally pulled from the indignity of his muddy prison.

Polyxena laid him on the ground and gently lifted his head to ease his breathing while he continued gasping for air. When he began to calm down and returned from the brink of his trauma, he attempted to lift himself up to a more dignified position.

"Are you all right, my lord?" asked Polyxena. "Are you able to stand?"

For the first time, Lord Zanar was without the angry and defiant look that was so much part of his persona. She sensed his feeling of embarrassment in front of a woman who saved his life with great courage, but there was nothing to be done about that at the moment.

Polyxena thought it best not to humiliate him with questions about his condition. She stood silently while Zanar began to move his body, first slowly and with some apprehension, then with more confidence.

In a few moments, he was back on his feet, if unsteady, and mostly uninjured. Apparently the same thick mud that almost took his life also prevented him from receiving fatal injuries by cushioning his fall.

The rain slowed to a mere shower at last, much gentler than the violent storm surge. Polyxena was so warmed by her sense of victory over the elements that she enjoyed the feel of the cool rainfall. A joyous feeling took possession of her and for a few wonderful moments she even attempted a few dance steps, whirling around the emerald greenery that surrounded the area like a lush carpet.

The euphoric sensation lasted for a few amazing moments, while all her fears seemed to vanish and give place to an unexpected sense of joy. Finally, exhausted by the rescue, she fell to her knees panting for air, then lowered her head and intoned a prayer of thanks.

She gazed at Hildebrandt with gratitude. The mount stood majestic and imposing with his splendid mane blowing in the wind and his intelligent, piercing eyes focused on her. Her loneliness and isolation disappeared in the presence of her amazing horse, so instrumental in saving her life. "Thank you, my beautiful Hildebrandt and may the good Lord reward your courage and loyalty."

A high-pitched neigh reverberated and Hildebrandt seemed to rejoice in the reward of Polyxena's affection.

She crossed herself at the end of her devotion, and approached Zanar. He remained aloof, tormented and unable to reconcile with the fact that he had been forced to beg a woman for his life. This constituted a great humiliation and loss of personal honor.

However, even in his resentment, he was impressed by the amazing rapport Hildebrandt had with Polyxena, since he had considered the Friesian a wild and uncooperative horse. At a time he had even contemplated having him destroyed. Now that the splendid steed had saved his life, everything about this strange turn of events bewildered him.

They were both breathless and overwhelmed, their strength depleted. The horses also needed a rest before the journey could continue. Zanar pointed toward the location of the safe house, which he insisted was visible from where they were standing.

To Polyxena, the place looked minuscule at that distance, nearly lost in the horizon. It took another hour of grueling travel across the rocky terrain before the exhausted duo was finally able to reach it.

Upon arrival, the house was larger and more attractive than Polyxena would have expected. It could easily shelter a hunting party and house a custodian. It boasted a simple stone tower behind a timber-framed facade and was crowned by stained glass windows that reached to considerable heights.

Rustic elegance coupled with European splendor in the design of the place, which must have once belonged to aristocracy. Plumes of smoke wafted from several chimneys, enticing the weary travelers in their soaked and muddy clothing with the prospect of dry warmth.

The main house was flanked by a large stable and Zanar guided Polyxena straight to it. She noticed that he was now moving across the grounds of the place with the easy manner of someone familiar with it.

An old man with a white beard appeared by the stable door. He made an odd impression, attired in a long gown and a cloth head cover patterned in black and white plaid, secured around his head by a black rope. His face was leathery and deeply wrinkled as from many years of exposure to severe weather, but there was a distinguished aura about him.

He appeared startled by Zanar's sudden appearance and his disheveled condition, but he rushed to assist Zanar in dismounting. As soon as Zanar was safely on the ground, the man bowed with great deference to him. He made a wide arm gesture with hospitable elegance inviting him toward the main house. Contrary to the reverence bestowed on Zanar, he completely ignored Polyxena's presence until Zanar instructed the man to give her aid.

She sensed the man's distaste for the presence of a female from a different culture, one not under his approval. She quickly dismounted her horse without relying on the helping hand of the elder man, which she didn't need anyway, and followed Zanar into the house.

They were greeted inside by a woman dressed in a black burka. Polyxena noted that although the woman was completely covered by the garment, her body stance and movements revealed that she was no longer young. She was obviously the wife of the older man, and they were caretakers here. They were obviously Muslim in faith and Polyxena knew enough to understand that her position as a European duchess would get her no respect here.

The woman bowed with respect to Zanar, but like her husband, she appeared startled by the presence of Polyxena. As they entered, Polyxena was impressed by the crafted atmosphere of comfort that filled the place. In the middle of the main wall, a large stone fireplace from a roaring fire produced a warm glow.

The vast room was sparsely furnished with rustic elegance. High-backed chairs surrounded a long wooden table, with copper candelabras resting on the surface. The western style of the room's decor sharply contrasted with the Muslim attire of the elderly couple, who appeared to be in service to the house.

Stuffed deer heads were displayed on the walls, while an assortment of sharp-edged iron and steel weaponry glinted in the light of the fire. She glanced up and saw large wooden chandeliers hung from a cathedral ceiling formed in intersecting arches that had been beautifully engraved with hunting scenes.

The place was nothing like any travelers' inn that Polyxena had ever seen. Several coat-of-arms hung over the fireplace—they appeared old and faded, stained by the smoke from the fireplace.

Because of the poor condition of the images Polyxena was unable to recognize the symbols to determine if they belonged to noble families of the Royal European Gotha. She assumed that the original owners were westerners and wondered how Zanar was connected to them.

The aroma of food filled the air, stimulating Polyxena's senses and making the place more inviting in spite of the Muslim couple's cold reception.

Zanar introduced Polyxena with great aplomb to the elderly couple, ignoring the cold reception toward her, "This is Aashir and his wife Muna. They have been in service to this house for many years." To the couple, he added, "I present her grace, Polyxena of Nemours, Duchess of Lorengard-Lorraine. It will be your responsibility to make her comfortable and welcomed in the house."

Aashir bowed politely to Polyxena, but it was apparent that he found her presence unwelcome. Nonetheless, he signaled to his wife to care for the Duchess. Promptly, Muna escorted Polyxena to the staircase and the upper floor where they disappeared from sight.

Aashir hastened to escort Zanar to a lavish bedroom adjoining the center hall, a stately fire place warmed the surroundings with its burning embers, beautiful tapestries on the walls depicted hunting scenes. A large four-poster bed framed by crimson velvet curtains was the centerpiece of the room.

The old gentleman helped Zanar remove his mud drenched clothing and placed a warm blanket around him. He filled a large basin with warm water and invited Zanar to bathe.

Two hours later, Zanar was comfortable seated by the fire, cleaned, refreshed, and elegantly dressed in warm lounging clothes from the lavish assortment of garments in the wardrobe of the house.

Aashir displayed constant concern in attending to Zanar, serving wine from a silver carafe with assorted candied fruits to delight his palate. Finally, Zanar got up and returned to the great Hall, where he sat by the fireplace waiting for Polyxena.

Finally, the duchess made her entrance, descending the grand staircase in a splendid velvet garment of fine fabric, but which was cut in a masculine style. There was nothing suitable to the Duchess's rank in the house, so this deep purple lounging gown was chosen by Muna.

It did have exquisite gold embroidery on the oversized sleeves, which were lined with ermine. Whether or not it was proper for her to wear, the luxurious attire was most becoming. Her long, dark hair lay softly on her shoulders and framed the beauty of her features.

Once again Zanar was rendered breathless by the sight of her. Even Aashir was stunned by the unexpected appearance of such beauty. He realized that his only other sight of her had been tainted by all the mud and the dreary, drenched clothing.

Polyxena noticed that Lord Zanar appeared considerably refreshed, almost oblivious to the recent turmoil. She concealed every reaction, except for the fine hairs that stood up on the back of her neck—a lustful look was present in his eyes. As a woman of beauty, Polyxena knew that look well.

In an instant, her survival instinct sized up her situation. The indignities and sexual overtures she had to endure because of his obsession with her were made possible for him by hallucinatory drugs. She feared the way they effected her and her usual inhibitions, but calculated that they would not be available in the dignified environment of the house. Even if Zanar brought them along and somehow retained them in usable shape in spite of his drenching, the presence of the conservative elderly couple was reassuring. Surely his pride would prevent him from allowing them to see him taking advantage of her in such an ignoble way.

So she greeted Zanar with a calm smile while Muna escorted her to the opposite end of the long wooden table. Her place faced him from a considerable distance, adhering to the etiquette of the western world. Once again, it seemed that they were in a moment of Zanar's better nature. She knew it could depart at any instant.

Polyxena couldn't understand why Zanar's behavior changed so radically. Here in the confinements of the house, he openly enjoyed European comforts and behaved like a western aristocrat, uncharacteristic of the true Muslim he professed to be.

She noticed that Zanar seemed amused, as if enjoying her uneasiness in the strange surroundings. He did not bother with an explanation, so it was left as one more mystery to unravel.

For a while, there was an uncomfortable silence while they prepared to partake of a lavish meal offered up on precious china plates beautifully decorated with images of exotic birds. The food was served with efficiency and style, adhering to the protocol of the European courts, and Zanar seemed at ease and comfortable in the western environment and familiar with the elegant eating habits of the aristocracy.

The mini feast consisted of roasted mutton, venison and stuffed pheasant, accompanied by honey-glazed potatoes, candied apples, and a lavish assortment of precious wines.

Polyxena indulged moderately in the beverage, hoping to warm her body with it. Though the heat generated from the fireplace was complimented by her comforting bath, she still shivered from the intense cold she had endured that day.

She noticed that Lord Zanar drank at a fast pace, gulping several cups of the enticing nectar with obvious pleasure. Polyxena only sipped at her wine, pondering why he continued to remain uncommunicative and aloof. What was the issue now?

She decided that it was time to break the silence and raise a few issues of her own, starting with questions about the manor house and the unusual decor. "This is a very beautiful place, my lord. Does it belong to you?"

His answer was curt, "It does now. It used to be part of my family's estate."

Zanar's answer only created more questions in Polyxena's mind. It seemed unusual for the western-styled lodge to belong to members of his family, since she thought Zanar was a Muslim, unrelated to the western world and its fashions.

He continued to remain silent after that brief bit of conversation, but he greedily drank in her beauty. His persistent stare felt as if his eyes were licking her skin. Polyxena struggled to appear calm and retain her dignity.

Finally, Zanar slowly got up from his chair and walked with a confident stride toward her at the far end of the table. With a commanding motion of his hand he dismissed Aashir and Muna, who immediately disappeared through the doorway.

Zanar stood erect in front of the young woman, bold and handsome. The elegant caftan enhanced his manly appeal.

Polyxena remained seated, disturbed by the aggressive stance, having experienced his volatile nature and sexual appetite. She sustained his stare boldly, trying to deflect his passion with her innate sense of dignity.

He smiled, openly amused by her rebuff and leaned forward toward her, close enough to let his burning breath caress her face. "There is a feeling of romance within these walls," he whispered. "Don't you find it so, my lady?"

Polyxena let a moment of uneasiness slip. It was evident to Zanar.

"No need for alarm, my lady. You have nothing to fear in this house. I give you my word that you are safe and no one will offend your honor." Lord Zanar paused for a brief moment and then looked into her eyes. "Let us say, dear Duchess, that you have earned my respect with your valor and this is a form of recompense for your courage on my behalf."

She was stunned, but greatly relieved by words that expressed gratitude, whether or not it was real, and she lowered her head in appreciation. However, she thought it would be prudent to remain silent and not address the delicate issue of having saved Zanar's life.

"I spoke of romance, my lady," he continued. "...not as a personal matter regarding the two of us, but with respect and deference, because these walls have witnessed great love and passion in their history, with people closely connected to my family."

Polyxena listened with genuine curiosity, hoping to know more about the mysterious place. However, Zanar disclosed no more information. Instead he extended his arm as an invitation to join him by the warmth of the fireplace.

She decided to comply and attempted to rise from her seat, but Zanar didn't budge from his standing position. He was uncomfortably close to her and there was little room available. Once she stood, they were definitely too close for comfort. She felt the warmth of his breath on her neck and his dark eyes were intimidating.

A strong aura of sexuality exuded from him while he stared at her with longing ignited by his volatile nature. But he surprised her by remaining faithful to his word and retreated to a more respectful distance instead of taking her in a passionate embrace.

A rainbow of conflicting emotions went through the room while Zanar and Polyxena walked to the stately fireplace. Each one feigned calm and decorum that was mostly inspired by the solemnity of the house, while their truer selves were in turmoil.

He lamented the loss of passion, but Polyxena held to the desperate hope that since she saved Zanar's life, he might be receptive to the idea of letting her return to her to family instead of forcing her to continue on with him.

They sat quietly by the fireplace, allowing the warmth of the burning embers to calm them. A strong sent of cedar permeated the house, soothing and enticing, disturbingly sensual.

Zanar remained silent, so Polyxena decided to take some control by speaking up on the issues. Aashir and Muna had left the room for the moment, so this was the perfect time.

"Please tell me, when do we leave the manor house? And where are we going, my lord?"

There was a long, uneasy pause. Zanar looked up at her and feigned surprise at the pointed questions. "Why, we are going to our destination, my lady. Where else did you expect to go?"

Polyxena hid her disappointment and continued with her usual assertiveness, "There has been no change in your mindset my lord, despite the recent occurrences? Coming so close to death has not given you a greater clarity and understanding about life?" She shook her head, distressed and angered by his uncompromising response, but her tone continued in a calm and deliberate manner.

"We have been given the amazing gift of a new day, my lord. Why not use it to a greater purpose?"

"There is no greater purpose than the completion of one's quest, my lady." Zanar smiled. "Since you live by the code of chivalry, you must understand the importance of fulfilling your mission, regardless of the consequences...As for me, I pledged my life to that end."

"There must be justice connected with the quest, in order to archive the honor of chivalry. There is no justice in abduction and captivity."

"I see...And are you so innocent? Are you so confident in the goodness and the worthiness of your disposition?"

Polyxena was stunned by the strange answer and confused with what appeared to be disparaging words toward her character.

"What sin have I committed in your eyes? What wrong have I done to merit such a condemnation?"

"I am not judging you," answered Zanar, raising his hands in a sign of denial. "I am leaving it to your own perception. However, I believe you are guided by strong emotions rather than rational thinking and self preservation. And so far, the impetuousness of your feelings has not served you well."

"Are you begrudging me for having followed you in the mud pit?"

"Of course not, I am very glad you did it. I was talking about the impulsive behavior you displayed in order to save your father's life. But I believe your effort to rescue me was less altruistic, since without my guidance you couldn't find the way out of the forest. You needed me alive for your own survival."

Polyxena's face flushed under the force of her disdain. She took a deep breath to regain her composure before responding.

"I didn't expect appreciation from you, my lord. It was, as you said, the impetuousness of my nature that compelled me to act in such a reckless way. However, I could have survived in the forest, somehow, with the help of Hildebrandt, and possibly found the way out. But inside that mud pit, for you, there was only the certainty of death."

"Then why did you join in on my risk? If memory serves me, you appeared frightened and even uncertain at times."

"Because you were dying and needed my help. I witnessed the terror and sorrow in your eyes. I was moved by it and decided to act, placing all my trust in Hildebrandt's intelligence and ability to save us."

"Perhaps that is true," he answered with a skeptical smile. "I already mentioned that you are an emotional woman, but I believe calculating as well, because by saving my life you hoped to buy your freedom."

Polyxena stood up from her chair, but conveyed an air of dignity in responding. "You know that it is dishonorable of you to make such an assertion."

Zanar was surprised to feel himself affected by her disdain. He had deliberately broken boundaries with his ungrateful words. But he was deeply conflicted by the desire to wound the haughty Duchess that had humiliated him with her courage and independent spirit, but harbored true feelings of appreciation for her. He lowered his head and mumbled as if to himself, "I didn't really mean it, my lady."

But his monumental ego didn't allow repentance. Zanar was now eager to regain his control and took a defiant stance. "The reason why you saved my life is of no importance. It was done by your own volition and you must face now the consequences of your actions whether they are what you intended or not."

"Can you at least tell me the name of the person who has ordered my abduction and with such hatred, disrupted my life?"

"It is not for me to say. We are only a few days away from our destination. You will soon face the judgment reserved for you."

It was obvious that she would get no satisfaction from the ungrateful and uncooperative man. She felt suddenly tired and overwhelmed in spite of her fighting spirit.

"There is something I am at liberty to say, my lady, which might bring you some solace to your distress."

Polyxena looked up and stared intently at Zanar as he continued.

"Maybe your circumstances are not as dire as you perceive them to be. Perhaps there is even room for hope. Although I can assure you, I have no knowledge of what destiny has in store for you, or the severity and manner of your punishment."

"Punishment.? What crime have I committed? I have been indicted by a cowardly enemy who hides in the shadows and will not allow me the justice of a proper defense. I find no solace in your condescending words, meant to clear your conscience of any feelings of guilt, since apparently you don't know, or don't want to know if you are taking me to my death."

She took a deep breath to slow the pounding of her heart and continued, "I believe it unlikely that anyone who exhibits such contempt toward me will show mercy."

Zanar shook his head. "We will remain here for two additional days to regain proper strength and rest the horses. After that we will be on our way and you will know the answers."

†††

CHAPTER ELEVEN

EAGLES DOMAIN

Two days later, Polyxena was again on horseback traveling toward her forced rendezvous with a mysterious destiny. This time an escort of heavily armed guards followed, dressed in black with the same Islamic style of clothes of the men who invaded the palace in Lorengard-Lorraine. Each man wore the dreaded ivory skull of the Crimson Amulet around his neck.

It was evident that there was no avenue of escape available to her and she was now truly a prisoner. Thousand of thoughts worried her mind and no answers among them. Her distress was debilitating and she fought to project a sense of strength that she could not feel.

Zanar, as usual, flanked her during most of their travel, but he remained aloof. She had long since grown tired of this cruel and relentless game. It had tormented her for so long by this time, that she was conflicted as to whether to cooperate simply to postpone her death another day, or face her enemy and end the uncertainty quickly.

Arsenio was always on her mind and her love gave her the strength to go on fighting. His image was her only source of relief now, and she could almost feel the warmth of his arms around her, so comforting and protective. She realized that this could be as close to him as she would ever be again, but even his memory lessened her despair.

"Where are you Arsenio, my love?" she whispered. "Please God, help my husband find his way to me. Guide me home to my child."

When she was abducted, she had entertained a slight hope that one of the men who had invaded her castle and were now prisoners, might reveal her whereabouts to Arsenio. But the grim reality of the difficult situation forced her to recognize that this was unlikely. Her sense of helplessness became even more acute.

The weather gave her some solace, since it was noticeably better than before. Only a few fluffy clouds marked the bright blue of the sky. The air was cool and invigorating, and at least she was now properly dressed in warm traveling clothes. The presence of the splendid Friesian, Hildebrandt, was also a source of comfort. He had proven to be a true friend and saved her life. To Polyxena he was like family.

"Is our destination very far now, my lord?" she finally asked Zanar, to break the uncomfortable silence.

He replied this time with appropriate deference, "Not far my lady, we shall spend the night somewhere within the forest and if the weather continues to be stable, perhaps at midday tomorrow we arrive."

A cold shiver went down Polyxena's spine. She had faced death before, but always on her own volition, spurred by her heroic and chivalrous nature. She now faced an unknown and mysterious evil, and the feeling was far more unsettling than meeting an adversary straight on, in battle.

She kept her fears hidden well enough that only her bold demeanor was evident. In spite of Zanar's natural reluctance, he remained impressed by the young Duchess's courage and resolve as well as her generosity in saving his life.

His respect for her daring mixed with his resentment toward a woman who possessed such amazing gifts. It left him feeling angry and conflicted.

The challenging travel route kept them in thick forest vegetation for several hours. They pushed their mounts as hard as they dared and otherwise proceeded in silence.

As dusk gave way to darkness, they reached the edge of the forest. Zanar slowed down the pace and pointed the escorting guards toward a nearby clearing. With sunset already done, it was time to prepare shelter for the night, and the spot was ideal.

The guards spurred their horses toward the chosen spot and there secured them to the surrounding trees. They brought forward a large cart from the rear of the caravan and unloaded the necessary provisions.

Polyxena looked on with interest while the guards removed folded sections of dark, sturdy cloth and placed them carefully on the ground, preparing to build a pavilion for the overnight comfort of the Duchess and Zanar. With expertise borne in repetition, they secured a center pole to the ground to support the guy lines that would stabilize a freestanding structure, and quickly slid the canvas panels into place.

In a short time the pavilion was free standing and quite lovely to look at. They even added the decorative touch of a fringed strip of colorful fabric to the top edging of the elegant structure. To complete the job, a large leather cone was guided into place at the peak of the pavilion to prevent rain from coming in at the center pole. It was now a luxurious shelter.

Polyxena was amazed by the zeal of the men, hard workers and experts in their task. They were soon putting finishing touches to the interior decor with the same sense of dedication. For a moment she forgot her grievances and enjoyed the lovely sight of a team of workers performing with skill. It was almost like watching the magic feats performed at major celebrations.

Nearby, Zanar noticed Polyxena's interest in the work of creating the pavilion. He marveled at her courageous and proud demeanor, that she could set aside the impending danger and the uncertainty of her future to admire skillful work. Her rank as a duchess came through, even when she wore plain clothing.

Polyxena was aware that despite the elegant tent built in her honor, she was ignored by the Muslim guards. Their complete rejection of her was apparent. The effect on her was to escalate the sense of impending doom regarding the hostile world she was about to enter.

Lord Zanar smiled. "I am certain the accommodations will be to your liking, my lady. I hope it will be helpful for a good night's sleep." He extended his arm to her and gallantly escorted Polyxena toward the tent.

She had no alternative but to go along in his parody of a courtly gesture. Despite her concerns she was amazed when they entered the pavilion to discover a large, inviting interior.

The uneven ground had been covered by a thick, colorful carpet and pillows were scattered on the floor. Plush fur wraps rested against the canvas walls to be used as makeshift beds. A metal chandelier bearing a cluster of candles hung from the top of the tent and infused the area with a soft glow.

Several trays of food lay waiting with an assortment of salted meats, sweets, and an abundance of fresh fruits. A decanter of wine and two silver cups stood ready. Polyxena was perplexed by this new twist of luxurious treatment, as a prisoner who might soon be facing death. She wondered if Zanar's recompense for having saved his life was to give her a few more hours of comfort, before the end.

He stood very close to her in the pavilion and she could feel the sexual tension like heat from flames. He suddenly took hold of Polyxena's hand and kissed it in his best imitation of chivalry, as if preparing to take his leave for the night.

"My lady." He looked deep into her eyes. "This is the last time we shall be alone before we reach the final destination. You must know how much I desire you." He took a deep breath. "This is a feeling I have had from the moment we met. I have never experienced such intensity of passion for any other women. It is unsettling to me. I perceived it as a sign of weakness in myself, but I confess that I hurt you because of it, by treating you with the disregard shown to a concubine."

Polyxena lowered her head at his words. "Why do you burden me with such memories?"

He seemed to think it over for a moment. "I really don't know why. Perhaps because I wish for you to understand that although you are my enemy...I respect you."

"You chose me as an enemy. My husband welcomed you in our house with friendship...and our reward was betrayal."

Zanar ignored her words and stepped closer, looking with obvious longing at this beautiful woman who stood proud and defiant before him. With a sudden compulsion he threw his arms about her waist and pulled her close to him in an embrace filled with passion.

Polyxena was stunned by the unusual behavior and felt a shiver down her spine when he placed his lips upon her neck.

"There is so little time left," he whispered seductively. "Kiss me Polyxena, kiss me for once, of your own volition. For just a few moments, let us forget our grievances and find joy in each other's arms."

Polyxena was stunned and recoiled from him, alarmed by her weakness in the equation. She was tempted to put her feminine wiles to work and appear to succumb to the moment, just to find some way to exploit his attraction to her. His new found respect and gallantry toward her might be manipulated to a better end if he believed she was drawn in by the charismatic allure of his presence.

Within herself, she ached to have her husband's arms about her and feel safe there. She was so eager to let their rediscovered love play itself out, but all the beauty of those dreams was about to be forever lost.

She was in the hands of mysterious, ruthless people who had disrupted her peace and taken control over her life, there was a desperate longing to go on living. She needed, for just a few moments, to forget the fear of death. And in that need was born a desire to lose herself in the passionate embrace of the handsome stranger, to feel the burning sensation of his lips upon hers, and slip away from the unrelenting distress.

The change in her was evident to Zanar. He clutched her closer, feeling the silky softness of her skin and the curvy perfection of her body. He relished this moment of unexpected openness. He realized then that he had never expected her to comply. He had been finding stimulation in debasing her with his lust. A receptive response seemed unreal and overwhelming.

Zanar realized it was due to her fear, but he didn't care and kissed her deeply, hungrily. This time she responded with the same passion, although hers was made of exhaustion and despair.

The moment was fleeting. Polyxena shocked herself with her behavior and made a complete turn of direction, attempting to move away from Zanar's arms. Although the moment of passion ended abruptly, it helped her to regain strength from her embarrassment at her weakness.

Wantonness of the flesh outside of marriage was unforgivable in her life. Much was expected of the Duchess of Lorengard-Lorraine, and explanations of weakness were not invited. The ersatz love scene quickly changed from passion to bitter tears.

For Zanar, it was worth losing that brief moment of compliance from her to see an indication of vulnerability in this strong-willed woman. Her courage was intimidating and she appeared able to make herself impervious to danger in spite of her fears. Now, at last, she no longer hid behind the veneer of honor and dignity. She had finally allowed her human frailty to come forth.

He was elated by the passionate kiss they shared. It was a riveting memory. He could still feel the softness of her ripe lips against his and the aroma of her honeyed breath that had been so intoxicating and enthralling to him. In that fleeting moment of ecstasy, he believed to have truly experienced the hidden, sensual wants of the elusive and volatile Duchess.

Polyxena's abrupt about-face left her concerned about the consequences of her reckless moment. She struggled to free herself from his arms and to her great relief, he made no move to stop her. He appeared to be truly understanding of her distress while he released her.

"There is no need for concern." He stepped back politely to savor the anguish in her eyes. "As promised, I will not force myself upon you, my lady. It will be your choice if you wish for me to remain here in the pavilion, or camp outside with the rest of the men. However, you must understand that if I remain here at your request, I will be much more than a simple comfort to you."

Polyxena was relieved that he left the choice up to her. She tried to regain her sense of dignity and purpose by standing tall in front of him and extending her hand in sign of parting.

Zanar exhaled, then kissed her hand with aristocratic deference in spite of his discontent. Without another word, he turned and stepped out of the pavilion to join his men.

Polyxena was relieved to see him go. She was exhausted by the day and needed to find refuge in the blessing of sleep. She lay down on the luxurious fur wrap, relishing its warmth and the rare privacy she had finally been afforded.

Her slumber was unusually deep, without the distressing nightmares that had lately tormented her. She was awakened early in the morning by the sounds of birds chirping while dawn broke and the reddish light of the rising sun imbued the surrounding area with a warm, golden glow. She looked outside, and the morning dew sparkled on the greenery. For the moment, she felt at peace, ready to face the unknown with her customary courage.

Zanar and the entourage were already up and prepared for the journey. After everyone had a frugal breakfast, the men dismantled and packed her pavilion with the same smooth teamwork they used to erect it. It disappeared from the beautiful landscape as if it had been a dream.

Lord Zanar greeted her with a restrained manner, and extended his arm to help Polyxena mount her steed. She thanked him politely, trying with some effort to remain calm and dignified with her emotions in turmoil. But she noticed that Zanar avoided making eye contact. She had no way to tell whether he was displeased because of her refusal to spend the night with him, or because he knew what was in store for her.

However, despite her trepidation, she enjoyed their fast riding pace in the cool of the morning. The countryside they passed through became more open. There air was scented by the pine trees and colorful wild flowers that were abundant everywhere. The scenery seemed familiar. She remembered traveling through Bavaria, admiring the amazing beauty of the region with its majestic Alpine foothills and lakes that glistened like deep blue sapphires in the sunshine.

"Is this Bavaria?"

"It is," answered Zanar. "We are entering southwest Germany and we are growing very close to our destination."

A moment later, Zanar pointed to the horizon where a castle was now visible in the distance, obscured by the morning midst and the reflecting rays of the sun. It was a grand structure, perched on one of the higher elevations. The massive structure appeared ominous to Polyxena, with mighty towers and turrets aiming boldly toward the sky.

The arduous climb over the rough terrain continued and the castle became more defined despite the haze and the bright sunshine. Polyxena was now able to see a multitude of eagles flying in circles above the battlements of the castle, appearing as vigilant as guardians of a fortress.

More eagles stood upon the many turrets and perched in great numbers on the battlements. Polyxena noted the intimidating appearance of the birds. She had never heard of eagles clustering in such large numbers—they could prove quite dangerous if trained to attack. She looked anxiously toward Zanar. "I have never seen eagles flock before. Why do so many surround this castle, my lord? The birds are not friendly by nature and usually favor nesting on isolated mountains tops far away from manmade structures."

A smile brightened Zanar's face. "You are right, my lady, it is most unusual and yet befits the place. That is the castle of Berchtesgaden, a mighty bastion built centuries ago by medieval warlords. It sits in the middle of a region of the mountains called...Eagles Domain."

Polyxena shielded her eyes to gaze up at the intimidating birds. "They seem to have regained sovereignty over their domain by treating the castle as just another mountain top."

"Fear not my lady. There is no danger as long as you remain in our company...Of course, we are soon to part ways..."

Zanar spurred his horse to a gallop and soon arrived at the castle. Trailing behind, Polyxena noticed that Zanar was greeted with great deference by the guards at the entrance, who dressed in flowing black mantles. Each wore the traditional headscarf tied at the forehead.

Lord Zanar quickly dismounted and she saw him giving orders to the men, pointing out toward her. Moments later she was surrounded and escorted to the imposing entrance to the forbidding castle.

They entered a large courtyard fully posted with armed guards. The grand structure was cavernous and gloomy. Polyxena winced at the distasteful odor permeating the air;

unsightly mold patches stained the walls. An icy draft made the dank interior feel colder than outdoors.

She clung to her woolen mantle while she was led to the foot of a large and imposing stairway. Her horse was brought to a stop, then the guards stepped back and respectfully waited for her to dismount.

She hated to leave the company of the loyal Hildebrandt. She hated to leave her friend alone under the control of these people. Dread formed like a ball of ice in her stomach at the simple act of stepping down and away from that reassuring presence.

Zanar noticed her distress and spoke with a gentler sound than usual, "Do not be concerned for the welfare of your horse, my lady. He will receive the best of care in the castle stable."

She caressed Hildebrandt's head and flowing mane, soothing his restlessness. The intelligent animal seemed to sense her discomfort. He continued to toss his head and appeared unusually nervous and uneasy while the guards led him away.

Tears that she could not shed for herself came easily upon saying good bye to her friend, the brave animal who steadfastly saved her life. During the journey to this grim place, he had been more to her than a source of comfort—he had been a living force of hope that she could feel in the movement of his muscles and the heat of his body. Habit reigned. Her steely resolve quickly returned. She dried her tears and stood tall with great poise while she addressed Lord Zanar, "I request a favor. And I respectfully appeal to your honor to provide it."

"That will depend on the request, of course."

"I need your promise that no harm will come to Hildebrandt, regardless of my fate here. It is all I ask at this difficult moment. Please give me your word that he will be treated with kindness."

Zanar had come to expect her altruistic nature to show itself, although it was increasingly more intimidating than inspiring. He sighed and nodded. "You have my word. I swear that no harm will come to your horse as long as I live."

Polyxena took a deep breath and resigned herself. Without further reticence, she placed her hand on Zanar's extended arm and followed his lead deeper into the cheerless castle.

The interior of the massive structure seemed like a living body in a state of decay. Isolated touches of former splendor were still visible in the exquisite carvings in the archways and walls. Giant wall tapestries retained some of their former beauty, but the look of neglect was in all directions.

Several winding staircases connected to the central hall, impressive with its high vaulted ceiling and striking gothic style. Oil lamps hung from iron chandeliers and gave off a puny light that barely abated the darkness. A deep gloom reigned in the massive hall.

A musty odor rose from the decaying remains of the furnishings. Rusted pieces of fighting armor were scatted throughout, looking eerily like pieces of the men who wore them. The strongest reminder of the former power and glory of this place was the coat-of-arms of the Noble House of Berchtesgaden. The golden image of an eagle's head was embroidered below the ducal crest. Several banners also graced by the family crest were displayed across the stone walls. Their presence was not enough to bring genuine elegance to this unreal place, but it served as a vague reminder of the idea.

The rest of the area looked like a badly kept military compound, an impression heightened by those armed sentries posted everywhere in and around the massive hall. When Polyxena looked at this scene through the eyes of a duchess who had repeatedly risked her life for her people and their culture, and was doing so again at that moment, she found it completely unreal to be a captive of Muslims warriors who were occupying a European castle. The castle itself was built by forces who would have been just as hostile to Lorengard-Lorraine as the worst of them. To her, the place felt less like an old castle and more like an old tomb.

Try as she might, she could imagine no other reason for this abduction than her knowledge of the Templar's treasure. She speculated that this was some sort of vengeance from the Muslim world against the Knights Templar for looting and occupying the Holy Land.

Except that it was strange to abduct her in favor of her father, who ruled over a far larger dukedom than her own. He was also a true Knight Templar, directly connected to the treasure and to the Crusades of the Holy Roman Church. Yet they released him in favor of her. If so, how could the Templars' treasure be the reason for her abduction? She had seen nothing that explained it yet, and none of it made sense.

Zanar had been detached and remote since they entered the castle and while he squired her toward the imposing central staircase. They climbed the many steps, and at the summit they entered a maze of corridors and stairwells that ran off in all directions. She wondered how Zanar was able to find his way in the intricate labyrinth.

The area was now much darker, lit only by the weak yellow light of a few candles. She was able to make out elaborate paintings on the ceiling of the corridor while several full suits of armor reflected points of the dim light. In the distance, she could see the brighter glow of torches.

Zanar walked her to an elegantly carved wooden door with an armed guard posted on either side. The guards threw back the doors upon their arrival, inviting or commanding them to enter.

CHAPTER TWELVE

CAMILLA OF BERCHTESGADEN

To her great surprise, this room was a beauty to behold. The splendor of the surroundings was dizzying, so different from the squalid appearance of the rest of the castle.

Lavish matched furnishings filled the area, each inlaid with precious stones. Magnificent tapestries graced the walls and softened sounds enough to kill the hollow reverberations of the stone walls and floor. The place was like a wonderful cocoon, superbly cared for by someone.

Zanar seemed intent on allowing the impact of the place to work on her. He stood back and folded his arms.

THE CRIMSON AMULET

Polyxena noted the astoundingly beautiful frescos painted on the ceiling, illustrated images of young women in varied stages of undress. They lounged seductively on cloud formations in an Olympian paradise.

The nymphs emanated a vivid aura of desire in their voluptuous nudity, the details of their sex barely shielded by transparent veils. Obviously the artist had been commissioned to depict a vision of human seduction and desire, rather than the chaste images of classical ethereal beauty.

Brass chandeliers held a wealth of burning candles, perhaps a thousand of them, more than enough to brighten the room. The golden light enhanced the beauty of the silken wall coverings and their gilded moldings shimmered in the light. The stately windows were framed by drapes of exquisite brocade in shades of blue and gold. The room's color scheme was predominantly in shades of blue and emanated a peaceful, relaxing aura.

The pungent scent of lilac wafted through the air and there was an additional something that made the enticing aroma mesmerizing. Polyxena decided not to fight the sense of well-being that washed over her. She needed it whether it was real or not.

The focal point of the stately room was a large painting on the center wall, depicting a lovely aristocratic lady. It was enhanced by a splendid, sculpted frame.

The portrait was unusually realistic, superbly detailed, and executed by supremely talented hands. It showed a woman in her twenties, with attractive aristocratic features. The focal points in her face were her large, gray eyes, enigmatic under strong arching brows. A small aquiline nose and a well-defined jaw line depicted a strong and determined personality.

There was an unusual pallor to her face, reminiscent of a porcelain doll. But no doll ever came with hair so fine. The face was framed by a mantle of flaming red locks that flowed freely upon her shoulders and rested below her waist.

The mysterious woman was elegantly dressed in a black velvet gown, simple in style and without embellishment. Her beautiful, aristocratic hands rested on an open book, as a symbol of her intelligence and knowledge, since in those days only chosen women in the aristocratic circle had the ability to read.

Her sole personal decor was a small gold cross on a chain around her neck. But the simplicity of the attire did not diminish the air of distinction in her elegant bearing.

The coat-of-arms of the noble house of Berchtesgaden was prominently displayed above the painting, and Polyxena assumed that this woman had been in a position of power, possibly the lady of the castle. She doubted she was still alive, since the styling of her attire was somewhat dated.

Polyxena gazed intently into the woman's gray eyes. They seemed strangely familiar, reminiscent of someone else's.

But in that moment, she was struck by the strong sense of a maleficent aura around the woman. Polyxena had the unsettling feeling of being watched by some mysterious entity, hidden from sight and looking at her from behind the painting. She knew well that it was common for castles and other halls of power to have hidden observation points into certain rooms, for distrustful nobles to spy on suspicious guests or possible traitors. The subterfuge could be built from a need for protection against enemies—or simple voyeurism.

Polyxena felt certain that someone hidden from sight was looking at her, but decided that it didn't matter at this point anyway. She stifled her dread by continuing to investigate the luxurious surroundings.

Zanar had remained silent throughout, almost disengaged, while allowing her to explore the area at her leisure. At last she turned to him.

"Who is the lady in the portrait, my lord? I suppose she was the owner of the castle, no longer living?"

"She is very much alive..." Zanar smiled. "...and you are a valued guest in her home." He pointed to the portrait. "I am honored to introduce Lady Camilla of Berchtesgaden. She is the descendent and heir of a great dynasty."

The answer clarified nothing for Polyxena, since it told her nothing about who the woman was and why Polyxena had been forcefully brought to her castle. She had grown tired of the secrecy and chafed under the feeling that some sadistic person was making a cruel game of tormenting her. Whatever the consequences, she wanted to know who her enemy was, and find out why any stranger could despise her so.

"I am not acquainted with Lady Camilla," Polyxena replied in an even voice, controlling her displeasure. "I might have heard about the noble house of Berchtesgaden, but I don't fully recall. I believe they are well known in the area of Bavaria and members of the European Gotha. However, I have no knowledge of any connection between them and any members of my family."

She stood defiant while speaking and her voice was resolute. "This is the time for truth, my lord, to finally understand the reason for my abduction and who my enemy really is? Since I am facing possible death, I deserve that small kindness."

"You are right my lady," answered Zanar, surprisingly receptive. "This is indeed the time to face the truth. I am now prepared to satisfy any questions you might have to the best of my ability."

Polyxena inhaled deeply to steady her heartbeat, aware that she was dealing with a ruthless force. She felt it then—the true cost of having her life stolen. In that instant, she felt her need for the love and contact with her precious child and her beloved husband, all the people she loved who had been so cruelly taken away. It seemed impossible that everything she knew of them was to be stolen from her forever. "I am puzzled, my lord, and in need of clarification. Lady Camilla is a western woman, judging by her appearance in the painting and since her golden cross depicts her as Christian. However you declare yourself a devout Muslim. Why would you follow and apparently obey, orders from a western woman? A Christian? She must have come to you as a stranger."

"She is no stranger to me, my lady. I have known and respected Lady Camilla the greater part of my life."

"Yes, yes, you 'know and respect' her, but it does not explain why you follow her, a female who does not appear to be one of your people."

"You are wrong in that assumption. She is very much part of my life, since her noble blood flows through my veins as well. She is my own grandmother." He laughed as though this was a fine joke indeed.

Polyxena held silent, looking at Zanar and comparing his bronze completion to Lady Camilla's pale skin.

"I know there is not much of a physical resemblance," he said, still smiling. "But I assure you that she is my natural grandmother, from my father's side of the family."

"Your grandmother," Polyxena parroted. "It is hard to believe that western blood runs in your veins while you profess to be a true son of Allah."

"I am a true son of Allah," Zanar said proudly. "But I am also honored to be her grandson. And it is now time to learn who Camilla of Berchtesgaden really is."

"Good. I am eager to learn why a total stranger should go to such measures to secure my abduction."

"Perhaps you will learn that you have more in common with her than you think."

Polyxena held her breath facing the fatal moment of truth, which she desired and dreaded at the same time. She sat on a nearby divan and prepared to listen quietly, while Zanar told the story.

"Lady Camilla is the only legitimate daughter of the late Maximilian of Berchtesgaden, Duke of Bavaria. A noble family that for centuries was one the most powerful in the southern region of Germany…the house of Berchtesgaden was feared and respected by friends and foes alike, until constant wars and reverse of fortunes eroded the power and prestige of the family causing a destructive decline.

"Lady Camilla was born during that challenging time and witnessed the humiliation suffered by her family because of their impoverished conditions. She understood early on that power and wealth are the only necessary ingredients for a successful life. It is essential to subjugate the weak and useless members of society who can only drain the resources and diminish the strength of the country, while it is vital to earn the fear and respect of the powerful."

Zanar seemed entranced while he spoke those uncompromising words, a cruel and violent ideology. "Camilla was a very unusual child, born with amazing gifts of clairvoyance…Blessed with the ability to foretell the future."

Polyxena was surprised to hear him entering the field of the occult and superstitions. Her upbringing was not easily influenced by claims of supernatural powers.

Zanar continued, "Such great talents were misunderstood by the ignorant masses. She was soon feared and shunned, even by members of her own family…also branded a witch by the religious establishment. And this all at the tender age of ten. However, by virtue of her powerful family, she was able to escape the ultimate punishment reserved for people accused of the heinous sin of witchcraft. Human immolation was the prescribed penalty for those unfortunate people…burned at the stake.

"She was spared that terrifying death, but they compelled her to appear in church, where a prelate performed an exorcism to remove the so-called evil from her. After that, she was ordered to wear black at all times and a cross was placed around her neck to prevent the evil spirit that had possessed her from being able to reenter her body."

Zanar paused and pointed to the painting. "As you can see, even as an adult, Lady Camilla wore the required black garments and the golden cross."

"My lord. Did she wear the crucifix out of devotion? Or only because she was compelled?"

Zanar ignored the question. "Camilla was often isolated and unable to interact with people of her own age. She spent an inordinate amount of time in the sprawling palace gardens, where she was compelled by her genius to explore the mysteries of nature...With so much solitude, she began studying the various plants and flowers of the gardens and found that she had an innate understanding of their proprieties.

"She was something of a self-taught alchemist. Early in her life she began to work with mixing various plants to create potions with medical benefits. Some of them have mind-altering effects. She was helped in that endeavor by the domestic animals...the dogs and cats in the castle. She studied their instinctive use and consumption of different plants, which they used at times to heal themselves from different maladies.

"She gained many insights into the powers of certain potions, but the strong condemnations aimed at her caused her to be frightened by her own abilities. She had always been told they were a source of evil.

"Her family perceived her to be a curse and feared that rumors might spread about her peculiarities. This would destroy any possibility of an advantageous union and an alliance through the marriage bed...Camilla was a virtual prisoner in the palace, unable to communicate outside of her inner circle.

"Her only recognized position in life was to become the bride of a powerful ruler of any European country and thus create an alliance to bring the Dukedom of Berchtesgaden back to its former glory.

"She was very young, and pretty enough, with her porcelain skin and flowing red hair. And so, according to aristocratic protocol, paintings of this young girl were sent to several rulers of European countries, in the hope that she would attract the proper husband.

"Beauty is persuasive everywhere. In a short time several marriage offers were presented to the Duke of Berchtesgaden for the hand of Lady Camilla, who was delighted by the response and, after much debate with family members, chose the most advantageous proposal. She was promised in marriage to Arthur Francis, the seventh Duke of Saxe-Hanover."

"Saxe-Hanover?…Is there a relation between Lady Camilla and the late Ludwig, Duke of Saxe-Hanover?"

"Yes, my lady, there is. She is his grandmother…"

The revelation hit Polyxena hard. The name of Ludwig of Saxe-Hanover was connected with too many awful memories, beginning with her arrival in Lorengard-Lorraine as the princess bride. Then the shocking news of Arsenio's death, an apparent victim of assassination. The Dukedom of Lorengard-Lorraine had fallen into the hands of Arsenio's first cousin, Ludwig, Duke of Saxe-Hanover, when he overthrew the government in a vicious coup d'état.

The Duke of Saxe-Hanover was long in his grave and yet his evil hand was still able to torment her. It reopened the painful wounds of the past and the loss of her great love, the chivalrous Knight Duccio Degli Uberti, whose life was cut short by the hand of a cowardly assassin at the Duke's command.

Life had been painful and joyless, then. She only weathered the storm through her faith and her sense of obligation to her crown. Her unforeseen blessing to her sorrow was the discovery that Arsenio was still alive, not killed, but secretly imprisoned down in the dungeons of his own castle.

Polyxena recalled how the Duke spoke to her about his grandmother, a woman he deeply admired, believing that her wisdom and clairvoyance would propel him to the pinnacle of power and success. He had been warned by Camilla not to kill members of his own family, for fear their blood would fall upon his head in vengeance.

Ludwig decided to follow his grandmother's advice and not to tempt fate. He chose to have his cousin disappear with everybody in the Dukedom believing in his death, instead of actually killing him. It was because of this twist of fate that Polyxena was able to find Arsenio and ultimately save his life.

"Now I understand who Lady Camilla is…But I still don't comprehend her contempt for me."

"What? You still do not see? You interfered with the course of destiny when you saved Arsenio's life. You were instrumental in bringing him back to power in Lorengard-Lorraine. It had already been ordained otherwise, by Camilla's prediction…You made a liar and a fool of her."

It was evident that Zanar placed his grandmother in a God-like position and that put him under her control.

"It was not my interference that saved Arsenio, my lord,

but a higher, benevolent power...I was only a conduit."

A gasp resonated through the room at Polyxena's challenging words. The malevolent aura felt stronger in that moment and the anger of the hidden entity was even more tangible. Zanar seemed unsettled by it.

"You are defiant to no purpose, my lady. You show no respect in your words for my grandmother's clairvoyance and her amazing abilities."

"I know very little about the woman and even less about you, my lord...Believe me, I am eager to know how a son of Allah is the natural grandson of a Christian lady. I would like to know more about Lady Camilla before she became the Duchess of Saxe-Hanover and learn about all the amazing talents she obviously possesses."

Polyxena thought it wise to display some respect to his grandmother. "I plead ignorance, my lord, since I had no idea that Lady Camilla was still alive when the Duke of Saxe-Hanover spoke to me about her."

"She is very much alive, Polyxena, and you are here to be the recipient of her justice."

"It is amazing that you mention justice. There is no justice without honor. I am at the mercy of Lady Camilla's perception of righteousness...I don't even know what she is accusing me of. I have only been the recipient of her grandson Ludwig's cruelty, not a perpetrator of violence against him."

Hearing her say that, Zanar was again struck by her courage.

He answered her, deeply conflicted, "I do not know what your punishment will be. It is not my place to judge and I will abide by my grandmother's justice."

"You don't think I have been punished enough? Everything of value has been taken from me...my child, my husband, my people. I wish to save my life if I can, but I will not beg to keep it...At least, my lord, while we await for her arrival, tell me about the lady who has ordered me captured."

In truth, Polyxena wanted to know everything she could about Lady Camilla, to understand her reasoning and her aspirations—to find a weakness.

Zanar bowed in consent. "Camilla was promised in marriage to Arthur Francis, the Seventh Duke of Saxe-Hanover, and at the tender age of twelve she was sent to her husband's realm to become his bride. She was frightened and unsure of her destiny, even if she was leaving a home full of strangers, who had never loved or understood her brilliance. But she was now about to enter a more uncertain world completely alien to her.

"Her new husband was much older than Camilla, even older than her parents. He was a cruel and lustful man who was very attracted to his child bride and terrorized the young girl on their wedding night with his sexual aggressiveness...She became a mother at the tender age of thirteen. Her son was named James...the heir to the Dukedom of Saxe-Hanover.

"James was taken from her and given to the care of a nurse and elder members of the court. They had the task of raising the future ruler of the Dukedom and to prepare him for his high position in life.

"Camilla was once more alone, although she was too young and immature to truly feel like a mother, but she had hoped that the child would belong to her in some way. She dreamed of sharing some of the power he inherited by birth. But she was alienated from him and her role at court was almost nonexistent. Her husband had little use for her except sexual gratification.

"The only solace was the refuge she was able to take in her extraordinary gifts as an alchemist. Now, at least, she was free to experiment and study nature without interference. Like her parents, her husband placed no value on her abilities, but he allowed Camilla to follow her interests.

"A special room was built at her request and there she began to research the mixing of powdered plants to create potions. She experimented on the available domestic animals, and even on herself, not caring very much if she lived or died.

Polyxena interrupted, "Was the powder used in my abduction an invention of Lady Camilla?"

"Yes it was," Zanar proudly replied. "Perhaps you are gaining a clearer understanding of her power."

Polyxena lowered her head, but remained silent, overwhelmed by a sick feeling of dread.

"Camilla, Duchess of Saxe-Hanover was tired of her unfulfilling existence and despite her success as an alchemist, her life was joyless. Her husband Arthur was growing older and more disagreeable each day, while their son, James…who was now nearly five years old, was a virtual stranger to her. They hardly spent time together…But great changes were about to take place in her life, with the sudden appearance of a powerful and handsome Sultan. He was an acquaintance of her husband, there on a goodwill visit to the Dukedom of Saxe-Hanover. The name of the Sultan was Dashan…known as the philosopher.

"He was young, handsome and wealthy in his own right as the leader of El-Cabir, a prosperous Middle Eastern Sultanate. Although there was no real friendship or trust between the Muslim Sultan and the Christian Duke, they shared a common interest connected with power struggles in regions of Europe. They had mutually decided to put their differences aside, for a common goal.

"Their first meeting was brief, but the young Sultan was struck by the young Duchess, her porcelain skin and flaming red hair. Camilla felt the connection, too, drawn in by his dark eyes, tall stature and his striking appearance.

"Since Arthur was very busy with the affairs of state, he had little time available to spend with the unwelcome guest. However he made certain the Sultan was treated with proper respect, to protect their tenuous alliance.

"Arthur elected his wife to entertain the Sultan in his place. She eagerly responded by arranging lavish banquets, long gallops in the verdant countryside, hunting parties, and pleasant walks in the palace gardens for her and the visiting Sultan.

"For the first time in too long, the young girl felt truly alive, enjoying the company of a person closer to her age who was handsome and attentive. He made her feel beautiful and desired, after all the rejections and solitude she endured.

"Although Dashan's attraction was apparent, he behaved like a gentleman with proper deference for the lady of the castle. But it was during one of the many hunting parties that destiny took charge and the fatal attraction between them took a decisive turn.

"On that day, they were galloping in the great open spaces, speedily moving ahead of the rest of the hunting party. A storm started brewing, quickly threatening clouds to gather. They found themselves at the mercy of a torrential rainfall.

"Camilla was familiar with the terrain and aware that her husband's hunting lodge was close. She guided the sultan in that direction and soon they were able to take shelter there…The hunting lodge in question, my lady, is the place where we took refuge from our own encounter with a deadly storm."

"I remember it well."

"Since they were alone with no available servants, Dashan took immediate charge once they entered the lodge. He built a fire, which began to warm the frigid air inside. He then placed a large fur wrap around Camilla's shoulders. Despite lacking the usual comforts in this place, she felt free of the stifling court etiquette while she sat unceremoniously on the floor.

"Keeping close to the warmth of the fire, she began to remove her wet clothing…Although shielded by the fur wrap, she was aware of Dashan's eyes looking at her with passion and desire. It made her joyful in that liberating moment, to allow her rounded white arms to become visible in the firelight."

At that point in the story a strange and powerful feeling filled Polyxena. Zanar's voice began to sound muffled, as if coming from a great distance. She got the impression of being transported in a dream world and she found herself witnessing a love tryst that took place in the hunting lodge decades earlier.

She wasn't certain whether she was awake or had fallen into a deep slumber, while images played out. She was not only transported to the hunting lodge, she felt herself blend into the environment. The scene was so vivid she could smell the musty odor of the great room and the cedar logs crackling in the fireplace.

She was an invisible witness to a moment of passion. She could see Dashan's tall figure and handsome face, which strongly resembled Zanar, walking toward Camilla. She waited with a look of longing in her gray eyes—lovely in the soft golden light as she extended her arms toward him. He hastened by her side burning with desire and caressed her long, red hair with a sensual touch that brought shivers down her spine. They looked deeply into each other's eyes and seemed unable to control their overwhelming attraction.

THE CRIMSON AMULET

It had been constrained before, but was now suddenly coming to the surface. The scent of her skin, barely shielded by the fur wrap, intoxicated him. He slid his strong arms about her, pulled her in and held her so close that she could barely breathe.

Polyxena felt an overwhelming warmth and desire taking over her body, as well. The couple's lingering kiss was volatile. Their bodies united in ecstasy on the floor. Even though they were covered by the fur wrap, their fiery passion permeated the room.

Polyxena felt young Camilla's emotions, so intense and overwhelming, during the volatile sexual encounter. She was drawn in to their climactic moment and was able to sense Camilla's rapture. It was captivating to feel such passion from a young girl who had never experienced such ecstasy before. Finally it subsided and their bodies relaxed, exhausted by the intensity of their lovemaking.

Polyxena was shocked that the graphic imagery and all the accompanying sensations were projected so clearly into her mind and her body. They seemed so real, almost tangible. But she could not understand why she was subjected to the spectacle. She had the awful feeling of being a voyeur. But at the same time she now had a greater understanding of the passion experienced by those two young people of long ago.

Just as mysteriously as the spell had come upon her, it now drifted away. Her mind began to clear. She found herself once again in the company of Zanar in the palace of Berchtesgaden.

263

She was left astonished and frightened by the experience and wondered if she was losing her mind.

Zanar continued recounting his tale, as if nothing unusual had happened. If he noticed, he chose not to react. "Camilla experienced love and true passion for the first time in her life. It was addictive. After all the loneliness, rejection, and self loathing, she had found an unexpected sense of joy in her unusual gifts, which made her so different from others.

"She felt elated and never thought that such happiness could be possible. She lived for the moments they spent together in the hunting lodge, their chosen trysting place.

"For Camilla, every available instant was spent in reckless pursuit of pleasure in the arms of the man she loved. Dashan was equally attracted to her. Their desire for each other made them oblivious to the looming danger caused by their reckless behavior.

"They knew that since Arthur was a very powerful and ruthless man, who ruled one of the most influential Dukedoms in Europe, it was unwise to challenge his anger and blemish his honor. In addition, Camilla's intuitive power also signaled a looming disaster. But such was the power of her intoxication that she chose to ignore her own feelings of doom in exchange for a few more moments of ecstasy.

"Young love…She had never experienced such fulfillment. It made her so elated that she wished to believe in her ability to alter an unkind destiny…To do that, young Camilla reasoned that she must avoid repeating the kind of manipulation she had suffered at the hands of her family, her church...and even her husband. The memory of it all made her feel weak and afraid all over again...It was because of those feelings of helplessness that she gravitated toward the power of darkness. Kill or destroy any obstacle. The only way to be safe and fulfilled in life is to gain total control over it."

Polyxena found Zanar's descriptions of Camilla and her aspirations distressing, since they depicted a highly intelligent but also unbalanced personality, someone prone to violence and murder to achieve her aims. "But how did Lady Camilla come to terms with her feelings of passion? Her lust for power?"

"It was a difficult process," answered Zanar. "However, she decided to open her mind to different possibilities, so long as they included Dashan, who had to be always by her side.

"Together they made plans for the future, hoping to consolidate a workable strategy that would propel them to the pinnacle of control in Saxe-Hanover...At first, they took in consideration Arthur's advanced age, that he might die soon and free their path to success. The uncertainty of the waiting period disqualified it as a practical consideration.

"A more workable solution was to hasten his demise. In order to achieve power in Saxe-Hanover, one needed to eliminate Arthur by any available means. Once he was gone, the Dukedom would be inherited by his son James...Ah, but James was only a child and unable to rule. Therefore, Camilla would be elevated to power as the regent in his place, with Dashan by her side.

"The plan was daring and reckless, because even with Arthur out of the way, bringing a Muslim sultan into a position of power in a Christian Dukedom would certainly send shock waves in the European courts and perhaps bring about lethal repercussion to the people who perpetrated such a course of action.

"However, despite their passion for each other, Camilla and Dashan each craved political power with the same intensity. They ultimately decided that in order to remain together and achieve their coveted goal, they had to eliminate Arthur. If they ever hoped to take control of the Dukedom…it was the only possible solution.

"Dashan's influence as a sultan, although considerable, was limited in comparison to the Duke of Saxe-Hanover, who was one of the most powerful rulers in central Europe. However, the Sultan had many loyal soldiers at his disposal, men who would give up their lives without hesitation if he ordered it.

"Since Dashan was a guest of the Duke and resided in the castle of Saxe-Hanover with his entourage, he and Camilla decided it was best to implement their plan as soon as possible by having his soldiers entrap the Duke in his own house. The Sultan's men could overpower Arthur's personal guards by his bed chamber, enter the room, and kill him.

"The scheme appeared to have a fair chance of success. The

drawback was the likelihood that the assassins sent to do the job would be unable to escape the castle after the murder. They were likely to sacrifice their own lives in the mission.

"Dashan knew his men would gladly volunteer. They coveted the idea of becoming martyrs in the holy quest of killing an infidel.

"The die was cast. The murder had to take place while they were away from the castle, to deflect suspicion, perhaps taking part in a hunt. They could find refuge together in the hunting lodge while the assassination took place. According to the existing laws of succession, after Arthur's death she would immediately take control of the Dukedom and the army. Her position would be secured as regent to the child James, and she would be able to eliminate anyone who interfered with her path to power.

"She could even break all the rules and place a Muslim Sultan as the Co-Regent."

To Polyxena, Zanar's tale of the lust for power validated her fear about the ruthlessness of her captor. Once again she felt as if she were losing her sense of reality. A wave of strange sensations washed through her and carried her off to places far removed from the castle.

In her mind's eye, she clearly saw the inside of a palace, resplendent with marble floors and precious tapestries. The place was alien to her. She was once again an invisible spectator, who had somehow traveled through time or in a hypnotic trance, to witnesses events from decades before.

She perceived an older gentleman pacing the stately hall. His long, white hair framed his patrician face, marked by deep wrinkles. Regardless of his advanced age, he stood tall and erect, with the broad shoulders of a warrior.

He was elegantly dressed in a black garment trimmed in silver and gold. A heavy leather belt cinched his waist and held a sword in a scabbard by his side. He projected an aura of confidence and by his demeanor he was surely lord of the manor. Polyxena assumed he must be Arthur, Duke of Saxe-Hanover—Camilla's husband.

The man appeared greatly agitated while he loudly addressed a couple of people who were standing by. They both seemed deferential and intimidated by his presence.

"Are you absolutely certain that the Duchess is implicated in an attempt to have me assassinated and take control of the Dukedom?"

"Yes, my lord," the Duke's minister answered. "We had to make certain of our findings before coming to you with this report. For some time we have been following the Duchess, since we were suspicious of her unusual behavior toward the Sultan, which appeared problematic, to say the least."

The minister took a deep breath, staring with trepidation at the Duke who was full of ire and clearly ready to explode.

"We discovered they were lovers for some time and were together often and alone in the hunting lodge. We took great precaution to investigate them, since they were unaware of the spying system within the lodge, and through the hidden openings in the walls we were able to see and hear their conversation, along with all the detailed plans they made to assassinate you."

"Dishonor!" Arthur's face flushed with rage. "Bring those traitors here, they must face my justice."

"Perhaps it would be wise, my lord, to wait until they try to implement their plans," interposed the minister. "I believe it's the best way to capture every one of the conspirators that might be evolved and be certain we arrest them all. We must leave no more assassins lurking about the castle."

The Duke lowered his head in consent, acknowledging the wisdom of his minister. He removed his shiny sword from the scabbard. "I will abide by your words, Ministers and wait for the assassins to show their faces and foul intentions. I look forward of plunging my own sword in their hearts as proper punishment for schemers and traitors."

Polyxena was dismayed by the sound of those words and wondered why she was chosen to witness such violence, since there was nothing she could do to alter the shadows of the past and the course of destiny. Perhaps, she thought, it gave Camilla some perverse pleasure to inflict such horror to someone she clearly despised.

She was aware that some hypnotic force was projecting images into her mind and making her an unwilling spectator to a bloody moment in history. She could clearly envision what happened to Dashan's guards when they walked into a deadly trap during their attempt to assassinate the Duke in his own bed chamber.

She saw them boldly enter the room, where the Duke lay sound asleep on the bed. At first, they were glad for the apparent ease of their mission. But in the next instant they were overwhelmed by a massive presence of palace guards, who had been waiting in the gloom to capture them.

After a short, uneven scuffle, the unfortunate assassins where disarmed and put to the sword, cutting them to pieces. The brutality of the confrontation turned the splendid room into a battle scene, with bodies strewn everywhere, while crimson blood spattered the ornate furnishings and every one of the precious tapestries on the walls.

In a twist of fate, Dashan's men achieved their coveted goal of martyrdom with their gruesome deaths. But those who died slowly enough to have a moment for thought knew that they had failed in their mission to kill the infidel Duke.

The horrific scene began to fade and slowly blurred before Polyxena's eyes. Her last glimpse of this foreign play was of Arthur's triumphant expression. He gazed with satisfaction upon the dead and dying assassins. She barely heard him call out to them, "I am the last voice you will ever hear, in this world. And while you die, I tell you that you are not martyrs. You are merely failed murderers. I tell you, you are dying for nothing…For nothing!"

✝✝✝

CHAPTER THIRTEEN

THE HUNTING LODGE

The mystical trance continued and Polyxena found herself by the hunting lodge, with aerial views of the stately manor. It was surrounded by heavily armed guards, led by Arthur with his sword in hand, ready to vindicate his honor.

She knew that Camilla and Dashan were guilty of the sin of adultery and of conspiring to commit murder. According to law and the code of chivalry, this was punishable by death.

It felt inevitable that she was soon going to witness more violent scenes of vengeance and bloodshed. But as a trained knight, she found it harder than enduring battle itself, to observe the brutal force of sword play as an invisible entity in a strange dream, with no power or ability to warn the victims or fight for their lives.

Now she saw the interior of the hunting lodge, brightened by the golden light of torches. The lovers came suddenly into view, passionately embracing and unaware of the trap being laid out for them.

Their naked bodies lay in a soft fur wrap on the stone floor, shielded from sight and warmed by the burning embers of the fireplace. They were oblivious to danger and drunk with lust and their dreams. In their gluttony for power, they thought it natural to assume that they had been victorious and their men had assassinated the Duke of Saxe-Hanover. In their reckless appetite for sexual gratification, they also thought it natural to ignore the possibility of retribution in the intimacy of the hunting lodge.

Camilla's clairvoyance apparently failed her, this time. Perhaps it was lust that impaired her judgment. If she was aware of her destiny at all, she refused to acknowledge the specter of death in order to prolong her moments of ecstasy. The pair held each other close, with kisses long and volatile.

A strong aroma of lilac permeated the area. It was Camilla's favored scent and this particular mixture appeared to be infused with one of her potions that enhanced their desire. Their bodies were so attuned when they reached their climactic moment, that they were one in their ecstasy.

Polyxena sensed the joy in their fatal attraction and their mutual desire. But it was at the peak of that moment that the Duke's soldiers broke into the lodge, with huge crashing sounds and the splintering of the doorway. Dashan awakened from his dreams of power and grabbed for his scimitar while Camilla reached for an available shawl to shield her nakedness. It might have made more sense to reach for a weapon instead, but on this night it was not going to make any difference to the outcome.

Dashan's attempted defense against the Duke's guards was a futile gesture, hopeless at the start. He was overpowered and disarmed by the men, then stood stoic and helpless while Arthur entered the lodge brandishing his sword and with hatred in his eyes.

He sneered at the sight of Dashan's naked body and then with great dexterity flicked the point of his sword toward Dashan's garments on the floor. He threw them toward the Sultan, signaling him to dress.

"Have mercy!" Camilla cried, beset by dread and falling at Arthur's feet. The Duke pushed her away with contempt, as if his anger was only enhanced by her pleas.

"Restrain him," Arthur ordered, pointing to Dashan.

The Sultan was now dressed, but shivered with cold and his sudden sense of doom, leaving him undignified in the face of approaching death. Camilla continued to cry for mercy.

Ignoring her irritating pleas, Arthur pointed his weapon toward Dashan's chest, ready to impart the fatal strike.

"No!" screamed Camilla as she rushed toward her lover, desperately trying to shield him with her body. She stared at Arthur, her husband, with defiance and contempt. She held on tightly to Dashan, with her body trembling but her voice strong and determined. "Kill us, my lord, if you will, but please kill us together. I favor death over spending one more moment of my life in your presence or in your home."

Arthur was so startled to hear this that he lowered his arm. He had never known that such fire burned inside the submissive young woman he married. For a long moment, silence reigned in the hunting lodge and all held their breath, waiting for Author's rage to explode.

"Death is the easy way out, Camilla," Arthur said in a strangely gentle voice. "You will not die, adulteress, but instead you will witness the death of your lover, as I plunge my sword in his treacherous heart. I will not be debased by the shame you inflicted upon my honor and that of our son, because no one will know what transpired here today." He raised his voice to fill the room and added, "And everyone here will face the penalty of death if they speak of it to anyone."

Without further delay, he buried his heavy sword in Dashan's chest. A scream of agony erupted from the young sultan and even though that first blow would have surely killed him, the Duke went into a killer frenzy and plunged the cruel, cold steel into him, over and over.

Polyxena could not escape the sound of Camilla's screams of despair. They reverberated in the stately lodge for a long time, until trauma and exhaustion took her. She fainted and was still unconscious when she was carried away by the Duke's guards.

Polyxena felt her clarity of mind returning. She was once again in the palace of Berchtesgaden, a place she was certain never to have left in the first place, since her travels in the shadows of the past were surely induced by another of the hypnotic potions used by these people. This one had somehow forced her to share the violent history of Lady Camilla.

She opened her eyes and was relieved to see Zanar. He looked at her with interest, since she was breathing heavily from the experience and perspiration had appeared on her brow.

"Are you all right, my lady?" He handed her a golden goblet filled with wine, to steady her nerves. She turned it down and asked for some water instead and took several deep gulps while slowly returning to a more stable condition.

"I say again, are you all right?" Zanar persisted, taking in the paleness and anguish in her face. "Has your awareness returned?"

"I am not sure. These mind games are debilitating and I don't understand why I have to be subjected to them."

"It is necessary to understand the situation."

"What is there to understand, my lord? And what purpose does it serve for me to witness such horror? No one has the power to change the course of destiny and the shadows of the past."

"I was not privileged to share your visions," answered Zanar. "...but I am certain you are not expected to alter anything, but to witness and understand."

Polyxena's self-control was at ebb. She had been greatly challenged and was not predisposed to diplomatic answers. "Even if you did not share with me the tragic visions of the past, I am certain you are familiar with the violent episodes in Lady Camilla's life and the Duke of Saxe-Hanover's gruesome sense of justice."

"Yes, the story is familiar and represents a dark episode in my family's history...my father and my grandmother both told me about it."

"I know it was a tragic time for your family, my lord. I also realize that consequences were appropriate for the crime, since adultery is a sin punishable by death. But in this case it was compounded by the conspiracy to commit murder against a royal Duke."

A loud hissing sound permeated the area in response to her words and although she was alone with Zanar, Camilla's presence was very much part of the environment. Polyxena understood that she might have gone too far in openly admitting her true feelings of justice.

"Despite the circumstances, I understand the great love Camilla and Dashan had for each other and their desire to be free from the autocratic control of the Duke. But what happened to the Duchess after Lord Dashan was killed? Did she return to the castle of Saxe-Hanover and continue living by her husband's side?"

"Oh no. She was immediately sent into exile and returned to her ancestral home in the castle of Berchtesgaden. It was not an act of clemency on Arthur's part...he feared a scandal that would stain his honor in the eyes of the citizens.

"She was forbidden to return to Saxe-Hanover or to ever see her son again, for as long as she lived, since the magnitude of her crimes would have also stained young James' honor, when was time to take power over the Dukedom.

"I guess he had his own sense of justice. But what happened to the remaining escort and guards of Lord Dashan who took no part in the attempt to assassinate the Duke? Were they also executed?"

"They were not. The Duke was a shrewd diplomat and knew how to deal with people from other cultures, so he decided to let them go as a sign of good will toward the people of El Cabir."

"Highly unusual." Polyxena shook her head in disbelief. "The men were not conspirators, but they could have been bent on revenge for their friends, regardless of the sins of their Sultan."

"The remaining men were grateful to have their lives spared, and actually escorted Camilla back to Eagles Domain and the castle of Berchtesgaden."

"Then how is it that Lady Camilla is related to you, since Lord Dashan was already dead at this point?"

"She found out that she was with child and members of the Sultan's escort knew that Dashan was the real father. They worshiped his memory and hoped to bring the infant back to El Cabir as the heir of the sultanate. But they could only do that if the child was a son and could became the natural heir of Dashan and be raised as a Muslim."

"What about Camilla? Was she willing to give up her child?"

"At first she objected to the idea, not wanting to be alone in Berchtesgaden. Her parents were dead by now and only a few servants remained in the decaying castle. She also hoped that the child would be a son and resemble Dashan and in some way keep her lover's memory alive."

"The child was born in this castle?"

"Yes my lady, my father, called Aashif the Bold and Courageous, was born here. At first she wanted the child to remain with her, but since Aashif had fair skin and strongly resembled Camilla instead of Dashan, the situation became problematic. She was still legally married to the Duke of Saxe-Hanover and since she had not been repudiated by him, she could have made the legal claim that the child was his son and thus second in line as heir to the Dukedom."

"I am sure she was not that foolish?"

"No, my lady," said Zanar. "The Duke would have never allowed the bastard son of a Muslim to make a claim on a Christian Dukedom. The move would have caused certain death for the infant."

"Did Camilla finally decide to give her child to the people of El-Cabir?"

"She had no real choice, since the child would have been in mortal peril without proper protection in the castle. Besides, since he didn't resemble Dashan, she wasn't sure she wished to be a mother."

Polyxena was appalled by the lack of maternal affection. She wondered if the woman had the ability to love anybody, since she seemed to have no real affection for her first son. Her overwhelming attraction for Dashan was more related to lust and power than true love. "Did the people of El-Cabir ultimately accept her child...even if he was the son of a Christian woman?"

"My grandfather, Dashan, was beloved by his people, and since Camilla had been willing to share the Dukedom of Saxe-Hanover with him, she was embraced as one of their own. Aashif became the natural heir of the sultanate of El-Cabir."

"I am aware that the guards of the castle appear to be Muslims," asked Polyxena with increased curiosity. "They also carry the symbol of the Crimson Amulet around their necks. How it is connected to me?"

"You will have all the answers soon...Now after she was exiled in the castle of Berchtesgaden, Camilla was alone and terrified. She could only depend on a small group of servants who still resided in the palace. However, since she had no wealth to procure an army of mercenaries, her only strength was her ability as an alchemist.

"Since Eagles Domain was home to hundreds of eagles, she decided to find a way to bend and control their will."

"Trained eagles?" interrupted Polyxena with contempt. "I have met and killed one such beast. He was named Attila and he belonged to Ludwig, Duke of Saxe-Hanover."

"Attila was my gift for Cousin Ludwig." Zanar answered with surprise. "And you are correct, he was very vicious and trained to kill. How did you manage to slay him?"

"I knew about his viciousness because I had just witnessed him murder an innocent child." Polyxena recalled the terrifying episode. "And since you trained him, your hands are also tainted with his blood."

"You continually fail to weigh your words, my lady." Zanar said, angered by her retort. "You have not forgotten that you are a prisoner here, have you? You should display more deference to your captors."

"I will not bargain for my life. And you do not intimidate me. I am a prisoner with no future and have nothing else to lose."

Zanar ignored her. "Lady Camilla had two sons, but twists of fate alienated her from both of them. However, the only one that really mattered to her was her legitimate son James, in order to regain prestige as a Duchess.

But even after the death of Arthur, James refused to see his mother and as the new Duke, he continued her exile from the Dukedom. My father Aashif was quite willing to meet his mother and visited her occasionally and even extended the invitation for her to be an honored guest in the sultanate of El-Cabir, though she never accepted. The relationship with my father was not very satisfying to Camilla, since he was unable to elevate her position in life.

"Despite the rejection, my father tried to love and respect his mother. He made great efforts to ensure her safety and sent many of his own soldiers to protect the castle of Berchtesgaden, which was in a state of disarray. Thanks to my father's devotion and help, through the years she managed to develop a small, army. They respected her abilities as an alchemist and considered her a great sage. They were ready to die for her, if need be."

"But if your grandmother was forbidden to return to Saxe-Hanover, how did she manage to meet her grandson Ludwig?"

"Her son James found that his attitude softened at the birth of his own son and he decided it was time to include Camilla in his life. When the child was old enough, he was allowed to meet his paternal grandmother in the castle of Berchtesgaden. Young Ludwig found an immediate rapport with his grandmother. They were very much alike and shared the thirst for power. He truly admired her and her great gifts of clairvoyance, believing that Camilla would help him to become the true force in Europe and build an Empire, with Camilla as the dowager Duchess sharing his glory."

"I truly believe in Ludwig's desire for conquest," said Polyxena, "considering his violent takeover of the dukedom of Lorengard-Lorraine. But I am not certain about your role here, Lord Zanar, since it would seem you also have no ability to enhance your grandmother's status in the world."

"I am considered illegitimate in the eyes of the European Gotha, and I have no abilities to improve my grandmother's stature. But she knows I am loyal to her commands. However, I also bear a great resemblance to my grandfather Dashan, and believe that to be the real reason I was welcomed in her world."

"You are satisfied with having such a low position in her eyes? You are like any other servant. I see very little honor in being accepted, simply because you resemble her lover."

The doors of the room abruptly swung open. Two guards entered and stood respectfully aside, giving clear passage to the lady of the castle.

THE ELUSIVE DAWN

A frigid burst of air preceded the arrival of the elusive lady of the castle and the many candle lights flickered, giving a darker, gloomier appearance to the room. Polyxena retreated against the back wall, instinctively intimidated by the malevolent energy she could feel entering the room.

She held her breath in that culminating moment, face to face at last with the unseen enemy who so cruelly disrupted her life. She fought back her fear while trying to understand her mysterious captor's charismatic power over so many people. How were they lured in? The charisma was nothing more than beautiful icing over a poisonous cake.

Zanar bowed deferentially when the womanly figure appeared in the archway of the stately room. She was not particularly tall, and yet her demeanor was somehow intimidating. Her head was crowned with beautiful red hair, long tresses that swayed within the cloud of frigid air that followed her into the room.

She appeared surprisingly young, perhaps in her late teens, with an unusually pale complexion and lovely aristocratic features. She wore a simple black garment with a flowing cape, a severe outfit that contrasted sharply with her youthful appearance. And she looked exactly as Polyxena had seen her, while she was in the mysterious state of trance that revealed so much.

And still, the events she saw in her vision had taken place decades before. This girlish woman appeared untouched by time.

A sense of wrongness fired a sour arrow through her. It was wrong. It was not of this world. She felt as if her heart turned cold and began to shoot out frigid blood, flushing the icy liquid into her arteries.

Polyxena had no more time to study her. The luminous gray eyes focused on her with a stare that was at once inquisitive and malevolent.

She spoke in a tone of mockery that Polyxena instantly recognized in Zanar's taunts. "Welcome to the palace of Berchtesgaden, Polyxena, Duchess of Lorengard-Lorraine." She managed to smile and sneer at the same time.

The voice. More wrongness. This was not the voice of a girl. It was deep and raspy, completely out of line with her appearance.

Polyxena responded with deliberate dignity, through she politely bowed her head. "Thank you for the greeting, your grace."

Camilla stared at her like a snake hypnotizing a mouse. The silence in the room grew thick. When she spoke again, there was venom in it. "Your treacherous beauty appears untouched by your recent difficulties. The same beauty that deflected the true course of destiny, for many people."

Polyxena did her best to appear undaunted. "You are much too generous my lady, since I have no power to alter the course of destiny for anyone."

Camilla's response was delivered in loud and prolonged laughter. The unpleasant resonance of it contrasted again to the innocent physical appearance of the dowager Duchess. A wild look of madness came over her eyes. "You are brave indeed, in challenging my words. Are you too high and too mighty for fear?"

"Would fear alter the course of my destiny, your grace? You have all the power here. While I would save my life if I could, I will not beg for it against your perceived sense of justice."

Camilla emitted a sharp hissing sound that belonged in the throat of a snake. Polyxena realized that she was again under the manipulation of a powerful mind and that the girl before her was an optical illusion.

Beneath the appearance was a madwoman driven by rage, and no eloquence and reasoning from Polyxena would mitigate her hatred. She guessed that this monstrous woman lived for many years in total seclusion in that decaying castle, surrounded by people from a different land and of a culture foreign to her. Her only companionship appeared to have been supplied by her trained eagles.

Camilla's exile after the execution of Dashan, along with the terrifying memories of his violent death, combined with the loss of her status as the Duchess of Saxe-Hanover to ensure a mental breakdown. And yet, wondered Polyxena, beating back fear with curiosity, what if Camilla's thin line to reality was only maintained through her work as an alchemist? It might be that these abilities lay so deeply in her, not even madness could corrupt them. If so, she might have become expert at creating the medical potions and mind-altering drugs Zanar employed.

Polyxena faced Camilla with defiance and since she was considerably taller, for a brief moment the lady of the castle appeared to be intimidated by her boldness and took a step back in surprise.

But in the next instant she confronted Polyxena with vicious anger. "You will pay with your life for the untimely death of my grandson Ludwig, Duke of Saxe-Hanover, ordained by me to become the ruler of the world. And if not for your interference and seductions, I would have shared the glory by his side."

"I had nothing to do with his demise. His own evil doomed him."

Camilla whirled around and angrily walked toward an imposing sculpted armoire set against the gilded walls. She pulled opened the heavy doors and retrieved a large cup made from a human skull. It was hard to tell at a relative distance if the cup was made of ivory or actual bone.

After she placed the skull cup on a nearby table, she poured liquid from a small bottle into it, then produced another bottle from the folds of her clothing and added a dash of white powder. The mixture flared and produced a greenish plume of smoke that undulated over the open skull like a belly dancer.

Camilla picked up the cup and held it over her head, standing erect, staring ahead in concentration. A cold draft swept into the room, extinguishing several candles. The frigid air plunged the room into deeper gloom. In the darkness, a soft glow was visible inside the cup. The macabre skull was almost translucent and the two splendid rubies that graced the eye glinted in the flickering light of the remaining candles.

In that instant, Polyxena realized what she was looking at. The words came from her mouth on their own, "The Crimson Amulet..."

"Yes. The Crimson Amulet. A symbol of power worshiped by one and all in the castle of Berchtesgaden. You are gazing upon our sacred idol and it is ready to implement proper justice to you, Polyxena, Duchess of Lorengard-Lorraine."

Camilla brought the skull very close to Polyxena's face, wafting a bitter almond smell through the air.

Polyxena recoiled from Camilla and the symbol of death. The dowager Duchess cackled loudly at that and the sickening sound of her voice was so disturbing that Polyxena brought her hands to her ears to stifle it. Camilla did not seem to care.

"Beautiful Duchess, you finally show your fears because there is no place to run," her venomous voice crackled. "Do you know what the crimson amulet idol represents? And who the Crimson Amulet really is?"

Polyxena struggled to retain her composure, there alone in the hands of a mad woman. Zanar was nearly invisible in a corner of the room, passively swallowed by darkness and deferential to his grandmother's wishes.

"I don't know who that skull represents," she finally said, gathering her remaining strength. "But if it's my death you wish, I am prepared for that moment and my soul is at peace. Though I still have no idea why I deserve such vengeance."

Camilla stared at her with dead eyes for a long moment, than flatly intoned, "Do you know how my grandson, Ludwig Duke of Saxe-Hanover died?"

"I do. He was killed in a duel with my husband, Arsenio, Duke of Lorengard-Lorraine. The duel came out of a revolt by the citizens of the Dukedom, who had risen against his unlawful takeover of their realm."

"Unlawful?" parroted Camilla with scorn. "His takeover was ordained as the beginning of his consolidation of power. He was meant to be the ruler of the world, and would have succeeded but for your interference and manipulation."

The dowager Duchess took a deep breath before pointing a shaking finger at Polyxena. "You released Arsenio from the dungeons of the castle, where he was intended to remain until the end of his days."

Polyxena was stunned by Camilla's knowledge. It was plain that she possessed amazing powers and at least some portion of true clairvoyance. That made her even more ominous.

Ignoring Polyxena's reaction, Camilla continued, "I was the one who suggested to Ludwig that it would be wise to bury Duke Arsenio alive in the dungeons of the castle, instead of killing him outright. The blood of vengeance would fall upon his head if he killed a member of his own family. However, death itself was not necessary."

"But your grandson's death was not caused by Arsenio," Polyxena insisted. "He was hit by lightning during a thunderstorm in the battlement of the castle, while they were fighting a duel to the death. The power of nature took him."

"I am fully aware of the circumstances," Camilla screeched. "And you are responsible for it, because through your effort and interference, Arsenio was released from the palace dungeons. You forever changed the course of destiny and caused the untimely death of Ludwig."

Polyxena stared back in defiance. "There was nothing holy about the cruelty of your grandson, Ludwig. He betrayed his cousin Arsenio by unlawfully seizing power and he caused death and destruction among the unfortunate people of the realm. Even without my interference, they would have revolted against him and eventually brought down his regime."

"Silence," Camilla whispered the word. Her tiny voice was so faint that Polyxena had to strain to hear her, even though the act of straining to hear felt like leaning into a knife point.

Camilla brought her lips close to Polyxena and barely breathed the words, "Your useless talk will not stop the hand of death. Your end is coming and Ludwig will have his just revenge."

Camilla approached the table and reverently placed the Crimson Amulet idol there. The little plume of green smoke continued to riffle and roll from the deathly cup and dance in the air overhead.

"I know how my grandson died," Camilla said. "It was not by the vile metal of your husband's sword, but by a burst of lightning that incinerated him and plunged his body from the battlement of the castle, trapped in his warrior's armor. His body was destroyed, but for his skull. It somehow remained miraculously intact, white as snow. Amazing perfection."

Camilla took a deep breath and leveled a sour gaze at Polyxena. "I ordered the holy skull to be brought to me and I swore upon my grandson's remains that he would not only be avenged, he would be instrumental in the destruction of his own assassin. If you think that isn't possible after his demise, you are quite wrong. This beautiful cup which rests before you was forged with Ludwig's skull. It is filled with a special nectar I concocted for this grand occasion. You, my lady, will drink the burning poison inside this holy vessel that I dubbed the Crimson Amulet." Camilla paused and stood silent for a long moment, relishing the torment she was inflicting.

"Do you know why I chose this name? Why I called it the Crimson Amulet when the skull is white? Because crimson is the color of blood and crimson is the color of your family coat-of-arms. Blood is the only necessary ingredient to wash away the infamy you perpetrated."

Camilla laughed, rejoicing in the younger woman's helplessness. "Zanar. Come forward and join us."

He immediately responded and approached them, but he appeared uneasy and made no eye contact with Polyxena. She took it as a sign of hope that his inner conflict might be exploited. Zanar was no longer the brash, confident man she witnessed on their journey.

"Take the cup, Zanar," Camilla insisted. "Bring this holy vessel to our honored guest's lips. Then make her drink every drop."

That's when it happened. Instead of pushing Polyxena out of this world, Zanar remained immobile, as if confused.

"Have you heard my command?" she called. "Take the cup!" Her words appeared to startle Zanar and snap him back to action. He reached for the Crimson Amulet.

But in that heart-pounding moment, a palace guard rushed into the room and spoke with great concern. "Forgive me for the interruption, my lady, but an army of heavily armed soldiers is approaching the castle. We are under siege."

†††

CHAPTER FOURTEEN

THE CHAMBER OF DEATH

For a moment, Camilla was unable to speak, shaking her head in disbelief. She pulled herself together and spat to Zanar, "Fool! You were followed. How did you manage to bungle so badly?"

"It is not possible that we were followed, grandmother," Zanar exclaimed with assurance. "I am certain of this fact. Surely one of the guards of my escort who were left prisoners in Lorengard-Lorraine betrayed his oath to you."

Without answering Zanar, Camilla hurried to a window and pushed aside the heavy drapery. The room they were occupying was located high up in the castle. From that great height they could see an imposing army marching toward the castle darting around the mountain like a mighty snake. The many banners of blue and gold clearly signified the Dukedom of Lorengard-Lorraine.

Polyxena was close enough to the windows to see the army and recognize their colors. The name flowed out of her, "Arsenio."

Her heart began beating so that it seemed to burst in her chest. She was elated by the sight, but at the same time her concern for her husband's safety raised her sense of danger and helplessness. She said quick prayers for all the valiant soldiers marching forward so bravely against an unknown enemy, in the attempt to save her life.

Camilla regained her composure and cried out to the guard in her strongest command voice, "Prepare a defense. The interlopers must be stopped."

The guard bowed and hastened to leave the room, but she stopped him with an additional command, "And release the eagles as soon as they approach castle grounds. Be certain the birds attack all at the same time, to cause the greatest damage to soldiers and horses. Death to the intruders who would dare to defile this sacred place."

"It will be done, your grace," the soldier answered and hastily exited the room.

Polyxena was terrified at the specter of the aviary attack. She had already experienced the devastating power of a trained predator eagle when she fought with Attila and that was only one creature. A whole flock would attack like a chaotic storm cloud made of fish hooks and knives.

Camilla took on the role of a capable battlefield general and imparted orders to her soldiers, who were so well dominated by her powerful hypnotic abilities that they appeared not to have a true will of their own—an ideal army. She was amazingly strong-willed, considering the dire circumstances and the fact that she was just as vulnerable as her prisoner.

She called out to her guards, "I only request the presence of two soldiers and Lord Zanar. They are sufficient to protect me. All others will defend the castle. Bolt the doors of this room as you leave."

Camilla's orders were immediately implemented and the great doors of the room were bolted, effectively trapping them just as much as offering protection. She quickly returned to the lookout spot at the window, followed by Polyxena and Zanar, who shared her interest but not her goals.

Arsenio's army was more powerful and better equipped than Camilla's forces. Several catapults were brought forward to destroy the walls of the bastion. The giant siege engines would be deadly and effective at bashing through the battlements by hurling dense metal balls and heavy stones.

And yet despite of the weapons superiority of Arsenio's larger army, they confronted a fanatical defense by fighters who appeared not to fear death. The battle was engaged and the attacking army grew closer to the castle walls. From the battlements, cannon blasts and clouds of arrows were hurled against Arsenio's incoming forces.

Dead bodies began to dot the icy roads leading to the castle gates. But with each passing moment, greater casualties were suffered by Camilla's soldiers, since most of their arrows were ineffective against the armored cavalry.

Horses stumbled and fell in the icy conditions and the great altitude labored the breathing of the attacking army in the midst of battle. Both sides engaged with fierce courage and the bright sunlight glinted on their swords as they flashed through the air, severing heads and limbs, coloring the white snow with the bright crimson that was the namesake of the amulet.

Polyxena looked on, feeling devastated by the deadly confrontation. Even from the considerable distance of the castle window, it was easy to distinguish the black garb of Camilla's soldiers from the forces of Lorengard-Lorraine. "How many must die to save one life?" she silently prayed. "Dear God, bring a swift end to this horror and protect Arsenio and his valiant men."

Camilla stood transfixed by the battle. She saw her men falling by the dozens while inflicting only minimal damage on the attacking army. She shouted useless screams of encouragement to her suicidal soldiers, who continued their desperate defense but merely succeeded at dying in escalating numbers.

The attackers found that their climb toward the castle was laborious and many valiant lives were sacrificed in the process. But they relentlessly advanced. The invading army marched on until the soldiers finally reached the summit.

Camilla clenched her fists. "The eagles. Now is the time to release them."

Polyxena saw that this mad woman had no concept of compassion and seemed void of human emotions. The evil crone had sent so many men to their deaths without hesitation or remorse, driven by nothing more than her delusional need for vengeance. Even now against a powerful army of superior forces, she remained committed against all odds.

Polyxena felt certain that even the killer eagles would not be enough to stop Arsenio's army. Eventually they would take over the castle. But at what price?

The sounds of shrill whistles filled the air and a moment later a swirling black cloud of eagles filled the air above the battlefield. It seemed like magic. They commenced circling the castle as if they were trained soldiers marching in a holding pattern, awaiting the order to attack. Their multitude obscured the sun like a dark and ominous cloud.

For a long difficult moment and for different reasons, all present in the stately room held their breath. But instead of another signal blast from the whistles to commence the eagle attack, the sound of trumpets echoed among the mountain peaks. In response, the invading army took to their crossbows and pointed the lethal weapons toward the sky. They immediately commenced decimating the birds under the practiced aim of the marksmen.

"Crossbows!" Camilla wailed in despair. "Somehow they knew about the eagles." She screamed orders to anyone within earshot, "Blow the whistles! Signal the attack, you fools. Now. Before my birds all die."

But except for the window, there was no way for the sound of her voice to penetrate the walls of the stately room. She attempted to open the doors, but they were securely locked and at that moment she had no power to open them.

Again at the window, she screamed for her eagle handlers to blow the whistles and recklessly extended her body so far out that she was in danger of falling. Despite her efforts, her voice died in the wind and the attack against the birds continued with deadly precision.

At last Camilla heard the whistles, but by now the birds' numbers were greatly reduced. A few were able to reach their prey and caused chaos with the horses and a few of Arsenio's soldiers were maimed or killed by the birds who managed to elude the crossbows.

Thanks to Sulima's warnings, Arsenio and his men had arrived prepared for an attack from above. As a child, she had heard the rumors of the vicious eagles protecting the castle that would kill anyone who dared to trespass. In spite of having no proof of the rumor, to be on the safe side, Arsenio made sure to include the best marksmen of Lorengard-Lorraine in his frontline forces.

Now the attack moved toward the facade of the bastion and focused there. Instead of trying to invade the castle by breaking down the massive doors, Arsenio avoided the usual ladders to scale the walls, because they left the men vulnerable to attacks by arrows, boiling water, oil, or simply being thrown to the ground as the ladder was pushed away from the wall.

His stroke of genius in the plan of attack was to push the siege towers close to the walls. His men could climb up inside the safety of the armored tower to the necessary height, then leap across the castle wall.

The defense of the castle had the advantage of being situated on the battlement and many of the first incoming invaders were ejected from the parapet. Their screams were lost in the violent skirmish as they lay still on the ground in pools of sacrificial blood, shed in the heroic attempt to save their Duchess.

Camilla's soldiers were nonetheless unable to stop the superior force of the Duke's army and were left to defend the castle in hand-to-hand combat. It was an impossible task against a trained army of superior force, but still, the useless defense continued.

Arsenio was unable to understand why they refused to surrender and stop the suicidal resistance, since it was obvious they could not win. The invading army had taken control of most of the castle.

As soon as he was inside, the Duke of Lorengard-Lorraine focused on finding Polyxena's whereabouts. He realized that Camilla's guards would die before revealing where to find her. The bastion was massive and a thorough search would be laborious, plus any castle was littered with secret passageways that were almost impossible to detect.

The first thing to do was to contain the situation. He shouted an order to pass down the command that the men surround the castle and keep a constant vigil to make certain no one escaped, whether they used a secret exit or not.

With the invasion still taking place, Camilla finally had to acknowledge the desperate situation. Hundreds of soldiers were overrunning her castle. The clashing of swords was audible even through the thick walls of the chamber and a sense of hopelessness took over while she tried to stifle her panic.

She paced the floor like a caged animal, alternating between haughty grandeur and childlike fear. The side of Camilla who believed in her power and invincibility contrasted sharply with the part that understood she was doomed.

Hundreds of soldiers were overrunning the castle. The resonance of clashing swords was audible even through the thick walls of the chamber. She had dared to abduct the Duchess of a powerful realm. Considered an act of war in the era of chivalry, she was now faced with the dire repercussions of her actions.

She finally stood tall, with the attitude of someone who has come to a difficult decision. She turned toward Zanar and invited him to move closer. He responded immediately to the request and approached, waiting for her command.

Polyxena was filled with dread, understanding that the moment she feared was fast approaching. She was helplessly trapped with no possibility to defend herself in spite of her years of training. To add irony to insult, her husband's mighty army was right there in such close proximity, but with no power to save her in time.

She noticed a faraway look in Zanar's eyes. That same blank stare was apparent in all the people who served Camilla. It was hard to understand how she managed to control and dominate so many people with the sheer power of her mind and no one seemed to have the strength or desire to contradict her and take control of their own lives. Perhaps a castle water supply spiked with one of her mysterious potions was keeping them under her spell?

Camilla walked toward the symbol of the Crimson Amulet and once more held it in her hands. The gruesome object became almost translucent in appearance, glowing softly under its own power while the splendid rubies in the skull's eye sockets sparkled in the room's candlelight.

The dowager held herself still, keeping her energy focused. Her hair was nearly the color of blood and a malevolent aura distorted the beauty of her face. She turned to Zanar and placed the ghastly cup in his hands.

"Take possession of your cousin's mortal remains. The hour of reckoning is here. We will defeat this powerful army that has invaded my castle and stained this holy place with their presence by depriving them of their goal. They will liberate a corpse."

Camilla took a deep breath. "Zanar, this is the moment of retribution. You hold the skull of your cousin Ludwig right there in your hands. It is your privilege to avenge his death. Let our lovely Duchess Polyxena, drink the burning poison that will finally end her wretched life."

Sounds of armed conflict grew loud, just outside the door. The approaching army had finally entered the corridor and had engaged the remaining defense.

Zanar moved like a sleepwalker toward Polyxena.

She knew it was the end of her life. There was no power left to her but to gather her strength and face her executioner with all the courage she could muster. "I am ready to face my maker. I only hope that my people will not be ashamed in the manner of my death."

She turned to Zanar in defiance. "But you will end your life in disgrace, having murdered a helpless and innocent person. You will be known as one who blindly followed orders from an evil woman, poisoned by hatred."

"Zanar!" Camilla shouted. "Make her drink the poison."

He was so conflicted between his grandmother and a resurgent sense of rebellion, that a mighty struggle exploded in his psyche. He had, after all, been dominated by the maleficent Camilla for such a long time. And the valiant Polyxena had influenced him by example, with her steadfast sense of honor in dangerous situations—she had earned his respect.

"Zanar. What are you waiting for? Make the great Duchess of Lorengard-Lorraine drink the poison."

That was enough to stir him. He stepped to Polyxena and quickly grabbed her by the waist. With all the strength of his powerful arms, he brought the deadly cup close to her mouth. Polyxena tried to turn her face away and wiggle out the strangle hold, but his strength was too great.

"God have mercy on my soul," she whispered, preparing to succumb.

She fixed her chatoyant luminous green eyes on Zanar's face and bored into him with contempt. She managed to humiliate him by refusing to cower.

Zanar again pushed the fatal cup toward her mouth, but he noticed that his hand, for some inexplicable reason, couldn't move forward. Some invisible power was preventing movement.

His hand shook with the effort. "I cannot do it," he finally exclaimed. He deposited Ludwig's skull on a nearby table.

"How dare you disobey my orders? Don't you understand that justice must be put into action? All our efforts were designed for this glorious moment of revenge. It will validate and reward the rest of our lives."

When Zanar replied, he spoke quietly to her, showing respect, "There is no justice without honor." He glanced at the Duchess for an instant and looked away.

Polyxena was stunned to hear Zanar defy his grandmother's wishes by repeating her words. She had no way of knowing how deeply her personal chivalry and sense of honor had affected him. Her example introduced him to a sense of justice he had never experienced. For the first time in his life, he questioned his own path.

Camilla focused the hypnotic illusion of her eyes on Zanar. "Don't you understand that you have the singular honor to avenge Ludwig's death?"

"No," Zanar spoke loudly this time, turning away from her stare. "The lady is not responsible for my cousin's death. You are! You instilled in him the power of evil, and then you induced him to destroy anyone in his path."

Zanar's breath was becoming labored. He pointed toward the bolted door and the sounds of battle in the corridor that were ominously near. "Your evil permeates this castle. Right now, it is causing the death of so many of my men who have succumbed to your destructive power."

"You are a fool to allow her treacherous beauty to destroy you in the same manner it destroyed your cousin."

"True, the lady is fine to look at," answered Zanar. "…but there is an inner beauty and an innate sense of justice in her…That is her true power."

"You are bewitched by this woman and your desire for her has twisted your reasoning. She must be destroyed at once or all will be lost." Camilla stared into Zanar's eyes, trying to again exhort her power of persuasion. "Make her drink the poison, or pay the consequences."

"What consequences? You evil old woman, we are trapped in your castle. It is already a tomb for so many of my men who forfeited their lives to no purpose, on your command."

Polyxena was surprised to hear Zanar openly refer to Camilla as old, in defiance of her projected illusion of being a young girl.

"Guards!" Camilla shouted, "Lord Zanar is too cowardly to follow our righteous path of revenge. Therefore it is your duty to take possession of the fatal cup and make certain the Duchess drinks the poison at once."

Zanar was defiant, but he was not out from under her spell He clenched his fists and did nothing while the two guards approached her. But once they reached Polyxena with the poisoned cup and attempted to force the lethal liquid into her mouth, he jumped forward and grabbed Ludwig's skull from their hands and and placed it with some deference on the table.

He pulled the scimitar from his scabbard while the guards attacked on Camilla's order. His skill and ferocity were enough to keep them at bay while he reached up and pulled a decorative sword from the wall. He slid it across the floor toward Polyxena and called out, "Defend yourself."

She snatched up the long blade with agility and positioned herself in a defensive stance. There was a sense of power in holding a mighty sword in her hand. After so much torment in captivity, she felt alive and hopeful. She now had the option of fighting to defend her life as an honorable Knight should, according to the code of chivalry. This was comforting even in the face of death.

Everything moved at great speed in the restricted boundaries of the chamber. Camilla recoiled in terror, not from the sharp weapons and the heat of battle, but of the awful consequences of her lust for vengeance and thirst for blood.

Zanar had already dispatched his opponent with relative ease, running the man through with his sword. He left him where he fell.

But for Polyxena the outcome of the conflict was in doubt, even with her prowess in the use of arms. She faced a heavily armed man. The guard was an adept fighter and confronted her with a blistering attack of wide arcs, attempting to overpower her quickly with his greater strength.

Compensating for brute strength, Polyxena countered with graceful feints and strong parries weaving a net of steel in front of her. Sparks flashed from their swords. She continued to sidestep with expertise, changing directions and confusing the guard. She confounded his defense moves and drew blood.

Frustration drove him to take the bait she offered and commit to a huge forward lunge, attempting to run her through. She sidestepped the thrust and left the tip to strike the stony wall instead of her.

The guard was confounded by this much resistance from a young female, an unworthy opponent who ought to be easy to overpower. But she continued to dodge his lethal strikes and to counterattack with great skill, even rolling catlike on the floor, and then leaping back to her feet to keep him off balance.

She shielded her body, using the furniture in the room, while he continued the attack with declining dexterity. When she saw him begin to tire, she shifted her grip on the sword's pommel to both hands, wielding the blade with added power to match her opponent's strength.

Camilla was alarmed to see this young woman holding her own and drawing blood from the guard, gradually weakening him. His inability to achieve a swift victory had left him gasping.

Polyxena's main strengths in the conflict were her stamina and her ability to move with great speed. She stumbled and lost her footing, crashing to the floor and for a moment she was vulnerable, almost helpless. Her opponent stabbed a killing blow toward her soft throat, but she rolled away and the blade hit the floor drawing sparks from the stone.

Camilla found refuge in a dark corner of the chamber. Nothing was going her way. Her guard was her last line of defense, but now he was struggling to take control of the duel.

Her men were still defending the corridor, but she feared the attacking army would soon break into the room. Her only objective in that moment was for the young duchess to die. Nothing else mattered in her vengeful mind.

She saw that Zanar was caught up in watching the duel, so she approached a nearby desk, pulled a dagger from a desk drawer and removed the blade from its casing. She placed the tip in the poisoned cup, allowing the deadly liquid to coat the point. Death would now follow any wound inflicted by the blade. She placed it carefully back in the scabbard, then retreated like a ghost into the shadows.

Zanar never saw Camilla's deadly maneuver and remained fascinated by the duel until the guard recklessly trust forward in another losing attempt to end it. Instead he presented Polyxena with the open target of his chest. Her counter-thrust was a blur of motion.

The guard stood still for a brief moment, and then grabbed his chest emitting a chilling gasp of shock and pain. He fell to the floor, breathing his last.

Polyxena stood panting and looked on with relief, but also repulsed by the cruel necessity of killing. She stood overwhelmed by her own emotions, panting and weary of the endless struggles destiny had placed in her life.

She has won, grandmother," Zanar shouted. "...and thus she is innocent. A greater power than ours has determined this.

Your accusations have created misery for too many people. But today you have lost, and the Duchess of Lorengard-Lorraine is the unquestionable winner."

Camilla stood in the shadows, her catlike eyes glowing in the dark with a maleficent stare. She appeared strangely composed and defiant despite her grievous loss.

Polyxena regained her composure and dropped her bloody sword to the ground. Although exhausted and overwhelmed by her endless struggles, she was self-possessed, beautiful and dignified, flushed from the arduous conflict.

Now she was tired of bloodshed and wished only for the nightmare to finally be over. She felt no need for revenge against the hateful woman. In her more compassionate mind, Polyxena looked upon Zanar's grandmother as a madwoman who had been swallowed up by evil when she lost her mind.

As for Camilla, her unquenchable hatred still simmered. She stepped out of the shadows and walked toward her. "You are indeed the winner, lovely Duchess and I congratulate you." She approached with feline steps.

"To the victor goes the spoils," she continued. "...and I am here to reward you, my lady with a proper gift." Using the full hypnotic power of her evil gaze, she removed the poisoned dagger from its casing and lunged toward Polyxena, aiming the poisoned at her heart. But Polyxena's sword lay in her path and she stumbled on it, causing the lethal blade to fall to the floor. It bounced and slid far away from Camilla's reach.

"You have lost and your evil reign is over," Zanar taunted her with contempt.

"No one will have power over me," Camilla cried. And before anyone could stop her, she moved toward the table and picked up the Crimson Amulet, eyes blazing.

"No, my lady," shouted Polyxena, just as Camilla brought the cup to her lips and gulped down the deadly brew.

She dropped the lethal skull to the floor and kicked it aside. For one moment, she sneered in triumph. But in the next, she collapsed to the floor and lay twisting in agony until death claimed her.

AURORA RISES

It seemed impossible to believe that the woman who caused so much sorrow and death was now forever silent. Her corpse lay on the cold marble floor, pitiful remains covered by the mantle of her splendid red hair, all that was left of her glory. The great metamorphosis of death now rendered the dowager Duchess in her true physical form.

Zanar was unmoved and even rejoiced at her death, but Polyxena's compassionate nature did not. She only desired to get away as soon as possible, return home and be at peace.

Now thundering sounds of freedom echoed in the vast hall. The heavy doors of the chamber began to give way and soon the liberating army would remove the last obstacle to secure her freedom.

What about Zanar? The thought flashed through her. He had been guilty of her criminal abduction and complicit in the death of many people. He had been purposely cruel to Polyxena many times over.

But he was also a victim of Camilla's hypnotic power and had clearly been brainwashed. Despite all the torment he had inflicted during her captivity, he saved her life at the very end. She admired his strength to rebel against an evil force that had controlled him most of his life. She felt compelled to forgive him.

Arsenio's army would never allow Zanar to live. By all the laws of chivalry, he would be executed without reprieve.

She was distressed that her station in life forced her to go along with the rules, even if she wished for Zanar to survive.

"I deplore unnecessary bloodshed, Lord Zanar," she announced. "I am grateful for your efforts in saving my life. And I don't hold you personally responsible for your actions against me while under this woman's spell."

Zanar watched her and had come to know her well enough to understand her thoughts. After all this, she still had it in her to be concerned for him, for his fate. He saw the sadness in her eyes instead of the joy and relief she should be feeling. He was humbled and ashamed in the presence of her forgiveness, after he inflicted so much pain.

He shook his head in disbelief. "I am amazed at your concern for an enemy. One who caused you much sorrow. You are indeed a favorite daughter of God, my lady. A true example of nobility."

Then he smiled. "And I thank you for your kindness, but I have a way out of my predicament. I must act with great haste. They will soon break down the doors to set you free."

"What can you do?" she asked. "We are trapped in this room and the doors are already blocked by Arsenio's soldiers."

"I am very familiar with this castle, even more than my grandmother Camilla. There are hidden passageways…and since I was in charge of her security forces, it was necessary to know the…secret escape routes."

Zanar approached Camilla's painting and placed his hand behind the elaborate frame, reaching for some hidden lever. Precious moments elapsed but nothing seemed to be happening. Finally, the splendid portrait pivoted on hinges and revealed a large opening in the wall.

Polyxena was taken aback, but decided not ask questions. It would be too late to attempt an escape once Arsenio's soldiers entered the chamber.

Zanar looked at Polyxena with deference and knelt before her. The young Duchess extended her hands and he kissed them with gratitude.

Then he was on his feet and at the opening. He turned back to Polyxena. "This path allows a secure exit from the palace, my lady. It goes all the way down toward the river, a safe distance from here. There are boats and with luck I will return home to a better life, after so much evil. Farewell my lady. May the blessings of Allah always follow the steps of your life. Please remember me and I pray that one day we will meet again."

He entered the opening and was swallowed by darkness. The painting slid back unto place. It was as if he had vanished into the air.

The sound of freedom drew near while the doors gave way to the liberating army. They would now find Polyxena to be the last one alive in the gloomy chamber, surrounded by the dead.

She looked at Camilla's remains, which lay pitifully like a macabre marionette. Her limbs twisted into unnatural positions by the agony of her death, the awful consequence of courting evil in the lust for power. She decided to position the body in a more dignified pose, something befitting her rank as the dowager Duchess of Saxe-Hanover.

Controlling her distaste, she knelt by the body with trembling hands and carefully pushed back the mass of red tresses that covered the remains like a bloody shroud. But she recoiled in horror at the sight.

Except for the flaming red hair, nothing left of the Duchess's beauty. The hair itself was nothing more than a well-made wig. And that lovely, youthful face—an optical illusion—was gone. Only the gruesome reality remained, flesh that was shrunken and aged, with skin now leathery and deeply lined, giving her the sinister look of a crone.

Polyxena looked all around herself with a newfound sense of reality, feeling as if she had just awakened from a nightmare.

She realized it, then. The beautiful chamber was gone. Now this room was as decayed as the rest of the castle. The splendid frescos on the ceilings were barely visible and covered with a layer of mold. A pungent odor permeated the area. The splendid furnishings were broken down and neglected.

Camilla was gone, but evidence of her perverse world was all around.

The heavy doors finally gave way and soldiers of Lorengard-Lorraine erupted into the room brandishing their arms. But at the sight of their Duchess standing in the middle of the room, they immediately lowered their swords and bowed with deference, clearly relieved to find her alive. They called for the Duke.

She smiled, but retained her dignity in spite of the excitement of the moment. Her heart pounded and she struggled to clear her mind.

Suddenly her father, Alexander, Duke of Nemours, appeared in the arch of the doorway. "Polyxena. God be praised. You are alive!" He exclaimed with infinite joy.

She found herself speechless at the sight, questioning the reality of the situation. Only the warmth of her father's arms about her brought about a sense of reality, a father confirming to his traumatized daughter that he was there for her.

"Father," she whispered softly. "It's really you? Dear God, I thank you for your mercy."

A flood of tears erupted and flowed down her face. Polyxena was suddenly very tired and rested her head on her father's chest, drinking in the sense of peace and protection after her punishing journey.

Alexander was also overcome, trapped within his regal dignity, but he lovingly caressed her hair while he held her in his arms.

"How is my child?" she asked him. "And Arsenio. Is he safe?"

"Yes, daughter. They are both fine and in the best of health, no need for concern. My grandson is growing so fast. More beautiful by the day. He waits for his mother's return."

Polyxena heaved a sigh of relief at the wonderful words. "God be praised. But where is Arsenio, father, is he here?"

"Yes, he is securing the castle and attending to the prisoners, but I sent word to him as soon as we found out you are alive. He will be here soon."

The Duke of Nemours uttered the words with a broad, satisfied smile. He relished this rare moment of joy and peace after enduring so much uncertainty and pain. "You are free, and soon you will be home again surrounded by the people you love. It was due to your husband's heroic efforts that you are at liberty

315

today. He placed his life in peril countless times, because of his great love for you."

The Duke's smile filled his daughter with bliss. "He is worthy of your love, my daughter. Arsenio is truly a valiant man…I am proud to call him my son."

"I thank the good Lord for the blessing of being able to see him again."

"However, he is not the only hero worthy of praise in the difficult and valiant quest to find you."

"Oh, I know, father. There is our entire army to thank, today."

"Surely, but I refer to Monsieur Ballon, the innkeeper. You remember him, yes?" The Duke chuckled. "He is now an honored Knight of the realm. He placed his own life in grave danger and was instrumental in saving Arsenio from certain death."

"Berthold?" Polyxena asked, eyes wide. "Saved Arsenio?"

"It is true. We owe him a great debt of gratitude as a valiant knight. What's more, because of his gallantry, Arsenio plans to elevate him as the First Citizen of the Realm."

"So the unlikely hero is a hero, nonetheless. Good, then. I am glad for any redeeming aspect of this madness."

Alexander took a few moments to look around the room, with particular attention to the bodies of the Duchess and her guards.

Finally he turned back to Polyxena. "I would surmise these are the remains belonging to Camilla of Berchtesgaden, the evil lady of the castle and two of her guards. But where is Lord Zanar? I thought he was in this room with you? Arsenio is eager to implement justice for his part in your criminal abduction."

Polyxena had never lied to her father about anything that mattered, but she realized that he lived by a rigid code of chivalry and was unyielding in matters of honor. He would concur with Zanar's death sentence for his role in her abduction.

But on this day, her independent nature won over her reluctance and she decided to trust her instincts rather than the rules. She was going to let Zanar escape.

"He is long gone, father," she said with conviction. "Perhaps this is the best way to resolve the conflict without additional bloodshed."

"Gone?" echoed the Duke. "Running away like a coward and leaving his mercenaries behind? When did he go?"

Polyxena remained silent, but held him firmly by the hand and looked into his eyes. "Please father, this is the best way out. Have faith in me one more time and believe there is no need for revenge, this time…Besides, Lord Zanar is truly long gone."

The Duke was reluctant. Zanar had committed a criminal act and in his rigid sense of justice, death was the punishment. However, on this special occasion, he elected not to question her motives and cause additional turmoil for her. He had learned to appreciate and admire her greater understanding of justice.

"Very well, Polyxena," he said. "I will abide by your wishes. There will not be a search party. Lord Zanar is gone, just as you say…He has escaped."

The Duke held his grateful daughter in a warm embrace, having made this concession out of love for her. He did not see how the elusive man could be truly out of reach, no matter what route he took. Perhaps he was still somewhere in the castle? The Duke addressed his men and pointed to the bodies lying on the floor.

"Take these corpses out of here, away from the sight of the Duchess, and bring some needed order here. And above all open the windows and allow some fresh air and light to brighten this dreary place."

Without delay, the guards implemented the Duke's order and enlisted all the necessary help to clear the room, pulling down the rancid curtains and throwing open the tall windows. Fresh air and bright light flooded in.

Polyxena breathed the clean air deeply, allowing her mind to get past the nightmarish memories of Camilla's dysfunctional world. She was happy that her father's generosity of spirit allowed Zanar to escape, and hoped he could find a better life, free from his grandmother's evil obsessions.

But as the guards in the room were getting ready to remove the bodies, another rushed into the chamber with a stunning announcement. "My lord, the surviving castle guards committed mass suicide. All of them. They took poison instead of surrendering. The bodies are all over the castle."

Polyxena lowered her head. Even in death, Camilla's fanatical reign of terror was not quite done. She had pulled all of her victims into the grave with her. It had been a death cult all along. At least the myth of the Crimson Amulet was over and done. And soon the macabre skull would be destroyed and buried along with its misguided followers.

Polyxena wished for nothing more than to go home to her family and get away from the reminders of her living nightmare. Her psyche had been strained during every day of her captivity and was still fragile.

Arsenio appeared in archway, breathing heavily, having run through the endless stairwells and corridors, overwhelmed with joy at the news of finding her alive and well. At the sight of Polyxena, he stopped, beset by powerful emotions. By some amazing miracle, she was alive.

Polyxena could see the great love in his eyes and was deeply moved by it. He had never looked more wonderful than he did now, as the grateful man who loved her, rather than the refined aristocrat always in control of his emotions. It was like a magical, beautiful dream, that the man who loved her had finally arrived to save her from her distress.

The Duke of Nemours was moved to see his daughter's happiness in that moment after so much sorrow. She and Arsenio were oblivious to anyone else.

He rushed to Polyxena and swept her into his arms. Their lips met in a passionate kiss and they became joyfully lost in one another. For the first time in her life, Polyxena felt a complete sense of happiness and true serenity of spirit.

Arsenio was the man of her destiny. They were together in spite of all the tribulations thrown at them. She felt completely safe in his arms. Although such fulfillment can be fleeting, they were fortunate to have experienced true perfection in life. No words were spoken in the idyllic moment, allowing passion to express their innermost feelings.

A dawn of their new life was rising, shining more brightly than ever before, as they looked at each-other with optimism and gratefulness. All the challenges and sorrows leading up to this moment emphasized their deep sense of happiness now.

He then pulled her away from that room's grim death scene and into the hallway, next to a great open window. No words were needed. They held each other for a long time, as if letting go might somehow allow them to be pulled apart again.

Polyxena took a step back and grasped his hand, then spoke so softly that no one else could possibly hear her, except for him, "Come now, Arsenio. Both of us have been away for far too long. It's time to go home."

TIMBER CREEK PRESS

PREVIEW OF

THE NEXT EXCITING NOVEL FROM

TIMBER CREEK PRESS

TEMPLAR'S REDEMPTION

The Third Novel in the

TEMPLAR TRILOGY

by

ADRIANA GIROLAMI

CHAPTER ONE

LORENGARD-LORRAINE

It was a day of great celebration. The many bell towers of the Dukedom filled the air with a festive sound in honor of their patron Saint Justin.

The yearly event was a traditionally joyful holiday, filled with fun and games. Throngs of excited citizens crowded the great square facing the gothic cathedral of Saint Justin eager to partake in the revelry. The stately procession was followed by the high mass and religious devotions. At completion the entertaining part of the celebration commenced.

To the sound of drumbeats a multitude of jesters and tumblers delighted the onlookers with their amazing dexterity and skills. Colorful carpets hung from stately porticos and balconies overseeing the area. Some of the habitants leaned from the windowsills favoring to view the many performers from afar. They marveled at the agility and perfection in which they tossed colorful banners to great heights into the air. With apparent ease they managed to recapture them in flight before they fell upon the ground.

The many activities comprise of the Joust of Bastions where the competing knights, horses and the public receive the holy blessings. This is followed by the Archery competition. However, the most awaited moment of the festival was the Joust of Saint Justin, where knights prove themselves in a horse race. During this competition they had to strike a helmet hung on a pole to win the *Gold Sword*, symbol of wealth and fertility.

Traditionally the rulers of the Dukedom would walk among the people for the grand occasion, dispensing gifts and good cheer.

Polyxena and Arsenio joyfully adhered to the requirements joining the citizens for the happy occasion. The little Prince Alexander was allowed to accompany his parents. He was now three years old and considered the proper age to partake in the event. His younger sister, Princess Vivienne who had recently joined the family to the delight of her parents and the citizens of

Lorengard-Lorraine, was only six month old and unable to join the outing because of her tender age. She remained at the palace in the loving care of her nurse.

The young prince was excited and delighted by the colorful festivities and looked on with wonder to the unfolding events. He enjoyed distributing gold coins to the attending artists, and reveled when the happy recipients squealed with joy.

He received from an attending vendor a golden donut. This traditional dessert for Saint Justin's celebration was wolfed down by Alexander with the same enthusiasm of any peasant child. With no regards for his aristocratic attire, he stained the garments with sugar and cinnamon while smearing honey all over his face.

His doting parents laughed happily at the sight, sharing the wonderful moment with their child and the good citizens of the Dukedom.

Polyxena was as always the center of the attention because of her great beauty and noble title of Duchess. She was beloved by the people for her kindness and generosity; however the obsessive attention she always received was a bit overwhelming for her unassuming and private nature. On this day her handsome son provided a reprieve, since much of the attention was now also focused on little Alexander who combined his patrician upbringing with a disarming innocence.

The sun was shining brightly in a cloudless blue sky, truly a special gift to enhance the celebration. Polyxena smiled to the kind citizens who approached her with affection and respect, grateful to be able to share with them the wonderful event.

Suddenly the figure of a young Muslim woman appeared in the midst of the surrounding crowd. Her attire was a traditional black abaya that covered her from head to toe. The sudden vision startled Polyxena and immediately a feeling of dread overwhelmed her at the sight. She recoiled slightly, but vigilant Arsenio noticed her distress and questioned her with his eyes. She responded with a bright smile in an effort to dispense any concerns. Reassured, Arsenio squeezed her hand lovingly.

The image had suddenly disappeared in the bright sunlight. She wondered if it was an optical illusion triggered by distressing memories. People in Muslim attire were seldom present for the Saint Justin celebration. However, all good people were welcomed in the Dukedom and treated with proper respect.

The Cardinal of Lorengard-Lorraine soon joined the royal family in the festivities. He dispensed blessings among the citizens and engaged many of them in lively conversation. He was truly a man of the people and greatly respected by the populace.

Suddenly she approached Polyxena while Arsenio was distracted by the performance of a talented tumbler. He whispered so softly that only she could hear his words.

"Your grace, I would appreciate if you could join me in the sacristy of Saint Justin, this evening…It's a matter of some importance."

Polyxena signaled her consent with a slight motion of her head. But she was alarmed by the request and wondered why her husband who was very close to the Cardinal was to be left in the dark. However, it was easy enough to fulfill the request, since she often ventured to the cathedral in the evening for devotions or to receive her confession.

Accompanied by her ladies in waiting, that very evening she went to the cathedral as requested, harboring some trepidation. She was met at the entrance of the sacristy by the Cardinal who squired her alone inside the sacred place.

Like the rest of the imposing structure, the room was beautiful in its simplicity. The focal point was a gold cross surmounted on a marble altar, shimmering in the light of a multitude of votive candles.

A young lady stood by the altar dressed in Muslim garbs with a black veil covering her head. The attractive face was visible, and she appeared to be a western woman by her light complexion and bright blue eyes. She seemed intimidated by the surrounding and a look of concern was visible in her face.

Polyxena immediately recognized her as the young woman she spotted in the crowd during Saint Justin's celebration and wondered who she was.

To break the feeling of uneasiness the Cardinal quickly introduced her to the Duchess.

"Your grace, this young woman named Melora has requested the sanctuary of our church. Her desire is to speak to you in private, since apparently you are acquainted with her."

Polyxena was stunned by those words, since the woman appeared to be a stranger. Despite of it, she extended her hand in greeting and addressed her.

"What brings you here my lady?...What do you request of me?"

Melora kissed the Duchess' hand with great respect and responded with a guarded voice addressing the Cardinal.

"Your Eminence, may I speak in private with the Duchess?"

Without answering the Cardinal quickly exited the sacristy giving the women the requested privacy.

Left alone there was an uncomfortable silence in the room, as Polyxena stared at Melora with curiosity and wonder. Finally the young Muslim said, "You don't remember me my lady?"

"I am sorry Melora, I have no recollection of you...Where did we meet?" replied the Duchess.

Melora took a deep breath and stared in Polyxena's eyes as she spoke.

"Your grace, do you remember Lord Zanar Mutamin?"

"Lord Zanar is here?" answered Polyxena shocked by her words. "It would be most unwise on his part...there is a death sentence on his head in Lorengard-Lorraine!"

"No my lady, he is not here...However it was in his company that we met."

With a sweeping motion of her hand Melora removed the dark veil, allowing her long, reddish blond hair to spill on her shoulders.

One of the maidens in lord Zanar's tent, Polyxena thought. The painful recall flashed in her mind. Polyxena remembered the only occasion she had been able to see the young women without the covering of their Muslim attire.

The recollection was shocking and debasing, especially in the confinement of a place of worship, Saint Justin's sacristy. The lustful imagery of communal sex, without boundary or restraint, quickly resurfaced in her mind with great clarity. She recalled with dismay the burning sensation in her limbs during the drugged induced orgiastic scene. The passion and desire she felt for Lord Zanar, was due to her lack of inhibition. Perverse pleasure coursed through her body as she experienced the smoldering passion of his penetrating kiss. She could feel the amazing sensation of ecstasy and it deeply disturbed her sense of morality and honor.

Melora, Polyxena recalled, was a standout in the frantic bacchanal because of the light color of her hair and sexual expertise. She had been prominent in the group and a favorite partner of debauchery for Lord Zanar.

Melora, blushing violently, understood by Polyxena's demeanor and apparent dismay that she was aware of her identity. The woman lowered her head and quickly retrieved the veil, placing it over her hair. This was done as a sign of respect was for the holy place.

"What do you request from me, my lady?" asked Polyxena with concern.

"I have run away my lady, and now fear for my life. However despite the inherited danger my greatest wish is to start over and have an honorable life."

"That is commendable Melora." Said Polyxena. "Do you have anyone out there, family, friend, who could come to your aid?"

"There is no one." Answered Melora somberly. "I have been sold as a slave when I was a child. My parents who were of European heritage were in financial ruin, and for a few gold coins they gave me up with no apparent regrets."

A pained look flashed in Melora 's eyes uttering those words.

"I have been abused by many men throughout the years...I tried to escape several times but was recaptured and beaten to within an inch of my life. In order to survive I became resigned to my tragic destiny..."

Polyxena was moved by the awful tale and looked with compassion at the young woman who appeared to be overwhelmed by dread and fear.

"In order to endure the indignity and squalor of my life I had to learn to be the best in my field." Melora added with emphasis. "It was important to attract and satisfy the lust of the powerful, not to be subjected to the cruelty of the masses. I endured the difficulties of my life by appearing receptive to the sexual aggressions of the mighty in hope they would treat me with less contempt."

Polyxena remained silent, while remembering with dread the orgiastic atmosphere of the tent during her captivity, and Melora's performance in the sexual games. She appeared to have mastered the art of lustful, perversion with apparent enthusiasm. How would she be able to change her ways now? It would be a hard, impossible road.

"Why do you fear for your life? Who wishes you harm?" Polyxena asked.

"Lord Zanar my lady. I have been his virtual possession for many years. He is an unforgiving, evil man who will enact revenge for my defiance, and his ultimate punishment could be worst then death."

"I don't think he will follow you," said Polyxena. "His life would be in grave danger if he enters Lorengard-Lorraine… Death awaits him here!"

"He will not be deterred," answered Melora. "The thought of having been outsmarted by a woman would be more injurious to his ego than fear of death."

Polyxena pondered those words which rang true to her ears and asked Kalina, "How can I be of help?"

The young woman was elated by the sound of those words, and fell upon her knees, kissing the edge of Polyxena's skirt. The Duchess helped her to her feet still conflicted with the situation at hand.

"Please my lady, calm yourself, you are in safe hands now under the protection and asylum of the church. No one will harm you here."

"I know my lady and I am so grateful…But I do not wish to be a burden or a charity case. I aspire to work at an honorable job, in order to bring respect and hope to my worthless life."

Polyxena remained somber and a bit overwhelmed—her kind heart was deeply touched by the desperate girl. However an unsettling feeling overwhelmed her, maybe because Melora was a sad reminder of terrible memories of her abduction.

"There could be employment in the castle…there are many honorable jobs available for a hard working person…However the structured lifestyle required might be difficult to endure for someone not used to it."

"You mean for someone tainted by my former life?" said Melora sadly.

"I don't mean to be unkind, my lady, through no fault of your own you have been exposed to situations alien to the people in the castle. Morality is a strict requirement there…"

"I know your grace…I have sinned in my life even if against my volition. I am not worthy to enter your honorable house…" Tears streamed down Melora's face.

"Calm yourself, Melora, dry your tears," said Polyxena, moved by her sorrow while touching her shoulder gently. "There is always redemption for those who desire it. We all sin in life and look to God for guidance and mercy…You are welcome in my house if you wish it."

Melora was overwhelmed by Polyxena's kindness. She kissed her hands with great devotion. "Thank you my lady, may God reward your kindness…I pray I will be worthy of your trust."

"I hope the transition in your new life will be rewarding and your future bright and filled with joy," answered Polyxena.

"Are you a Muslim, Melora? Do you require the traditional garments of the faith?"

"No my lady, I was born a Christian, however these were the only garments available to me. I have nothing else to wear."

"That will be easily remedied," said Polyxena. "I will make sure you are provided with the proper attire. One of my ladies will bring it to you in the sacristy. Present yourself tomorrow in the castle and you will be welcomed."

"Thank you my lady," exclaimed Melora with jubilation, while drying her tears.

"There is one more stipulation," said Polyxena. "No one must know how we met or who you are…no one, you understand?"

"I swear it upon my life, your grace, no one will ever know it from my lips and I will keep the secret as long as I live." But suddenly Melora's jubilation turned into a look of concern as she spoke.

"What about Lord Zanar, my lady? I know he will follow me out of vengeance. He might even try to get in touch with you since he suspects I am here...He is an evil man, and I fear his wrath!"

"No cause for alarm Kalina," said Polyxena. "You are safe among us, we will protect you. Only death awaits Lord Zanar in Lorengard-Lorraine. He had been given a chance at one time, by me, to survive and have a better life. But, since apparently he is back in his evil ways. I will no longer interfere on his behalf, and leave him to his fate if he suddenly reappears."

With a benevolent smile, Polyxena bid the grateful Melora good bye and left the room.

THE DISQUIETING DREAMS

Polyxena's faithful companion, lady Davina, was entrusted with the task of helping Melora. Her duty was to assist the newcomer to become familiarized with the palace etiquette and fit in the alien world that was opening to her.

She was provided with a suitable gown to integrate with ease in the environment and avoid attracting undo attention.

Melora was delighted with the simple, but elegant garment granted her by the generosity of Polyxena. It was made of silk in a light shade of blue to harmonize with the color of her eyes.

The young woman was in her early twenties and of middle stature. Her well molded figure possessed a sensual allure and, despite the modesty of the gown, sexuality exuded from her. Although her visage lacked exceptional beauty, was enhanced by lovely eyes and reddish, blond tresses that reached all the way to Melora's waistline.

At entering the splendid palace she was overwhelmed by its beauty and elegance. Her obvious amazement and visual delight had to be tempered by the vigilant Davina in order to detract attention to the unusual newcomer.

Melora displayed real aptitude and proved to be a quick learner, making Davina's job considerably easier. In just a few days, she was eligible to become a lady in waiting to the Duchess. This was a great honor coveted by many and achieved by few.

She received a wardrobe of beautiful gowns suitable for the important position. Polyxena's generosity was apparent once more, since all her ladies in waiting originated from aristocratic, families and supplied their own wardrobe.

Part of the duties of the ladies in waiting entailed more than just keeping the Duchess company. The position required participation in the many charities Polyxena was involved with, benefiting the citizens of the Dukedom.

The transition to her new life appeared to be sailing forward smoothly, until Melora's apparent inexperience affected the process.

While walking with lady Davina in the long corridors of the ducal palace, she noticed three gentlemen approaching. She was impressed by the sight of the elegant courtiers, inquiring with curiosity,

"Who is that tall gentleman in the middle with long, blond hair…He is so handsome?"

Davina smiled as she answered, "He is the lord of the manor, Melora. That is Arsenio, Duke of Lorengard-Lorraine…"

"He is the Duke?" asked Melora obviously impressed.

Before lady Davina had the chance to stop her, she ran toward the gentlemen and bowed to Arsenio. With great deference she exclaimed breathlessly, "Your grace, it is a great honor to meet you and to be a guest in your beautiful house."

Arsenio was startled and amused by the unusual greeting, but graciously replied, "I am pleased you are happy with your accommodations my lady, may I know your name?"

"My name is Melora…"

"I am pleased to meet you, lady Melora, what are your duties in the Palace?"

"I am lady in waiting to the Duchess. This is such a great honor for me. I am so grateful."

"You are welcome in my house, lady Melora. May you find pleasure in your employment."

With those parting words the Duke took leave from the exuberant guest, exchanging a surprised and bemused look with his companion as they disappeared down the long corridor.

Melora was soon joined by Lady Davina who said in reprimand, "My lady, that was unwise and contradictory to court etiquette. You should never address first the rulers of the Dukedom. You may respond to any question only after proper introduction."

Davina's displeasure was apparent and her cheeks were tinted bright crimson.

"I apologize my lady," said Kalina Melora. "I wished to express my gratitude to the Duke, but allowed my exuberance to take over. I meant no disrespect. However in the future I will take better care to abide by the rules."

"That would be wise," answered Davina with an indulgent smile as she squired Melora down the corridor.

That evening, Polyxena and Arsenio retired to their bedchamber exchanging the usual pleasantries at the end of a busy and rewarding day. They enjoyed the special pleasure of being alone after having so many people swarming about them because of court etiquette.

The young Duchess's beauty was as enticing as ever. Even after having given birth to their youngest child, Princess Vivienne, her allure remained untouched. The love and attraction her husband had for her was intense and palpable.

He kissed her with desire and she responded with ardor and warmth, snuggling happily in his arm.

"I had an unusual experience this day," Arsenio said with a bright smile on his face. "Actually it was quite amusing…"

"Really?" said Polyxena with apparent interest and a smile on her face. "Then please share it with me."

"Well, it had to do with a young lady," said Arsenio feigning some reluctance.

"A young woman?" answered Polyxena pretending concern. "Was she pretty?"

"I guess pretty enough," answered Arsenio. "But not nearly as beautiful as you. He added as he swept her in his arms kissing the young woman with added passion. Polyxena removed herself from the embrace, enjoying the titillating moment, but feigning jealousy.

"Tell me more about this mysterious woman, my lord, since you aroused my curiosity…"

"Well, my lady, in reality I know very little about the woman, other than her name," answered Arsenio. "She is actually one of your new female companions. Her name is Melora and I actually wondered why she was chosen for such a task. She displayed little aptitude for it."

Polyxena was startled by the words. The name Melora sent a chill down her spine. For a brief moment she was unable to answer. Quickly though, she regained her usual demeanor and said,

"Ha…Yes, Melora. She is very new at the job and still training with Lady Davina."

"Who is she?" asked Arsenio. "She seem an odd choice for the job, since she appears to have little knowledge of court etiquette."

"Please don't be such a stickler for protocol, my lord," said Polyxena with her heart in turmoil, while trying to present a jovial and calm demeanor. "She was recommended to me by his eminence the Cardinal. Apparently he is a friend of his family, and they wish for Melora to be more adept with the structure of court etiquette. She then could aspire to a proper marriage in the aristocratic circle."

The answer seemed reasonable to Arsenio, who smiled as he answered, "As long as you're pleased with her, my love. It is all that matters."

To Polyxena's relief no more questions were raised about Melora, but the anxiety triggered by the episode was overwhelming. She had never lied to her husband before. Melora represented a very dark episode in her life. She tried desperately to suppress her memories during her eventful return home from being abducted. She had been compelled to follow Lord Zanar in order to save her father's life. Polyxena participated unwillingly in debauchery under the influence of heavy drugs. Those orgiastic scenes brought shame to her honor.

Adriana Girolami

She had been unable to discuss the situation with her husband, despite the awareness that Arsenio must have wondered what happened to her honor while captive in the hands of those men.

Bound by the great love and respect he had for his heroic wife, Arsenio never questioned her on the subject, unwilling to cause additional distress. The difficult situation was the only shadow in their marriage that loomed ominously over them.

Polyxena was reluctant for the romantic moment she was about to share with her husband to dissipate, regardless of the reasons. She placed her arms around him to rekindle his passion and desire with a passionate kiss. The young woman wished to stifle in the heat of ecstasy all her concerns and deflect Arsenio's probing questions.

Unfortunately Melora's presence had opened the proverbial Pandora's Box, and it was impossible to close it again.

That night Polyxena experienced strange dreams. She envisioned herself in a place never visited before. Her body was in a state of semi-undress. Her limbs burned with the same unrestrained desire she experienced during the drug induced bacchanal in the fatal tent. Many men were present whom she never met before. They appeared to be encircling her. She was terrified by their presence and yet overwhelmed by her desire to be possessed.

The conflict was an intense burden even in her dreams—she was entrapped in a terrible nightmare and was unable to escape. Suddenly the face of Arsenio appeared. She ran toward the beloved image, hoping to find in his arms the protection she craved against her demons. He held her tightly against his body. The closeness made her burn with desire. She felt his hands caress her body with no restraint and it gave her a strange, perverse pleasure.

She looked up in order to stare deep into his eyes, but it was not Arsenio who held her in his arms. It was Zanar. All the other men had also disappeared. She was alone with the handsome sheik who had encircled her body with such force that it was difficult for her to breathe.

Strangely her desire even intensified at his sight, as their lips met in a smoldering passion that burned with destructive power. The closeness to Zanar almost paralyzed her with the strength of the pleasure it exuded. There was no restraint as he took possession of her body which was so predisposed to lustful gratification.

A sexual act had never been consummated between them in real life. Only passionate kisses had been exchanged. In this mesmerizing dream all obstruction had been removed. She was a willing partner filled with lust and unquenchable desires. The climatic passion of their bodies appeared endless and all consuming. The forbidden fruit emerged sweeter and more exciting than ever before. Honor, self-control were all obliterated in that fatal, moment of total debauchery and passion.

However, the awakening from the depth of desire was sudden, with nightmarish consequences. All her burning want was now turned into sheer terror. She gasped for air trying to control the powerful beating of her heart.

Arsenio was awakened from his sleep by her distress, as he tried to comfort her despair with loving words.

Although he asked her several times about the genesis of her fears, she was unable to answer. Polyxena struggled to reconcile with the lustful dreams that filled her with terror. She wondered why she was so attracted to Lord Zanar, even if only in a dream. Her lustful desires were so real during the nightmarish interludes that filled her with trepidation. Her family history was a sad reminder of lustful betrayal and attempted murder. The unholy acts were perpetrated by her beautiful mother Chantal, Duchess of Nemours, whom she physically resembled. Did she inherit her perverse nature as well?

For years she struggled with the knowledge of her mother's multiple assignations and attempt to assassinate her father. She managed for a while to suppress those unrealistic fears, which sharply contrasted with the nobility of her nature. However, Melora's sudden appearance reawakened dormant apprehensions which disregarded the true nobility of her soul.

Her overdeveloped sense of conscience was a trait present among people of character. It triggered an unjustified sense of guilt over shameful situations in which she had been forced to participate.

The dreams continued unabated for days and her anxiety was apparent to Arsenio. He was unable to diminish her sudden distress. She refused to discuss the situation. Despite this, he did his best to comfort her with love.

Even with all the upheavals her family was a constant source of stability and joy. Her husband and children were the reality that dissipated most concerns. With their love she was confident in the ability to surmount even her worst fears.

†††

TIMBER CREEK PRESS

www.ingramcontent.com/pod-product-compliance
Lightning Source LLC
Chambersburg PA
CBHW050915250626
47155CB00001B/245